A
Man in
Love

Also by Martin Walser

A Gushing Fountain

A Man in Love

A NOVEL

MARTIN WALSER

Translated from the German by
David Dollenmayer

Arcade Publishing • New York

For
Ulrike von Egloff-Colombier

First English-language Edition

This is a work of fiction. Names, characters, places, and incidents are either the products of the author's imagination or used fictitiously

Originally published in Germany under the title *Ein Liebender Mann* by Rowohlt Verlag GmbH

10 9 8 7 6 5 4 3 2 1

Library of Congress Cataloging-in-Publication Data

Names: Walser, Martin, 1927– author. | Dollenmayer, David B., translator.
Title: A man in love: a novel / by Martin Walser; translated from the German by David Dollenmayer.
Other titles: Liebender Mann. English
Description: First English-language edition. | New York: Arcade Publishing, [2019]
Identifiers: LCCN 2019006902 (print) | LCCN 2019011255 (ebook) | ISBN 9781628728743 (ebook) | ISBN 9781628728736 (hardcover:alk. paper)
Subjects: LCSH: Goethe, Johann Wolfgang von, 1749–1832—Fiction. | Levetzow, Ulrike von, 1804–1899—Fiction.
Classification: LCC PT2685.A48 (ebook) | LCC PT2685.A48 L5413 2019 (print) | DDC 833/.914—dc23
LC record available at https://lccn.loc.gov/2019006902

Cover design by Erin Seaward-Hiatt
Cover illustrations: iStockphoto

Printed in the United States of America

Part One

Part One

Chapter One

BY THE TIME he saw her, she had already seen him. As his eyes reached her, hers were already trained on him. That was on July 11, 1823, at five o'clock in the afternoon beside the Kreuz Spring in Marienbad. A hundred genteel guests were putting themselves on display, promenading while holding in their hands glasses of the water that was more extolled with each passing year. Goethe had nothing against being seen. But he wanted to be seen as deep in conversation rather than on promenade. In these July days, he was in constant conversation with Count von Sternberg, a naturalist a good ten years younger than Goethe. Although he couldn't get used to it, Goethe had come to expect that nearly all natural scientists had at best only a smirking pity for his theory of colors. If he encountered one who did accept it, he was so moved and grateful he often could barely contain his amiability. Count Kaspar von Sternberg was just such a scientist. He had written a book about prehistoric flora, which meant he could read what had been preserved in stone. And by this time, stones had become Goethe's favorite area of research. But now, in these July days, there was another circumstance quite apart from science that attracted Goethe to the count. The previous year they had both stayed in the palace run by Count von Klebelsberg as a spa hotel. And the Levetzows had stayed there, too. The two men had met in Amalie von Levetzow's salon. "But we know each other already," Goethe had exclaimed. "We've known each other from prehistoric times." That was an allusion to the title of Sternberg's book, and he had practically rushed over to embrace the count. People took notice because usually, when there was an acquaintance to be made, Goethe remained where he was and gave the other person—man or woman—the opportunity to approach him. "We both climbed the Donnersberg, Baroness, up by Teplitz, each from a different direction. And we both reached the pinnacle and wrote to each other about it." The count had called them two travelers, coming from two different areas of the world and of history. Encountering each other and comparing their experiences, they had seen the advantage of arriving at one and the same goal in different ways.

Now, on the promenade, Goethe asked Count Sternberg to tell him about the Swedish chemist Berzelius, who had just made the astonishing discovery that the volcanic rock in the Auvergne was closely related to the rocks here on the Kammerbühl.

It was the kind of conversation that shields its participants wherever it takes place. Today, it was Goethe who more than once peered around while they talked. Goethe was nearsighted but loathed spectacles. In the circles he frequented, everyone who wore spectacles knew that and took them off when paying Goethe a visit. "Spectacles put me in a bad mood," he had said, and whatever the famous writer said got passed on. At a distance, he would not have recognized the person he was keeping an eye out for, but Amalie von Levetzow and her daughters Ulrike, Amalie, and Bertha, who were nineteen, sixteen, and fifteen this year—this group he would have spotted at any distance, no matter how crowded the promenade. And that's just what happened, although the relative heights of the four figures had shifted. Ulrike was now the tallest, clearly taller than her mother.

Without interrupting the count's discourse on the relationship of the stones in the Auvergne to those on the Kammerbühl, he steered himself and the count toward the group of Levetzows and met Ulrike's gaze. She had discovered him when he had not yet discovered her.

A motion, a wave, coursed through him, an inner storm. In his head, it was heat. He thought he might get dizzy. Exhaling, he tried to release and relax his forehead and eyes, which felt frozen. It surely wouldn't do to celebrate this reunion—they hadn't seen each other for a whole year—with a grimace of astonishment, pain, or dismay.

There now, that's better. The salutations. The young mother was clearly livelier than any of her daughters. Ulrike's steady gaze—did he recall it from last year? Her eyes and his remained locked together. When they couldn't keep it up anymore, when something had to be said at last, he said, "Please understand, dear onlookers, I study not just stones, but eyes as well. What causes more changes in the eye, a new light from without, or a different mood from within? Since in the blink of an eye (and what a delightful gift that phrase is: the blink of an eye), the weather has just now slid a dense cumulus cloud in front of the sun for us, Ulrike's eyes are in the process of changing from blue to green. If the cloud stays, we'll be dealing with a green-eyed Ulrike. Count Sternberg, this double phenomenon—whether the external or the internal cause predominates—should interest us. A cordial welcome to you, dear lady, and to you, the most agreeable trio in the world. Welcome."

Sixteen-year-old Amalie, whose quick tongue was most like her mother's, said, "We're not a trio at all. We're individuals, if you please, Herr Privy Councilor."

"I'll say it pleases me," said Goethe and looked at Ulrike again. Ulrike was still gazing at him as calmly and steadily as when she first saw him. He stayed in her line of vision. He played at being the ocular researcher but wasn't one. The others might believe it. Ulrike did not believe it. And he didn't believe it, either. She looked at him only to show that she was looking at him. Before leaving the topic of looking, he said, "Ulrike, in the future some men will claim you have blue eyes. Others will say your eyes are green. I say: Don't let yourself be pinned down."

Afterward, he took her gaze with him, back to his room. They had all eaten together, chatted, and talked back into life their memories of last year and the year before. That miserable stretch two years ago when it didn't stop raining for a month! Without Herr Privy Councilor's thousand and one ideas for things to do, they wouldn't have been able to stand it! To be sure, his lectures about stones had scored a hit only with Amalie. He had a whole room with tables just for the stones his manservant Stadelmann had knocked together from all the surrounding country. To this day, Amalie was still a little insulted because Herr Privy Councilor put a pound of chocolate between the stones for Ulrike, to make them more enticing to her.

"And fresh from Vienna it was, too, that chocolate," said the Baroness, "from the famous confectioner Panel!"

"And there was a poem with it," said Bertha, who also had to get in on the conversation.

"Ah," he said, "a poem."

"She still knows it by heart," said Frau von Levetzow.

Before Goethe had time to say, Please tell it to me, Bertha recited what she called a poem with positively artistic flourish.

"In your own way, this is for you to savor.
If not as drink, may it as food find favor."

"I'd still like to know why there are blocks of granite around here with ocher-yellow veins running through them," said Amalie, to draw attention back to her interest in stones.

"Bravo," said Goethe. "Bravo."

The count rose to go, saying he wanted to put into better order what he and Goethe had discussed earlier concerning Plutonism and Neptunism. Waved to everyone, bowed, and was gone.

Goethe gazed after him. Two more like him and I would congratulate the dear Lord.

"What is Plutonism?" Amalie interjected quickly, looking not at the person she was asking but at her sister Bertha, whom she had beaten to the punch.

"And I want to know what Neptunism is," cried Bertha, trying to outdo her sister, two years her senior, in everything.

"And I'll tell you all," said Goethe. "The learned argue about whether the surface of the earth as we know it today was formed by fire (which then withdrew into the depths but still has volcanoes to remind us of its earlier role) or by water, which gradually flowed off to form the oceans."

"And you?" asked Ulrike. "What do you think?"

"I think we shouldn't decide what we can only conjecture about at present. But since one can't help leaning one way or the other, I confess to being a vacillating Neptunist."

"That doesn't give me much to go on," Ulrike replied rather severely. She said it only to Goethe, and with that look again.

Goethe asked if she wanted him to say more than he knew.

She said that since it was a question about science and not poetry, one had the right to expect decisiveness.

"Oh," said Goethe, "our Ulrike is breaking a lance for the *Critique of Pure Reason*, no less."

Her mother: "You should know that in Strasbourg, they've started calling her Contresse Ulrike."

An opportunity for Amalie to prove she gets all their jokes: "*Comtesse* and *contre*, it's all French in that school."

Goethe congratulated them on a school capable of such discoveries and confessed how happy it made him to be sitting and chatting in their family circle again. It was impossible at home in Weimar, where they were always lying in wait for him to say something profound.

"For which Herr Privy Councilor has partly himself to blame," said Ulrike.

"Admittedly, Contresse," said Goethe. "There, my life is more theater than life."

8

"And here?" asked Ulrike.

"Here," he said and nothing more, just looked at Ulrike. And she looked at him and said, "Yes? Here?"

"Here," he said, "I realize again that through two long Weimar winters I've been suffering from knowing too little about the Levetzows."

"Two years ago," said the always talkative Amalie, "we knew even less about you. We mustn't forget that in that first year, our older sister, who had already put seventeen springs behind her, confessed that she'd never read a line of Goethe. But—horrors!—quite a lot of Schiller."

"In German class in a Strasbourg boarding school," said Ulrike, "they assign only the honorary citizen of the French Revolution, of course."

And Goethe: "I took the liberty of reminding you I'm less fit to be a model for the young than Schiller, Gellert, Hagedorn, and Gessner."

And Ulrike: "You also said the French were more for idylls and stylizations than nature and reality."

"Yes," said Goethe, "that's why Salomon Gessner is much better known there than here. That's where he belongs."

"But so does Voltaire," Ulrike said.

"And it wasn't my friend Schiller who translated *him*; it was me."

"Twice, in fact," said Ulrike. "*Zaïre* and *Mahomet*."

"Not the greatest of plays," said Goethe.

"Since I've started reading your books," said Ulrike, "I'm bothered by not knowing even for a moment who you are. They are always such high-flown tall tales. They're full of wonderful talk, ideas, feelings, but who is *he*?" That's what she wanted to know. For that was the effect of reading him: an increasing annoyance, a common curiosity to get to know him, himself, what he was really like. So that he would be in some way accessible, so that one could reach out and catch hold of him if one wanted. One would like to touch him. But who was he?

"But you can do that with Scott!" Bertha broke in.

"You're right," said Ulrike. "It doesn't hurt not to make the acquaintance of Scott."

And Bertha, who obviously wasn't sure what this conversation was about, said that as soon as it rained again this summer, they could read aloud to one another. Read Scott. She'd brought *The Black Dwarf* along.

Her mother added that Bertha had been practicing and practicing what Goethe told her last year about reading aloud.

Bertha turned to her sisters. "He called me a fair rising star and said when I read aloud, I should always begin deep and then rise."

"As we heard today," said Goethe.

And Bertha immediately started intoning again, "If not as drink, may it as food find favor."

"Yes!" Goethe exclaimed. "Since it's the closing, don't let 'food find favor' fall off, but carry it up and out, 'food find favor,' equally strong and higher than all the other words."

"Excellency did nothing but criticize me," said Ulrike quite calmly. She never interrupted but always spoke up when she wanted to.

"Yes!" Bertha cried, "You were supposed to work on developing more energy and a more animated presentation."

"I have no wish to be another Tieck," said Ulrike.

Amalie: "What's that supposed to mean?"

And Ulrike: "Another elocutionist."

Amalie regained the floor: "We've already figured out that the Privy Councilor is no model for the young."

Goethe said he could hardly wait to hear what came next.

"Well, your game," said Amalie. "One person suggests a theme and the next has to make a story out of it, but everyone has the right to put in a word that has to be incorporated into the story. And which word did you insert into Ulrike's story? 'Garter,' Herr Privy Councilor. Rike blushed . . ."

"Did not. It never got that far," exclaimed Ulrike, "because when that word slipped out, Herr Privy Councilor immediately added 'the Order of the Garter.'"

"As if he'd never meant anything else," said Amalie. "We know better."

Since he found it unjust to be regarded by this circle of promising daughters as an utterly unsuitable model, he started to murmur—more to himself than to the circle—that he'd never smoked tobacco, never played chess, and had avoided anything else that wasted his time.

And Ulrike said, "That sounds like regret that you've lived such an exemplary life."

Since he had ended up in the bosom of the heavenly Levetzow family, he said, not everything he'd done could have been so wrong.

And so it went.

Actually, he had only been looking for opportunities to meet her eyes. He was aware of that, standing now across the street at the window of his modest rooms, which he loved, and looking over at the great mass of the Klebelsberg spa hotel, over to the windows in the third story behind which Ulrike now stood, sat, lay, read, thought. . . . How could he live with that gaze? Last year it was probably already too late. He'd been sick last winter, very ill. He had written to her, and she had answered. That was something, but only today did he realize what. The few letters she had written were already such that he couldn't show them to anyone. Only half of each letter he wrote to her was dictated to his secretary John. He had to add something in his own hand to every one, something that could not have any real content but was meant to reveal what was being kept secret by its lack thereof. It had to be addressed never to Ulrike alone, but to her mother as well. And yet, and yet, it was all bearable. He could look forward to another summer of banter. And then that gaze that changed everything. It dredged up memories of Sesenheim and Friederike's simple girlishness. Eyes full of passion, but everything changing so quickly, as if every mood had to be abandoned immediately in order to become clear. Friederike's mouth knew so little of what it was doing that you yourself had to supplement her ignorance and inquisitiveness with your own. And Charlotte Buff, the great sentimentalist who held and extinguished the universe in a sigh. He had then taken what she awoke in him and augmented it immensely: Werther's Lotte. Afterward, Charlotte rightly complained about what he had made of her in the novel. He himself was Werther's Lotte just as much as he was Werther. And Christiane, the great emotion that was never too self-absorbed for every accommodation. There was no situation she couldn't master through subservience. And then Marianne, who wanted to be a completely kindred soul and was able—with enormous spiritual energy—to adapt herself almost to the point of self-dissolution. But only as a costume ball, a cultural sensation, a splendid anecdote for the literary historians. And Ulrike. Two years of girlish enchantment composed entirely of entertaining indirection. Last year, still a delicate not-yet-awakeness, a lively desire to participate, always striving to do everything right—a landscape on which the sun had not yet risen. And now the sun is up, the landscape lives. Now, her gaze. There is no defense. And besides, what is there to defend against? You've been taken captive, a captive of that gaze.

He had to sit down at his desk. This Ulrike, Contresse Ulrike, belongs in his novel, in the very much behind-schedule second version of *Wilhelm Meister's Journeyman Years*. Hersilie is the figure he can enrich through the Contresse. But not a word about it to Ulrike. However much you'd like to let it slip that she's going to be in your novel, control yourself! You must never tell a source she's a source, because then she would cease to be one.

He couldn't go to bed. He wasn't ready for the self-abandonment known as sleep. If he could hope to dream of her, then yes, gladly. But as things stood? Exchange a wakefulness in which he could think uninterruptedly of her, imagine her, for a condition of slumber in which she probably wouldn't occur at all? Not yet.

Walk up and down. Stop at each window. Look across the street. Which window does she sleep behind? Last year he, too, had lodged in the Klebelsberg house, which was called a palais as well as a hotel. Apart from the fact that the young widow Levetzow was the mistress of Count Klebelsberg,

Ulrike's grandfather Broesigke had a permanent landlord's right to the palace. This year Grand Duke Carl August was also planning to take the waters in Marienbad, and since he was an old friend of the Broesigke, Klebelsberg, and Levetzow families, he simply had to stay in their house, on the second floor to be precise, in the prince's suite where Goethe had stayed the year before. It would soon be fifty years that Carl August had been Goethe's sovereign, Goethe's employer, and Goethe's friend. Goethe could have stayed in the Klebelsberg Palace again, but he decided instead on the Golden Grape across the street. And after what had just happened, he wondered what wise instinct had told him to do so. Being under the same roof now, but separated by walls and stories, he would have to invent some kind of noise that could reach her to announce that he was there and unable to breathe if she did not learn, sense, hear that he was there. There for her alone. She has a small face but a nose one would not call little. And plum-pit-shaped eyes that change color but always shine. He had already taken that fact home with him in the preceding years: those never weary, never dull, always shining blue and green eyes. Mostly, however, they aren't blue or green, but blue-green. He had to turn to her mouth. Her lips were no mountain range, but a full and harmoniously shaped upper lip that could rely on the modest services of the lower lip. Almost a bit lonely, this mouth in the lower half of her face. The nose keeps to itself. Just a hint, almost imperceptible, of a bend. It simply has no intention of running dully, boringly straight. Those who don't look closely think it's pointy. In reality, it ends in a point that is, in the final analysis, rounded. It ends, as a nose must, above her lonely, beautiful mouth: by pointing the way to it without infringing on its space. This face has a grandiose unobtrusiveness, contains the entire Ulrike. Now he regrets having always drawn landscapes and never people. To be sure, this Ulrike-face is the first face in the life gallery of faces he would have liked to draw. It is a landscape in the light. If he weren't a draftsman but a painter, he would have called it an unearthly, shining light. One could paint it, but not draw it.

He had to stand before the large mirror in the dressing room, lamps flanking it on both sides.

The proprietor of the Golden Grape was known in town as a lighting fanatic. He never missed a trade fair where he might come across a new kind of lamp. That piece of information could have been what made the choice of this hotel pleasant for the privy councilor. He clasped his hands behind his back, producing a practiced, stately appearance. He felt compelled to walk into the study and fetch from a drawer the Viennese journal sent him by a certain Herr Braun von Braunthal, a twenty-one-year-old poet, because in it he had described a visit to Goethe in Weimar. Goethe laughed every time he read the part of the report—and it was the only part he did read—that concerned his appearance.

For me in that moment, however, it was not the banal shell of a civilized man; as he paused a second at the door and his eyes fell on me, Goethe really seemed like a statue of Zeus carved from Parian marble. That head! That figure! That demeanor! Beauty, nobility, majesty! Already an old man of seventy-three, hair white as new-fallen snow cascading in waves about his sturdy neck, his noble features still strong, the muscles still firm, the high, rounded forehead smooth and pure as if of alabaster, lips with the expression of untroubled self-confidence, simultaneous dignity and gentleness, the lifted chin expressing strength, and finally the eyes, splendid, sky-reflecting, miniature mountain lakes of pure blue! Of all the likenesses of him I have ever seen, not a single one matched this admirable totality of greatness, beauty, and power. With the utmost artistic effort, one might very well recreate such a unity in a statue—as has been done—but never in a painted picture; no more than one would be able to paint Monte Rosa or Mont Blanc transfigured by the rays of the setting sun. Thus Goethe appeared, and my spirit revered him. How lucky I considered myself, being a still insignificant and as yet unformed young man; for I knew very well that he sometimes refused to receive important, experienced men, and I could see from his casual attire that he was either making an exception or not going to too much trouble for me. He turned his gaze upon me like a regal boa constrictor upon a doe. Except that he didn't crush me to death, but walked slowly to the divan—the "west-eastern divan"—inviting me with a gentle gesture to follow him and then (oh joy!) to sit down beside him. He began the conversation with a mild earnestness, and it coursed through all my limbs like a benevolent electric charge when the lordly old poet gently took my hand, a hand trembling

with rapture and veneration, enclosed it softly in both
of his, looked into my eyes, and said . . .

With conflicting feelings, he returned the magazine to the
drawer, walked back to the mirror, smiled a little, and saw the
gap where one of his front teeth was missing, missing for
thirteen years. He still hadn't gotten used to it. He had, however, disciplined his mouth so that the gap never appeared in
the presence of other people. He hoped. He had assigned his
daughter-in-law Ottilie to pay attention and report to him
whenever some excess of high spirits allowed the gap to be
seen. In his opinion, Ottilie always delivered her reports with
somewhat too obvious satisfaction. He didn't conceal the gap
from himself when he was alone. Now, for instance. As if he
had known ahead of time or feared what was happening now,
in his recently published story "The Man of Fifty," he had
written that with such a gap, it was quite humiliating to court
a young woman.

He went into the bedroom, lay down as he was on the
bed, and ran through the figures in his books, looking for a
sentence to express what now dominated him. There was
such a sentence. Fairly quickly he summoned it up from
memory. While still quite young, his Wilhelm Meister had
thought: So it's all for naught.

Chapter Two

IF HE, SEVENTY-FOUR, were to marry her, nineteen, then she, nineteen, would be the stepmother of his son August, thirty-four, and his daughter-in-law Ottilie, twenty-seven. He found himself preoccupied with such calculations while sitting at a breakfast table spread with everything one could wish for, procured by Stadelmann from the catering house.

Today he was sending Stadelmann—whom he had taught how to identify rocks during the past two years—to the Wolfsberg to break out some augite. A feldspar macle would be extremely welcome as well, he told him. To his secretary John, he said he wouldn't need him for dictation till eleven. The reason was that Dr. Rehbein, medicus to the Weimar court and also Goethe's personal physician (who had spent many hours at Christiane's deathbed as well!), had sent word of his arrival. Within the past year, Dr. Rehbein's own wife, his third, had died, too. Dr. Rehbein was probably the most beloved man in Weimar.

When Goethe appeared in the room where he received

guests, Dr. Rehbein was waiting and rushed up to greet him. He barely gave Goethe the chance to boast how healthy he felt here—completely free of last winter's miserable shortness of breath—he was so bubbling over with his own news: He intends to get engaged. He simply has to. If he doesn't propose at once, he will lose Catherina—yes, Catty von Gravenegg, thirty years his junior. Since he had to get here before the Duke in any case, there is nothing for it but to celebrate the engagement here in Marienbad. But it's impossible to imagine doing that without the presence of the Herr Privy Councilor. He apologizes for his unseemly haste. "But—Catty . . .You understand." He cannot pretend to act as His Highness's spa physician here. It's not allowed in any case, since the local doctors have that monopoly. All right, so he's just a spa guest in the entourage of His Highness, et cetera. But to spend weeks here promenading, seeing and being seen, while Catty rattled around Munich—it's unhealthy. So she's coming here and there's going to be an engagement. But he must confess how much it pains him to have just read in "The Man of Fifty" that a surgeon is the most venerable man in the whole world.

Goethe amplified: "He frees one from a genuine malady." Then he gently embraced Dr. Rehbein and said, almost whispering into his ear, that the praise for the surgeon was necessary to the action of his journeyman novel, of which "The Man of Fifty" constituted a part. And although it was published two years ago, that novel was anything but finished. Every day he was beset by characters and sentences begging to be included. And Wilhelm, the hero of the *Journeyman Years*, is meant to become a physician, a surgeon, once he has studied and sampled everything the world has to offer. And why? Because for the Wilhelm he had spent his life describing, the author wanted a profession tailor-made for his body and inscribed in his soul, one through which he could do the most good for mankind. "To be of use, Herr Doctor. From the useful through the true to the beautiful. That's the direction we all want to go, Herr Doctor." And he could have plausibly added that Dr. Rehbein himself was a prime example. When someone like him, a physician, can stand here at fifty, so truly hale and handsome, he's neglected nothing, made no mistakes. There followed a long handshake.

The doctor had left with the privy councilor's cordial acceptance of the invitation to the engagement party. Goethe sat and thought: thirty years his junior. It wasn't envy that he was feeling. He considered the visit a confirmation. Well, yes, some envy, too. For what is envy but a form of admiration condemned to misfortune? There cannot be enough fifty-year-olds getting engaged to twenty-year-olds! Let there be an outbreak, an epidemic of engagements. If only so that with his own enormous number—seventy-four minus nineteen equals fifty-five—he doesn't look quite so absurd.

He saw what an invigorating effect Dr. Rehbein's visit had from the fact that at the door and as casually as possible, he had asked the physician—who would just now be crossing the street and entering the Klebelsberg palais—to give his best to all the Levetzows, especially Ulrike, and tell her that this afternoon he could fulfill the wish she had expressed yesterday. At any time. He could tell that his courier, Dr. Rehbein, did not quite know how the message was to be understood, i.e., how he should deliver it, so Goethe added in a tone of extreme unimportance, "One has to educate children when they request it." Then he held on to the curtain and watched as Dr. Rehbein crossed the street and disappeared into the Klebelsberg palais.

His secretary John was informed that when the mail came, he should bring it into the study only if Fräulein von Levetzow had arrived and taken a seat. Perhaps Ulrike had forgotten that yesterday she'd said, "But who is he?" If she had forgotten, if it was nothing but an empty phrase, then everything was and is an empty phrase and he is nothing but an illusionist. Perhaps there's no such thing as her gaze; perhaps with her nineteen years she's the calmest, most composed, least moveable person in her family.

He had to emit a brief cry, a negation of the internal conversation that had just happened to him. And once more, a brief cry. And because it was his habit not only to allow to happen everything that happened to him, but also to make himself aware that it was happening, he allowed the conversation with himself to continue: When I let out a cry—a little cry, not too loud—then always such that only I hear my cry. I really do not want anyone else to hear me crying out. And besides, he didn't have to cry out yet, only sit and wait. If she doesn't come, he will sit here and never move again, a man frozen in waiting. He was surprised that the pain caused by waiting did not enable some kind of movement—walking up and down, perhaps. He wanted to demonstrate it to himself. That was his condition: Ulrike, or nothing. Just think of it: Last year, in that very family circle, he himself, sitting here right now (he who no longer knows how to draw a breath without Ulrike's encouragement) had trumpeted his wish to have another son, who could then marry Ulrike. He himself would like to train Ulrike to be the perfect match for his son. He no longer knew that person who had talked so big, with such paternalistic mendacity. For it was already dishonest even back then. Not morally dishonest, but an outbreak of weakness, of cowardice. He could never say something like that again. But Ulrike hadn't yet been Ulrike, either; she was still asleep in her girlhood. But now . . . but she still wore no jewelry. Her neck, her earlobes, bare. Hadn't she worn any last summer, either, or the summer before? Perhaps because the weather had been so bad. But now, in this stupendous summer! Did she want to differentiate herself from all the women festooned with jewelry?

Here she came. An almost colorless green dress whose many little buttons precisely traced her figure. The neck trimmed with lace. Her hair always a little looser than all the other women. He had no trouble standing up. She greeted him almost jauntily. It wasn't the mood he was in. At least, he couldn't maintain that tone. But once she was sitting on the sofa, in one of the sofa corners with her arm on the big yellow cushion, he was able to walk back and forth and speak as though to several people. Soon his secretary John came in and handed him the tray piled high with mail.

"Ah, here's the mail," he said. "Ach, no, my dear John, one can't read any boring letters when one has such a visitor. But don't leave. I want to show my visitor how things go around here. Oh, just a moment, here's something urgent. You see," he said to Ulrike, "we're so well coordinated, my faithful John and I, that he puts the only letter that can't wait on top of the pile. It's urgent, because His Royal Highness will be leaving Weimar in a week so a reply has to go out today. If you please, John." He turned to Ulrike. "May I?"

"You must," she said.

He paced back and forth in front of Ulrike, dictating: "Our most gracious Royal Highness has deigned to disclose to the undersigned that His Majesty has the intention of delighting Herr Lenz, our excellent Councilor of Mines, on the occasion of his imminent jubilee with a number of princely gifts, of which the following is a preliminary list. The celebration will consist of a banquet. My unpresumptuous suggestion would be: As pièce-de-résistance we present the erupting Vesuvius, under which the medal intended for the honoree could be placed." He paused and asked Ulrike, "Do you understand?"

Ulrike asked what unpresumptuous suggestions were.

That was a polite circumlocution for not wanting to make unauthorized assumptions.

"And what does that mean?" asked Ulrike.

"My suggestion is meant only as a suggestion. The grand duke must decide. You see, Councilor of Mines Lenz is a passionate Neptunist and for his jubilee he'll be served a volcano-shaped cake for dessert, at the bottom of which he'll discover the medal he's to be awarded. To be sure, the grand duke will take my suggestion into account when he decides."

Ulrike: "But only unpresumptuously."

Goethe: "Exactly."

Ulrike: "A wonderful word. I'm going to ask Mother not to wear her bright blue dress again today. My unpresumptuous suggestion would be the light beige one."

Goethe: "And she will obey."

Ulrike: "So, unpresumptuous is a kind of command."

Goethe: "The most polite kind of urgent wish."

Ulrike: "But even more important: It's a compliment. The recipient feels included. I give him credit for understanding exactly what I mean. It flatters him. Herr Privy Councilor is very subtle."

"That will be all for today, John."

John left. Goethe sat down on the sofa next to Ulrike and said he would like to call everything he ever says to her unpresumptuous. It will give him the courage to say more than he ought to. "May I unpresumptuously make you a Royal Highness for a moment?"

"My education has been in a postrevolutionary boarding school," said Ulrike. "Her Royal Highness is all ears."

Goethe jumped up and began to pace back and forth, declaiming, "There would be one more devoutly modest request. Would Her Highness favor me with continuing benevolence, think of me in the most generous light, and in the near future graciously grant me the opportunity to address her on a large variety of subjects?"

He stopped in front of her, would gladly have sunk to his knees but knew he might have trouble getting up again. She extended her hand to be kissed. He held her hand an unconscionably long time, but touched it only slightly with his lips. Almost not at all.

Ulrike jumped up. "Ah, your Excellency," she said, "how much has been wrecked by the Revolution!"

He answered offhandedly, "I want to say quite unpresumptuously that I'd like to spend time only with you."

"I don't yet know," she said, "what I should have against that."

"The way you talk to me," he said, "awakens something in me. I can't quite name it—don't want to, since it's barely stirred. But it feels invigorating."

She said she had to go over and give her mother the unpresumptuous suggestion.

"Yes, go. Every second in your presence is . . . a . . . revolution. I'm afraid."

She gazed at him, said nothing.

"Now your eyes are green," he said. "Pure green."

"Being afraid isn't so bad," she said in a loud, harmless, throwaway, casual tone.

And he: "It would be lovely to have someone who feels exactly the same fear as oneself. That would be closeness. The very essence of proximity."

"Oh," she said, "that's one of your sentences again. Having someone who feels exactly the same fear as oneself. May I say what I think, Excellency?"

"Whoever doesn't tell me what she thinks insults me," he said.

"Another one of your sentences. To me, they always have such a finality about them. No more thinking possible or necessary. It is as it is, or rather, as you've said it is. Physics and chemistry are my favorite subjects; they're the most inter-esting because things happen in them. They yield results because there's an experimental protocol. What if we—only you and I, of course—were to experiment with your sentences, or any sentences, that have that authoritative ring? Would that be forbidden or interesting?"

And he: "The more forbidden, the more interesting."

"Another one of those majestic sentences!" said Ulrike,

but laughed merrily. Then she said, "Well, before you decree any further decrees (perhaps you've been a minister of state too long?), I'm going to propose that all these sentences are just as valid when you turn them around."

Goethe was able to reply with no less merriment that Ulrike's sentence far exceeded all of his in its apodictic urgency.

"However," said Ulrike, "I shall immediately offer evidence that the opposite sounds just as valid. I don't say it is, but it sounds like it."

"If you please," he said.

She: "It would be lovely to have someone who precisely does not feel the same fear one suffers from."

He: "Don't stop!"

She: "Whoever tells me what he thinks insults me. And please, Excellency, don't consider if that corresponds to your experience, but only if it sounds just as valid as its opposite."

"Ulrike," he said, "you're starting to get dangerous in the most desirable way. And please, don't turn that sentence around. That's enough for today."

"Are you angry with me, Excellency?"

"Ulrike," he said, "at the moment I could consider my life bungled because I didn't have you."

Ulrike said that sounded heartwarming without having to be true.

Goethe remembered two years ago, bringing a copy of the just-published *Journeyman Years* to Marienbad for Ulrike and inscribing it "In friendly recollection of August 1821." And they met here last year, were meeting again this year, and she had never even mentioned the book. He knows what that means but doesn't want to spell it out. But it spells itself out inside him. For Ulrike, the *Journeyman Years* are unreadable. And if they're unreadable for Ulrike, they're altogether unreadable. He's got to be able to think that.

Ulrike said there was something else that couldn't be put off. As a reader of his work, she knew that he didn't allow situations to pass without having exploited them pedagogically, and that's why she was going to imitate him and for fun, offer him something instructive.

He made a gesture inviting her to continue.

She said that yesterday her ever lively sister Amalie had made the mistake of asking him how he liked her dress.

"Yes," said Goethe, "and I said it was very pretty."

And Ulrike: "'But Ulrike's is prettier,' you added."

And Goethe: "To which your sister replied, 'I didn't even need to ask that. Everything about Ulrike is always prettier.'"

"It wasn't necessary," said Ulrike.

"But it was true," said Goethe.

"'True' is no excuse for an embarrassment."

"Another one of those majestic sentences!" he cried.

"The assumption was that I would imitate you. If you criticize me now, you're criticizing yourself."

"I capitulate," he said.

"Please don't forget that Amalie is sixteen," she said.

"Barely, or already?" Goethe asked.

"Barely and already," said Ulrike.

And he: "I have to admire you, Ulrike."

"So many things one has to do!" she said. "But I'm glad. Of course. Very glad. Adieu." And left.

Leaning against the curtain, he watched her cross the street. Watched how she walked, how she seemed about to become airborne with every step. She walked as if walking uphill, but with utter ease. She was enormously light. Since he could not call after her to say what he felt, he got out the poem he had written her a few days ago because they had missed each other on the promenade. When he went to give it to her, she said she would like to hear him read it first. And he did:

> Beside the warm spring, there you pass your days.
> But that is troubling and unclear.
> For since I hold you wholly in my heart,
> I cannot fathom that you're there and here.

"Lovely," she had said.

And he: "Do you think so?"

And she: "It's lovely to be addressed like that."

He'd called her *du* in the poem, not the formal *Sie*.

Then she'd said, "We'll have to miss each other more often."

Now he sat down at his desk and wrote, "The loveliest of all the loveliest dancers." And had the pleasant feeling of having outdone himself again.

Chapter Three

NOW HE WAS never to be seen without her, nor she without
him. Everyone saw it. And Goethe saw that everyone saw him
with Ulrike on his arm. He enjoyed their looks, the heads
bent in whispering, and he always saw to it that Ulrike and
he were talking to each other. He presented himself and
Ulrike as a couple in discussion, a couple always enthused
about something, a couple with more to say to each other
than all other couples on earth. It had to be clear to anyone
who, glass in hand, had an eye out for someone to chat with
on the promenade that this couple was so caught up in conversation that they must not be disturbed. Goethe, however,
had not only to demonstrate their inviolability but also be on
the lookout for someone showing up among the strollers to
whom he could serve up Ulrike, simply because the person
was so important or so famous that it spoke well of Goethe
to serve Ulrike to such a celebrity. Last summer, he and
Countess Strachwitz had tried this out as a game. He told her
that she and he would now promenade while conversing so

animatedly that no bored stroller would dare disturb them.
That had been a game. Now it was serious.

Since she, a pupil in a Strasbourg boarding school, was
interested in all things French, he began to talk about her
situation when he spied the Count of Saint-Leu approaching.
This was Napoleon's brother, Louis Bonaparte. He used to
be King of Holland, but after a falling-out with his brother
he was then the Count of Saint-Leu. He'd been devoted to
Goethe for years because he made poems and every summer
waited to see what Goethe thought of his newest productions.
Goethe thought them not bad at all, and so he admitted the
count to their conversation, said something friendly about the
poems, and asked for permission to show them to Fräulein
von Levetzow soon, who as a boarding-school Strasbourger
had more sympathy for French literature than for German.
But Goethe also saw to it that such tolerated intruders didn't
stay very long. When they had bidden Count Saint-Leu adieu,
Goethe told Ulrike that his secretary John was currently at
work compiling a list of all his writings since 1769 for the
count, who was going to have them translated into French.
He would then be very eager to hear her opinion of them. Of
course, Ulrike wanted to hear about Napoleon himself more
than about the poet and former King of Holland. Goethe was
happy to oblige. On the day of the Battle of Leipzig, a plaster
relief of Napoleon that hung in his study in Weimar fell all by
itself from its nail. And Napoleon's eyes, had he mentioned
them? Napoleon's gaze that everyone feared? It was said to
be penetrating and sharp, piercing, that gaze. In his three
encounters with the Corsican, Goethe had not found that
to be the case at all. "He had a steady gaze," Goethe said,

looking at Ulrike. "He didn't blink, ever, as if his eyelids were made of stone. Yours are certainly not like that, Ulrike, but you have that steady gaze, too. You never blink. And the ancients relate that that's how you can tell the difference between gods and men. Men blink, the gods don't." And he looked at her, and she looked at him, on the promenade, a hundred paces from the Kreuz Spring.

She broke the spell. She said, "But he was always friendly to you."

"Yes," said Goethe. Napoleon had purportedly read *Werther* seven times. And of course, he'd found something to criticize.

"What could that have been?" asked Ulrike. "I'm all ears."

"He said I had mixed Werther's motives," said Goethe, "to have one reinforce the other. Werther's not just unhappy in love, his pride and ambition have also been wounded. One unhappiness reinforces the other, and Napoleon thought that was an error. He found it unnatural. It weakened the figure of Werther, who ought to be unhappy as a lover. Love, unrequited love, should have been the only reason for his ruination."

"I agree," said Ulrike.

He said he hadn't just disagreed with Napoleon, but had also told him that the artist needed to be concerned with the effect, and heightening—exaggeration—was called for.

"But Napoleon was right," said Ulrike. "The fact that Werther was also unhappy in his career means that as an unhappy lover, he wasn't so unhappy that he had to kill himself because of it. It makes him smaller, more mundane, less interesting."

"But more believable," said Goethe. "He's easier to identify with."

"And that's a shame," said Ulrike. "He should be a flagrant miracle of unhappiness from nothing but love."

"In fifty years," he said, "no one in all of Europe has seen that except Ulrike von Levetzow and Napoleon I."

"Napoleon had an unconditional character," she said. "Better no effect at all than a predictable one."

To inflate his importance for Napoleon, Goethe said that at any rate, the emperor had ordered a Brutus-tragedy from him. "His thought was probably to get a thorough besmirching of regicide."

"Napoleon," she said, "made it to St. Helena himself, without Brutus."

Goethe had to add that Napoleon had named him *officier de la Légion d'Honneur*, which offended his dear, respectable Germans.

Ulrike asked why he never wore his medal.

"Should I?" he asked in return.

"No," she said.

Such agreements were always sealed with a silent exchange of glances. He felt that with no other person on earth would he find such concurrence. A graybeard had just greeted them in passing, and Goethe told her that he had been a quartermaster in Champagne, and when Ulrike wrinkled her forehead in inquiry, he added: "Campaign of 1792." When he realized that that information had no perceptible effect, either, he added that it had rained for the entire campaign in France. That still made no impression. And so he went on to say that he had mostly been busy writing in his diary. Sometimes one just can't do anything right. After two more sentences in which he described himself as a darling of fate, but then found that excessive, he heard himself say without transition that he'd never had any enemies, but many adversaries. All contemporary physicists rejected his theory of colors and simply parroted Newton. And then had to give her a lecture about how his adversaries dissected light and the eye although in reality, they never occurred apart. He left light and the eye in place as the precondition of his theory of colors. Since he had celebrated Ulrike's eyes on that first day on the promenade, he thought she could still be won over to his point of view. On the other hand, when he listened to himself complaining about his miseries with the theory of colors, he knew he could not do himself greater harm than with these querulous remarks about the injustice of the world.

Then luckily, a thunderstorm began and so she learned from him what Seneca had written: that people struck by lightning always lay on the ground faceup. When Ulrike was amazed at how much he knew, he said he had heard about victims of lightning from Chief Detective Superintendent Grüner in Eger, whom he visited every year on his way from Weimar to Bohemia, and again on the way back. He'd climbed practically every single knoll, hill, and mountain around here with him, looking for unusual stones. Who else but this police official could have told him that the shawm was forbidden under Louis XIV because the Swiss were dying of homesickness when they heard it. And as soon as he stepped through Grüner's door, his first sentence was always: Well, my good fellow, what are your newest acquisitions? And Grüner would reply: Everything at your service, Excellency. I owe it all to you.

"*Ach ja*, Ulrike, if only one always associated with people who owed one everything."

And Ulrike: "What would that get you?"

"You could say," said Goethe, "whoever's grateful to me, I'm more grateful to him for being grateful to me than he could ever be to me."

"You always want to outdo everyone," said Ulrike.

"Only because I don't want to be outdone," he said.

"Only because you know you always outdo everyone."

"Ulrike," he said, "the way I can talk to you here and you to me—can you recall last year and the year before in the deep valley of Karlsbad, were we ever able to talk like this to each other?"

"There's something American about Marienbad," she said. He didn't get it right away.

"Just look at this wide pastureland. Up there at its highest edge, where the forest begins—one hotel next to another. Three, four gigantic hotels plopped down in the middle of a green wilderness. Four years ago, that's all there was here: green wilderness." That's what she thought was American.

"The Klebelsberg palais," he said, "is itself a provocation. Four stories with a hundred rooms and a magnificent façade fifty meters wide. Can that end well?"

"Excellency, if something must end well, it will," she said like a strict teacher. In his tone of voice, actually.

Goethe marveled at her and asked whom he was hearing when she talked like that.

"Me," she said. But whereas he got all his information about lightning victims and Seneca from a certain chief detective superintendent in Eger, she got everything having to do with Marienbad from her future father-in-law, Count Klebelsberg, and her grandfather, Baron Broesigke. The privy councilor ought to hear those two going at it some evening: Marienbad, the greenest wilderness in Europe that always got bypassed by Europe's rich and famous on their way to Karlsbad. Klebelsberg—whose main occupation was, after all, to be the Austrian minister of finance—and her grandfather Broesigke were calculators. Her grandfather had also built a house here. And by the way (she said it only to let Goethe know that her family also included more elevated as well as older members), her mother's father was a godchild of the great Prussian king, Frederick.

"Ah," said Goethe, "what a lovely bridge: from the great Frederick to the American Marienbad."

She said she was sure her grandfather would be pleased to show Goethe the certificate of godparenthood if he'd like to see it.

And Goethe: "I really would like to see it." Apropos, he said, at the end of one of his novels when the hero had the choice of investing money in Russia or America, he had him choose America.

"Change of topic, Excellency!" she announced.

And he: "What's this now?"

She said she'd just been trying to show off with America, but for him it was nothing new; he'd checked it off long ago!

"But sadly, only in a novel," said Goethe in his most melancholy tone.

Of course, Ulrike had figured out that Goethe was proud to be seen walking with her. And she understood that it was important to demonstrate to the Marienbad audience through lively conversation and all its accompanying gestures that they were simply not to be interrupted. That Ulrike appeared in a different dress every day pleased Goethe as much as if he had invented those dresses himself. All her clothes probably came directly from Vienna, from Count Klebelsberg, her mother's friend. All the Levetzow women dressed more vibrantly and indeed, with more thought than the other women, never in a piece of clothing that made its wearer into that piece's presenter. His daughter-in-law Ottilie could learn something from them. But he already knew that if he ever described the velvet and silk, wool and leather of the Levetzow women in Weimar, Ottilie would react with an explosion of nerves, i.e., she'd get sick or angry. Or both. Ottilie's sister Ulrike von Pogwisch had just written him a letter to say how things were going in Weimar. She had heard, she wrote, that Goethe was paying special attention to a namesake of hers. She wasn't the least bit pleased that her name was Ulrike. Back in Weimar, whenever he heard that name he would always think of the other, distant, pretty, amiable Ulrike. In a letter to his son, he had made friendly mention of the Levetzow family. He already had to treat Ottilie more like his own wife than his son August's. Because he was long since familiar with society, he was aware that he and this Ulrike here were known as a couple in rumors, gossipy letters, and diary entries from Zurich to Hamburg. A spa like this was a pot in which rumor was cooked and then shipped out to the whole world. He could imagine which ladies from the promenade wrote hither and yon to which other ladies about him and Ulrike. Out in the world, the rumors then get honed by their recipients. Bettina von Arnim will see to it that no address of any importance is overlooked: Goethe, seventy-four, a von Levetzow, nineteen, her mother, twice widowed and currently chasing a wealthy

Viennese career politician who even accompanies himself on the piano. And just a touch—but only a touch—more genteel: Caroline von Wolzogen, the sister of Schiller's widow Charlotte von Lengefeld and the author of thoroughly charming novels. She will report to her friend Caroline Number Two, wife of the great Wilhelm von Humboldt, in her purposefully ambiguous style, that while on one hand Goethe was no longer quite right in the head, on the other it was still quite impressive he still had enough of his wits about him to fall in love. The particular woman had never mattered much to him; he could always find one to trick out with his fantasies. These gossipy letters will say that the Levetzow women have the knack of staging themselves to their own advantage. And then some correspondent or other will show off with an ethical balancing act: Now that everyone was pouncing on Goethe with universal gossip, wasn't it more original to spare him, to make it a habit to defend Goethe? Maybe some woman in Frankfurt will see him as a natural phenomenon lacking in character. And one of the Carolines will write back saying much the same thing, but with a bit more subtlety.

There was no one he could tell how good it felt to survey the predictable moods of his circle. Whether in the cultured corners of Germany or here in the heat of the Bohemian magic cauldron, they needn't hold back as far as he was concerned. Let them shout it from the rooftops: A scandal! Bad taste! Infamous, dirty old man! A sad end to a great person! He was elated by anything that had to do with Ulrike. He experienced her as an influx of life. More than one unimpeachable observer had told him right to his face how well he looked now, how vibrant, how strong—really handsome.

With such effects, how could he help but worship their cause! After all, there was also plenty of unpretentious approval, which he and Ulrike took in just as unpretentiously. Those were the effects they talked about together. "Did you see that stately woman, Excellency, and how she pointed us out to her three children and waved to us herself until her children did, too!" They were even applauded—it was almost theatrical. To be sure, there were others who said that was going too far and turned away demonstratively from the applauders. The Marienbad Promenade had not been so lively in a long time.

When he brought Ulrike home, the two of them often sat down on the palace's raised terrace that was bordered with pots of flowers. Ulrike, who couldn't get interested in rocks, was drawn to flowers as if to a lost homeland. Again and again she would walk along the floral border, smelling the perfume, and then close her eyes and guess which fragrance belonged to which flower. "They have their own majesty," she said as she sat back down next to him.

"My favorite majesties are the lupines," he said.

"Mine are wolfsbane," she said.

And since he was sitting directly across from her, held fast by her gaze, he said that because Marienbad was so American he needed another round of their court etiquette game as an antidote. She nodded in what he took for pleasure.

And so he began: "First and foremost I owe a debt of thanks to Her Majesty for showing Her humble servant for many a day and in many gratifying ways evidence of Her most amiable notice, such that without delay the hope could arise that the flower—still in its childhood—that I have so tenderly raised from a secret seed may continue to find favor with Her Majesty, the only promise of its happy growth."

And Ulrike continued: "Since We love above all else everything that blooms, We wish it happy growth and condescend to measure what has been called into being with an incalculable yardstick, so that Excellency (in the truest sense) can continue to expect Our affectionate interest."

Now the church's six o'clock bells chimed in. It stood halfway up the hill between the Kreuz Spring Promenade in the valley and the incipient ring of palatial hotels. It still seemed too big for this green solitude. As long as the bells were tolling, no one spoke on the terrace.

Then, carried away somehow, or at any rate less composed than the time and place of their conversation called for, he said, "A trip to Eger with you, Ulrike, wouldn't that be something! With no audience. You and me from Eger westward, to Haslau and beyond Haslau along the mountain ridge, we would come to the forest they call the Kingdom of Heaven. And there, alongside the high road, is the giant quartz rock where I always sit down and do nothing but look. And to do that with you, Ulrike! Forgive me if my wishes sometimes tend to be immoderate." Abruptly he rose to go, but turned back again and said, "Until this evening, dear girl," and gave that gentle bow that was more implied than real. And he walked over to his Golden Grape, walked as well as he could. He knew about difficulties in walking only from hearsay. But the fact that Ulrike might be watching him made his pace uncertain, and so he exaggerated each step. That, however, could look comical. Entering the door across the street, he looked back—surreptitiously, so to speak. The terrace was empty. Ulrike had not watched him go. That didn't meet with his approval, either.

He knew he must write something now. And since he felt strong enough at this moment to present Ulrike even to the least sympathetic audience, he wrote to Ottilie. Ulrike must not be mentioned, but all the sentences that emanated his strength were sentences full of Ulrike. Even with all the strength he felt, he was in a conciliatory mood. Peace with Ottilie! A letter to lull to sleep all the bellicose moods engendered by gossip and rumor.

"It is all succeeding beyond my wildest dreams, gratifying to the heart, the spirit, and the senses, as the saying goes . . ."

It wasn't his style, but if he knew Ottilie at all, she wouldn't read what was on the paper, but what wasn't. She had sensed his feelings for Ulrike von Levetzow before he was fully conscious of them himself. Two years ago when he returned to autumn in Weimar from summer in Bohemia, Ottilie was already armed with rumors that at that point were really nothing but rumors. Lacking the courage to confront him with what Caroline von X or Caroline von Y had told her, she had appended a businesslike request to a note informing him about current household affairs: Would he please not enter into this kind of attachment any more, which his advanced age prevented him from conscientiously fulfilling. He had laughed at her. Back then.

Chapter Four

Dr. Rehbein took up a position in the middle of the ballroom of the recently completed catering house and opened the celebration of his engagement to Catty von Gravenegg by introducing his guests. First came Grand Duke Carl August, then Goethe—His Excellency Privy Councilor and Minister of State Baron von Goethe. Louder applause than for the Grand Duke. Goethe, sitting at the same table as the Levetzows of course, directly across from Ulrike, looked at her as he was being introduced. She didn't applaud until she noticed that Goethe was being applauded more than the Grand Duke. She applauded the applause, then looked over at him. Since the ballroom was not especially brightly lit, her eyes were green.

Dr. Rehbein melted a bit with the heat of his joviality, gratitude, and happiness at being able to greet Napoleon's stepson Eugène de Beauharnais—former Viceroy of Italy, today Duke of Leuchtenberg and Prince of Eichstätt—and Napoleon's brother Louis Bonaparte, former King of

Holland, today the Count of Saint-Leu. "And how fortunate I am in the knowledge that Julie von Hohenzollern is here among us, too. Out in the world, encounters occur in incomprehension, but in Marienbad, history encounters itself." Thunderous applause. Dr. Rehbein asked Catty von Gravenegg to join him. She came. Goethe was seeing her for the first time: a big strong girl, tow-colored hair that had never suffered under curlers or curling iron, down to her bare shoulders. The lace-trimmed décolletage of her black dress was an invitation to imagine the entirety of her considerable bosom. Goethe did so and saw right away how ineffective the image was. All he felt was that he belonged entirely to Ulrike. He wished he could show that to her more clearly.

Dr. Rehbein spoke as only a happy man can. How had he managed to win this girl? "Look at her and look at me." He belonged in the novella in Goethe's *Wilhelm Meister*—"The Man of Fifty." But Catty was not Hilarie, who first embraces the fifty-year-old and then falls for the wild young Flavio. "I'm only gonna fall once in my life," Catty was quick to interpose in her Bavarian accent. Loud applause. She didn't curtsy, she bowed like an actress. They stood there hand in hand, a glorious couple. He in curly black hair, she in a wave of blond, both beaming with happiness.

Goethe watched Ulrike. Because she had turned toward the middle of the room, he saw her from the side. She always made a very erect impression, as if it was easier for her to look up than straight ahead. What was going through her mind? It had not occurred to him that the difference in age of the couple would become a topic of the engagement party. He looked at the couple again, spellbound, moved by their demonstration of pure happiness. He did not fear being watched himself. It would make sense for the entire room to turn and look at him and Ulrike. Go ahead, be my guest. He was justified in calling the thing that now completely filled him a higher unconcern. Was Ulrike sitting up just a little too straight? Ah, if only she would cast a brief glance this way so he could show her his unassailable unconcern and encourage her to be just as unconcerned as he was. As long as he could almost reach out and touch her, or at any rate have her visibly sitting there before him, he was invulnerable. Yes, the world is always ready to wound you, but not here. Marienbad was not the world. Give us a quick look this way, Ulrike, so I can see that you're taking part, see what this heavenly performance of an engagement means to you. Are they playing us? He hoped she was following what was happening in the ballroom with the minimal smile that always meant she had nothing against it. What do you say, Ulrike? Later, when the party continues into the wee hours up in the Klebelsbergs' palais, we'll speak at length about every second we've witnessed together and ask each other, What did you think of that? And you, what did you think? He was happy through and through that together with Ulrike, he was witnessing a public event so beautifully expressive of its own significance. How wonderful were the warm, cozy sessions with her family. How gloriously engaging their dialogues before the watching public on the promenade. But in the end, an event had to happen that they could experience together! And one that seemed made to order for them. And don't go comparing the numbers that obtain here with your numbers. If Ulrike can enjoy this event, she can . . . she can . . . Ah, Ulrike, look at me for just a second.

When Dr. Rehbein had come to the end of his informal unceremonious speech—all the more authentic because it sprang from his feelings of the moment—there was more loud applause. Before he regained his seat, with Catty pressed close by his encircling arm, two servants dressed as carpenters brought in a cradle overflowing with colorfully wrapped and probably suggestive gifts. The grand duke came forward and congratulated the couple, gesturing toward the cradle with its contents as his present. Then he laid the couple's hands together and raised their four joined hands into the air like a trophy—Goethe recalled that ducks were the grand duke's favorite prey—and announced to the room that he had an interest in seeing his personal physician in good hands. Applause. Goethe clapped energetically and commanded his face to wear a knowing smile. Ulrike turned back toward the table, and Goethe nodded to show her that everything here was taking place to his complete satisfaction. Then dinner was served. Dr. Rehbein requested their attention once more. Since his fiancée was a vegetarian, they would eat no meat this evening. But he could promise them that their caterer, M. Charcot, had assembled and prepared the very finest ingredients from every corner of Europe, as only he could. There would even be meat-flavored dishes, but without meat. A few courageous bravos, including one from Ulrike.

For Goethe, Catty von Gravenegg was now twice distinguished—or rather, attractive: once for her Bavarian accent and once for her meatlessness. He was justified in thinking himself an expert in means of expression: this young woman, celebrating her own body in every move she made, and on top of that, a vegetarian. He said to Ulrike that he hadn't known she leaned toward vegetarianism. She raised her eyebrows, threw both hands in the air, and said, "I lean in general, Excellency." From that moment on, she never addressed him as anything but Excellency. And then in fact they experienced a variety of tastes that could not be equaled by any menu with meat as its main attraction. Frau von Levetzow was delighted by the witty way Dr. Rehbein had worked "The Man of Fifty" into his speech and with the white wine from the Loire proposed a toast to the Man of Fifty. Everyone near enough to hear drank a heartfelt toast to the poet. But not Ulrike. Goethe saw that she shook her head and silently mouthed "No wine." No alcohol at all, in fact. He put down his glass and thanked everyone who had drunk to him—or rather, to his Man of Fifty. He himself would have loved to drink along with them, he said, but since he couldn't do anything Ulrike von Levetzow didn't do and she had decided to close her door to wine, for today he'd close his as well.

"What about tomorrow?" asked a young man whose appearance suggested he came from far away. Goethe looked at him. Then he looked at Ulrike. Then he said, "Only the noble Ulrike von Levetzow can decide what tomorrow will bring, *mein Herr*. I'd like to drink to that if I may, Ulrike." She threw her hands into the air in his direction and cried, "*Ja, ja, ja*, Excellency." Goethe took a big swallow.

Then the party moved up to the Klebelsberg palais. They were greeted beneath the arches of the reddish vestibule by the head of the household, who had arrived from Vienna that noon. An even more attractive man than Dr. Rehbein, Count Franz von Klebelsberg welcomed Goethe with open arms, and in a voice that could only have belonged to a singer, he said that although the privy councilor probably couldn't stand to hear it any more, he was at that moment exactly forty-nine—he'd be fifty in January—and had discovered the frightful things in store for him from Goethe's book, which brimmed with the most beautiful details. Without his Amalie von Levetzow, he would flee from that birthday to the North Pole in the hope that there, all dates would be frozen. As soon as Goethe was near enough to be embraced, the count let his arms drop, took a deep bow, and added only, "A very great honor, Excellency."

"Franz," said Ulrike's omni-observant mother, "settle down." And so they moved on into the large ballroom that opened out beyond the vestibule.

The room, finished only a year ago, was a radically Romantic interior with all the necessary decorative excesses. Huge windows into which virtuoso glass cutters had incised floral patterns of differing translucency. In each corner and between every two windows, pairs of red marble columns with nothing to support but acanthus capitals. It was a ballroom of pure playfulness and boisterously dreamy atmosphere. Those who had never been here before congratulated the count. When the spa orchestra began to play, they were immediately in Vienna. Ever since the Congress of Vienna, if you wanted to be modern, young, beautiful, and happy in Europe, you danced the waltz.

Frau von Levetzow saw how the music affected Goethe. "No problem for the Man of Fifty, Herr Privy Councilor," she said. Reading his works, she had always remarked that Goethe never allowed the body to take second place to the soul. But now came the crowning glory, the summit: the Man of Fifty gets a *Verjüngungsdiener*—a valet for rejuvenation, a cosmetic advisor, as it said in the book. "It sounds so businesslike, so reassuring: cosmetic advisor and then valet for rejuvenation. I'd like to give you a kiss for inventing that combination, Herr Privy Councilor." And she kissed him on the cheek. All he saw was that Ulrike was watching her mother sternly, her high, rounded forehead knit into a frown. But her mother wasn't yet finished unloading all her high spirits. Goethe's most beautiful neologism, she said, was the *Schönheits-Erhaltungs-Lehrer*—the beauty preservation teacher—a verbal bouquet so lovely it all but embraced you! "It tempts readers like me to ask how much is autobiographical . . ."

A disapproving "Mama!" from Ulrike was all it took. "Come, Excellency," she said and stood up. It was clear she was asking Goethe to dance. Pointing to Ulrike, he asked her mother's forgiveness for his abrupt departure, which couldn't have been more opportune. On the way to the dance floor she walked close by his side, took his arm, slipped hers through his as she always did wherever she appeared with him in Marienbad. He drew her to him almost impulsively. She turned to look at him and said, "Please forgive her. Frau Amalie von Levetzow *est parfois un peu volubile.*"

Goethe had been avoiding balls and tea dances for the past few years. Since the Congress of Vienna, three-quarter time had come to be a creed. Of course, he was interested in what that meant and how it was expressed. Years ago, he'd had a dancing master show him the steps—in his private apartment—in case he ever needed to know them. And that was the case now. A custom that had survived from earlier times was cutting in. A woman or a man was permitted to tear a dancing couple apart by cutting in. He'd always been a dancer. It used to be that, if the nights acquiesced, he would often abandon a partner and pretend to—or probably really did—go crazy as a solo act. Now he was with Ulrike. At once she became a part of him, lying so lightly in his hands and arms and bent outward by the spin. They were one body. He wasn't the least bit fearful that something could happen. Their eyes were locked together so tightly that neither she nor he got dizzy. But he was cut in on, and by the young man who had asked "What about tomorrow?" down in the catering house. Now should have been Goethe's turn to cut in on another couple and get himself a new partner. But he could dance only with Ulrike. The whole world ought to understand that. Back at the table, his dancing skill and condition were admired. He found it offensive, and said so.

He asked Frau von Levetzow who it was who had cut in on him.

It was a Herr de Ror, perhaps a Greek, definitely not a Turk. He'd made his money in the Orient trade, was fabulously wealthy, and dealt only in the finest things. In jewelry, not in spices. There wasn't a queen, princess, or countess in Europe on whom he hadn't hung a necklace or placed a tiara. The ladies in Paris knew him, as did those in London and Vienna. And besides that, he was also a translator, translated poetry from many languages, especially Oriental ones. It was said he knew seven languages.

He asked how she knew so much about him.

"From Franz. He's the one who invited him. He lives here in the hotel, in the second-biggest suite." By which she meant that the grand duke was in the biggest. "What's curious is that he's a man without a given name. There is much speculation about that."

With the prelude "May I take the liberty of joining you for a moment?" the Duke of Leuchtenberg plopped down on Ulrike's empty chair. "We have an appointment," he began.

"I know," said Goethe.

"That's all right then," said the duke. "So I haven't ridden my coach up to Marienbad from Rome for nothing. The fact that you recall our conversation, Herr Privy Councilor, gives me reason to hope. It was right here in this house, almost exactly a year ago—we were still complaining about all the hammering going on. And now? All finished, a fairy-tale house. What a fellow this Klebelsberg is! My congratulations, dear Lady . . . That you remember, Herr Privy Councilor, tells me that we're going to keep going: The Rhine–Danube Canal will be built! I'm an Austrian—forgive me, a Bavarian by marriage—and you and I, Herr von Goethe, shall give birth to the idea. Others will build it . . ."

Goethe interrupted the voluble fellow: As impolite as it was, there was nothing he could do at the moment, he said, but watch everyone dancing at the Viennese command. Weimar was still dancing to the tune of the ancien régime and he felt it his duty as a retired Weimar minister of state to act as its spy here. While he spoke, he did not take his eyes off Ulrike and Herr de Ror for even a second. There was nothing for the Duke of Leuchtenberg to do but also turn his attention to the dancers. Goethe continued to play the schoolmaster. He thought it would be foolish, he said, to pass up, for inconsequential reasons, a proffered opportunity to learn something. "There, look at that."

And everyone looked. De Ror was positively slinging Ulrike around. At times, he was holding her with just one hand and her free arm flew freely through the air. Again, the fabulous independence of all her joints was observable. Her head itself seemed to fly along its own orbit on her long, slim neck. And Herr de Ror was the gentleman making it fly, while remaining comparatively still himself. Gradually, more and more people were watching this couple. Even couples still dancing gave up, stopped, and watched. Then a rather stocky young man stepped into their path and tried to cut in. But Herr de Ror ignored him, so the stocky man tried to trip him. Herr de Ror jumped over the other's leg and amazingly enough, took Ulrike with him, preventing them both from falling. He continued to hold Ulrike with his left hand, but with his right fist, he gave the interloper such an uppercut that he fell backward and didn't get up again. The orchestra struck up a brisk imperial march and couples returned to their tables with playfully military step, while four waiters carried the unconscious man out of the ballroom and Dr. Rehbein trotted along behind them.

"The poor man," said the Ulrike-mother.

"Do we know his name?" asked Goethe.

"The count gave him a lift from Vienna in his carriage today. He's his protégé, a young poet."

"A poet," said Goethe.

"Braun von Braunthal," she said.

Goethe jumped up, looked toward the door where the young poet had just been carried out. Braun von Braunthal, the gushing enthusiast whose hymnic description he had just reread. Braunthal wanted to reclaim Ulrike—for us. Goethe sat down and reproached himself for not doing anything for the felled young man.

Herr de Ror returned with Ulrike. Since Napoleon's step-son didn't realize whose chair he was sitting on, Ulrike now sat down next to Herr de Ror.

Ulrike said, "I'm so sorry for that man."

And de Ror: "The rule is always, that if you want to cut in, you wait until they finish the piece they're dancing to. Or doesn't that count anymore?"

Everyone confirmed that was still the rule.

Ulrike repeated how sorry she was for him.

Fortunately, Count Klebelsberg had sat down at the piano and attracted everyone's attention with a few virtuoso glis-sandi. Now in his lovely voice he announced that he was going to perform the newest setting of one of the most beau-tiful poems of our master here, since he assumed—knew for certain, in fact—that no one here had yet heard what Franz Schubert had done with Goethe's "*Nur wer die Sehnsucht kennt.*"

> Only the yearning know
> How much I suffer!
> Alone and cut off
> From every joy,
> I gaze at the firmament
> In that direction.
> So far away is he
> Who knows and loves me!
> My head is spinning and
> Inside I'm burning.

Only the yearning know
How much I suffer!

At first, there was utter silence. Then suddenly, as if a conductor had given the entrance, everyone broke into thunderous applause. For Count Klebelsberg first, but then for Goethe. He stood up, bowed, and raised his clasped hands in thanks to the singer. He had no defense against that voice. He saw that Ulrike had tears in her eyes, and her mother, too. He thought of Zelter's setting of the poem. Schubert—that name was now often mentioned by Viennese visitors or others who had been there. He was perfectly happy with Zelter's settings. As far as he was concerned, his poems didn't need to be set to music. And now he begin to feel some irritation after all. It was going a bit far, what they'd made of him.

Count Klebelsberg announced that he would sing the *Erlkönig* next, and whoever wasn't carried away by this song belonged in a museum among the rubble from the pyramids.

Laughter. He began to sing and Goethe felt defenseless. It wasn't right that this music could so usurp the text that the words became merely the occasion for enormous, truly demonic gestures. Tonal gestures. A frenzy of pain. Again, he thought of Zelter's straightforward serviceability. Zelter strove to perform the text. This Schubert fellow was trying to tear your soul out of your body, and the text was nothing but a convenient excuse.

"One more time," called Klebelsberg, "at the urgent request of a number of ladies who have never before heard such a thing, '*Nur wer die Sehnsucht kennt.*'"

Very clever, thought Goethe. The effect was ten times as

strong as after the first performance. Some women were openly weeping and embracing one another. Goethe again pumped his clasped hands cordially in Count Klebelsberg's direction. The applause went on and on.

"What now, Excellency?" asked Amalie von Levetzow.

Goethe nodded, gestured toward Ulrike, who now sat farther away than before. But it was clear enough that she had tears in her eyes. Then to dispel the heavy mood, he said, "He certainly has a voice—like seven celestial swarms of bees."

"You make me happy," she said. She would tell the count as much and he would probably die of pride and joy.

The Hohenzollern princess was standing by their table and from partly behind the glistening gold Japanese fan for which she was famous, she asked for the pleasure of waltzing with him if another waltz was to come.

He agreed with gestures learned in the previous century.

Napoleon's stepson had withdrawn with the declaration that he would continue to dog the heels of Herr Privy Councilor. Goethe had not been able to react appropriately, he was so eager to know what was being said at the other end of the table. Ulrike did not return to her now empty chair and sit across from Goethe. She stayed turned toward Herr de Ror and the men he was debating with. Even Amalie von Levetzow, who was sitting right next to Goethe, showed that now she was concentrating on de Ror and the others. And Ulrike! Like a sunflower, not just her head but her entire upper body—even her entire existence—has turned toward this newest sun. He can still just see her, half from behind. They were talking about literature, that much he could make out. Only two names mattered, whether in Vienna or in

Marienbad: Byron and Scott. Everyone agreed. Byron and Scott were the only authors people still read.

Frau von Levetzow interrupted the conversation to say, "And what did Byron say, gentlemen, about our Goethe? He called him the undisputed sovereign of European literature."

Herr de Ror thought it a two-edged compliment. Sovereigns were the ones who had fallen asleep on their thrones while Byron went to Greece to join the fight for independence from the Turks although—no, because his inferior government used its veto at the Congress of Verona to prevent the European nations from supporting the Greeks' war of independence against Ottoman authority.

"Byron just dedicated his *Sardanapalus* to Goethe," said Frau von Levetzow bravely.

"No question about it, Excellency. You are the most vivid monument that ever dominated an era." Everyone applauded this declaration of de Ror's.

Goethe found it necessary to say another word about the veneration for Walter Scott. "His magic, gentlemen, comes from the grandeur of the three kingdoms of Great Britain and the richness of their history. And what do we have to show between the Thuringian forests and the sandy wastes of Mecklenburg? Nothing. In Germany, a good novel will always be an exception. For my *Wilhelm Meister* I had only the most wretched subject matter: a troupe of vagrants staging plays for the provincial nobility."

No one contradicted him, but no one wanted to continue with the topic, either. Goethe was immediately annoyed at himself for tracing the fame and brilliance of Scott's novels to circumstances for which the author was not responsible. And then, too, for his laughable attempt to make his own novel great; look at what I accomplished with the miserable subject matter Germany had to offer. Nor had he said it in a tone that could continue to be played like a ball.

Without the least transition, Herr de Ror began to talk about being in the theater in Vienna day before yesterday: "The leading man enters, slowly removes his splendid helmet and places it on a table. The actor playing the hero is more than elderly. You could see the hands that had just released the helmet, and they were trembling, but then he raises them into the air, and of course they're still trembling. And to his left and right, the lovers both raise their own hands in the air and what do they do? They tremble. But wait, the best is yet to come: The hero's confidant slinks forward to stand beside the other three, raises his hands in the air—and of course, they're trembling—and so we end up with eight trembling hands in the air."

Now everyone at the table was laughing. Herr de Ror pretended he wasn't responsible for the laughter he'd just produced. His head reminded one of the Orient, but you wouldn't consider him an Oriental. A face on the brink of being adult, a manly face above all, a considerable nose, hardly the trace of a mouth, hair cropped close to his skull, dark eyes, a gaze that established distance—in sum: fairly insipid, although vouching for power. This still-young man will never immerse himself in others. He will remain self-contained. Such were the polemics racing through Goethe's head. He could not resist. At once he lost himself imagining de Ror. He had to leave. His gaze said mostly that he would still need to deal with the fellow, but not here. High time to leave!!!

"Until tomorrow," whispered Goethe into the Ulrike-mother's ear. "Many thanks for a lovely evening," and pressed her gently onto her chair so she would stay seated and not make a fuss over him. And he was outside before they had finished laughing about the eight hands trembling in the air. Ulrike had laughed, too, laughed along with the others, in all innocence, so to speak. Was he intending to prescribe what she was permitted to laugh about? Yes, said a voice within him. He tried to take it back and felt like a hypocrite. A last observation: In the meantime, Herr de Ror had laid his arm on the back of Ulrike's chair. Only on the chair? Or was it already around her back or her waist? In his self-imposed hurry, he hadn't been able to ascertain that. But he did hear what he said to her, as heedless of the volume as if they were alone. "*Il-y-a quelque chose dans l'air entre nous.*" And he'd leaned his face toward hers as if she were the doctor checking to see how bad the infection was. That's how overbearing his pantomimed proffer was. The last sentence Goethe heard was another of the theater-lover Herr de Ror's declarations, to the effect that the worst play was still better than the best bore-dom. That was Vienna for you. Then Goethe was outside and quickly across the street and up to his room.

What now? What to do? Where to go? Staying here was out of the question. Stadelmann was asleep and so was John. Should he pack himself?

To know exactly what was to be done and yet not do it, that was the catastrophe.

He knew every second of the day, but in no second did he admit to himself, that this could never be. Never, never, never. He was already lost after that first year. That certain something that is nothing and will always be nothing, and which, the longer it is nothing, becomes more and more important until it becomes what's most important, all-important, the only thing, and fills you up, defines you, makes you blissfully happy, lifts you up to any height only to hurl you down all the more cruelly. His heart was pounding in his chest, throbbing in his throat. He had to throw open a window, inhale fresh air, move his arms. He sensed that there were thoughts that can suffocate you. He could not inhale as much air as he needed. His breathing was short and shallow. His time-tested maxim when some slippery slope, something uncontrollable, some gravitational pull into impossibility made itself felt: Where is your foothold, the well-rehearsed fear of falling into lurid poverty? Nothing impoverishes like unlucky love. Write that down. A god gave you the power to say how much you suffer. What a miserable advantage; you have to be able to shoot yourself. It's torture to have to say how much you suffer. Lotte took the pistol down off the wall for your Werther, cleaned it carefully, and handed it to her Albert, so he could give it to Werther, so he could put an end to his filthy condition with a pistol cleaned by Lotte. Suffering is filthy, makes you filthy. When things get desperate, there's no other way to clean them than with death. You escape by writing. . . . You have never, ever suffered. Till now it was always the others who suffered. Frau Berlepsch: the twenty-page letters she's been writing you for twenty years. It's been a long time since you could stand to read one. The letters of a poor, tedious woman besmirched by suffering who claims to have been born to love you and awaits a response from you—if only for a second. Compassion is closely related to disgust. Now you can write a twenty-page letter to Ulrike von Levetzow and threaten her with further twenty-page letters, since you have to write instead of shooting. That fellow without a given name speaks seventeen languages. He must look down on you in every respect. The size of a guardsman, six feet two at a guess. Slim, but not in the least scrawny. And a face neither wide nor slender, where bones, not flesh, predominate. A massive chin balanced by a sweeping mustache on the rather modest upper lip. An almost too powerful nose, unenlivened by even the slightest curve. Derisively raised eyebrows. A green gemstone in his violet scarf, probably an emerald. The color of her eyes. How fitting. As soon as they're alone, both of them will remark it, celebrate and applaud it. You look handsome today—that's what she said day before yesterday when he came to fetch her for their walk on the promenade. She didn't say, You are handsome. He has stayed in shape, looks good. You can read in a hundred newspapers how good he looks. And yet, the way they're amazed and excited about his appearance is also a blatant insult. Even louder than the paeans to his still fabulous shape he can always hear, You still look pretty good for such an old scoundrel. At your age, any talk about how you look is always an insult. And not just about how you look. Think of Byron and Scott, who dominate the scene. You're *vieux jeu*. But there's nothing either new or bad about that. Bad maybe, but not lethal. You don't die just because you're old. Write it down. What's bad is not being permitted to love anymore. But you are allowed to love. You just have to get used to no longer, never again being loved. Write to Frau Berlepsch—Isolde, that's her name—write her that now you understand her, now you know how you've tortured her with your disregard and pity bordering on disgust. To love without being loved—it shouldn't be allowed. He'd never before suffered this most vicious blow of fate for which Ulrike von Levetzow was born and raised. It's not the only reason for her existence. In Europe she will be a brilliant success as Frau de Ror. And before that, she will have incidentally had the function of teaching you what many have learned from you: how it feels to love without being loved. Once as a cheeky greenhorn you wrote, "No one is currently in love with me and I'm not in love with anyone. Only death stands in the corner." The fact that no one is in love with you is only cruel when you are in love with someone and your love is not returned—or worse, it's rejected. If Creation was ever interested in making the earth and human life on this earth tolerable, then missing in the instructions the Lord gave to mankind via Moses was the most important of all: Thou shalt not love. That is Commandment Number One. Moses was probably so exhausted from climbing the 7,362 feet to the top of the Mountain of Legislation that he didn't hear the first commandment issued by the Lord, a tragic failure that can never be made good. If Moses had brought this commandment down from Sinai, mankind would be missing out on nothing except tragedy. The source of every tragedy has always been love. And how easy it would have been to get along without love! It has never been necessary for reproduction, so what is it for? So we notice we don't live in Paradise anymore. So no human life gets by without suffering. Not one. The Lord was clever enough. I am a jealous God, was his commentary.

Goethe needed to take his clothes off and throw them as

far away as he could. He'd have to burn all the clothes he'd ever worn in Ulrike's presence. You look handsome today. This single sentence in three years. He had seen every time, and enthusiastically confessed to her, how lovely she looked in that dress and that dress and that dress. In the years 1821 and '22 he was already dressing with more thought than ever before in his life. With loving thoroughness, he had assembled his vests and scarves, tailcoats and jackets. She never saw it. And now, this arrant sentence: You look handsome today. Yes, yes, yes, she didn't just say You look handsome, but You look handsome today. God forbid he should think he always looks handsome, to say nothing of being handsome. But a seventy-four-year-old is not handsome under any circumstances. And if he cannot live without being handsome or at least found to be handsome, then he shouldn't take refuge in writing, i.e., whining, but just go ahead and shoot himself.

He stood there in his dressing room before the floor-length mirror. The six lamps on the right and left once again provided the most favorable lighting. He was unable to find the naked man in this mirror repulsive or revolting in the least. He could not resist a sort of affection for this naked fellow. And the feeling was not at all for the person, only for the nakedness. Then, however, a storm arose, a nervousness, an impatience that almost shook him but in any case drove him from the mirror. He yearned for Ulrike to come. Nothing could be more grotesque than to wish Ulrike to come, her marvelous limbs swinging along fluidly, and stand beside this naked man whom someone—he couldn't remember who—had described as a youthful old man. When she had walked beside him, she sometimes had hummed and this almost-singing had directed her movements. Actually, she was always dancing. Now she lay in her bed and the guardsman-sized fellow without a given name lay next to her or on top of her. He doubted she would sacrifice her virginity on the first night, but who knew? This Oriental need not follow the local customs and he might try to persuade her that they were both born to revel—or perhaps perish—in the joys of the Orient anyway. Since he always carried all sorts of jewelry in his luggage, when they had closed the door to his suite behind them he would first see which piece suited her best. The fact that Ulrike wore no jewelry— her considerable neck bare, bare her at least equally considerable earlobes—had to present a challenge to the Oriental non-Oriental. You need some color, dear girl, or perhaps fire— some diamonds. It's clear he wouldn't go to Ulrike's room, but take her to his suite, the second largest in the Palais Klebelsberg. They've already passed the kissing stage. You great man. That's what she said to him once when they were standing under the colonnades, but she probably only meant as a poet. Now she could say it with more conviction. You great big fellow. In case they were past the first kiss. The windows of the ballroom across the way were dark. Here and there in the upper stories, a lighted window. No room really illuminated any longer, only a hint of light promoting all possible actions. *Il-y-a quelque chose dans l'air entre nous.*

Once his breathing had become involuntary again, he returned to the mirror in his dressing room. Wasn't it strange that he felt close to this naked man. He would have liked to caress him, but no, that would be going too far. But there between his soft loins longing to surrender: his genitals, which for his entire life had had the ambition to be all that mattered. His entire life he had had to tame the power-hungry ambition of this member, not always with equal success. There were times when that ambition possessed him more than he dared to admit, awakened by women, of course. He was supposed to wish for and perform solely what that organ wanted. And it had been like that right down to the present day. The fact that this member is not permitted to appear in the language in which life first becomes aware of itself—unless it be in Latin or corrupted—is a disgrace. A cultural disgrace, in fact, and one you've done nothing to overcome. Yes, yes, make excuses, boast of this or that act of linguistic liberation. But the genitals' claim to expression—and that is their claim to life—was still eking out an existence in exile, in a stupid, cowardly dungeon, and that was a deficiency. He again apologized to his member. He extinguished the lights and sat in semidarkness. He felt he couldn't go to bed. Anywhere now but bed. Into his study? No, into the salon. He sat down on the sofa where he sat when visitors came. Once without waiting for him to say where she should sit, Ulrike had gone over and sat down on the sofa. She was so easygoing, so ingenuous. He pressed his face into the golden yellow cushion with a pattern of pale pink birds that only flew in fairy tales. She had rested her arm on that cushion, but oh, how she did it: with a wide sweep ending in a gentle landing. He thought about Lucidor in *Wilhelm Meister's Journeyman Years*. Drowning in his sorrows, he had pressed his face into a cushion when he mourned his Lucinde. But then Lucinde was there, standing before him when he thought he had lost her. You are the only one I ever wanted to live with, he says. Lucidor, she replies, you are mine and I am yours. And she had embraced him and asked him to embrace her. Literatureliteratureliterature!

He took the cushion and hurled it into the farthest corner. From now on, read and write only books in which everything is as nasty as in real life. He longed for a novel where hopelessness reigned. Werther! No, he was able to kill himself and be released. He can't even fall asleep, sleep for an hour, find release for an hour! Wide awake—what torture! To be awake is to think of her. Goethe is rococo. Who was it said that? Was it little August, his son, his errant seed? Goethe was rococo, *he* was nineteenth century. That's what little August said. Ah, if only he were rococo. Ah, if that had never ended, that flirtatious terrain, that cordon of whim and jest, a fortress against the world. And so the world had to destroy it, so that only what was tolerable would occur. And then the Revolution with its slogans of happiness that made only the sloganeers happy while sending people down hopeful paths to disaster . . .

He was compelled to run through the moments he could recall from the years '21 and '22. Then their differences from the moments of the present summer. The result: If today's Ulrike were still the Ulrike of back then, he wouldn't be sitting here in the dark sorting moments like prehistoric artifacts. The Ulrike of last summer and the summer before had won him with her ingenuous vivacity, her carefree temperament, the irony with which she played mother to her two sisters. And frequently, when she'd again said something she thought clever, she almost made a parody of turning to him to ask if he thought what she'd said was good. It had become a charming habit, this turning to him and pantomiming the question, So—what do you think? Sometimes she was more explicit, "And Herr Privy Councilor, what does he think about it?" She even allowed herself little provocations: "Assuming Herr Privy Councilor was even listening, which we simple girls have no right to expect." Whatever the topic of conversation, she invented occasions to show that for her, he was the most important person in the circle. That often happened to him, but nowhere had it been a girl who wanted not just to honor him, but had this charming and amusing, constant need to have a bit of risky contact with him. But it was a girl. She obviously thought she had to make sure he didn't suffer even a second of boredom with her family. When her mother had told her that Goethe wished he had another son for whom he could train Ulrike to be an ideal wife, the next time they were together she said she was wondering why Herr Privy Councilor didn't want to train his make-believe son for her, instead of her for his son.

"And what was your explanation?" he asked.

"Two possibilities," she said. "Either Herr Privy Councilor thinks his son is in any case the ideal make-believe husband for any woman and any family, or," and she had looked Goethe in the eye, spread her arms, and continued in a cheerful tone, "or it would simply amuse Herr Privy Councilor to try and figure out how to train a restless girl like me."

Instead of answering, he turned first to her mother as if he hadn't expected her to pass along to her daughter the wish he had spontaneously expressed.

Ulrike exploited the pause to say, "Word has gotten around what a passionate pedagogue you are. And who would not long to be trained by you? The third possibility is that Herr

Privy Councilor thinks a von Levetzow has to receive special training to be worthy of a Goethe."

Everyone laughed. Then Goethe began in a rather quiet voice to make what he himself called a confession.

"Why shouldn't I confess," he'd said, "that all that business with a son can have occurred to me only because I wanted to say something that would show me in a situation where I'd be constantly occupied with you." He believed that both Ulrike and her mother had found this confession quite moving.

Of course, the ever alert sister Amalie had to remark at once, "And when Rike is trained, it's my turn."

And then Bertha, "What about me?"

At the end of the season, they bade one another farewell. *On s'est promis de s'écrire.*

All those hours had the effect of making him eager for this summer to arrive. A little bit eager. And now this bolt from the blue. The new Ulrike, her gaze, her demeanor. And he thought he sensed in everything she said and did that she was continuing what had begun the previous year. She showed that she was. But now as a different Ulrike. As she had last year, she again turned to him in the middle of conversation, wanted his opinion, his reaction. But she did it as if quoting herself from the year before. What had he overlooked or misunderstood? Where did he get the impression that he and Ulrike were moving toward each other? Whence his insouciance about numbers? And that the possibly scandalous nature of his appearances with Ulrike wasn't worth worrying about? Were there constraints or rebuffs he hadn't noticed? He must have misinterpreted not just this or that detail, but everything.

They had been living past each other. She would probably be appalled, and her mother, too, if they knew of the illusion he had worked his way into. He did not know how to find his way out, the same as it had been for years with his theory of colors, his anti-Newtonism. Practically every contemporary physicist makes fun of him or is concerned about his stubbornness. He cannot extricate himself from his color theory, however, which is more intuited than calculated. But he would much rather desert to Newtonism this very day and admit that his theory is a stubborn illusion than to accept the possibility that he could ever perceive Ulrike other than as he did. If she isn't the way he imagines her, then he's living in an illusion he cannot do anything about. He calls it love. He can feel it like a burn or an endless scream, or simply a total catastrophe. It isn't yet clear what has collapsed, exploded, been destroyed, the heavens a ruin, no fellow man to be seen. He stood there balling his fists and pressing them against his eyes. And he cried for a time. A fairly long time. And heard himself singing. He sang, sang the Schubert lied to his text:

> Only the yearning know
> How much I suffer!
> Alone and cut off
> From every joy,
> I gaze at the firmament
> In that direction.
> So far away is he
> Who knows and loves me!
> My head is spinning and
> Inside I'm burning.

> Only the yearning know
> How much I suffer!

He sang the line "Inside I'm burning" twice and drew out "know how much I suffer" into the upper register as if it would never end, just as Count Klebelsberg had done. He realized he was imitating him, and with the most intense involvement.

He went over and put on his white flannel nightshirt. Still, he could not get into bed, although sleep would have freed him from his obsessive thoughts. But he could not imagine lying down and waiting to find his way into sleep. If he lay down he would be the helpless prey of his worst imaginings. He had to sit down. Even better: Stand up, walk back and forth, hands clasped behind his back—his posture when on display. It had always helped him get through anything. He marched back and forth. These rooms were much too small for his backing and forthing. In Weimar, he had six rooms when he needed them, one after the other, doorless, a lane. But this imprisoned back and forth! When had he been so helpless, he'd like to know? He had to accept his thoughts. The stiffer his resistance to these thoughts, the more blatantly they dominated him. All right, stop putting up such a fight. What misery to have written it all out beforehand in a novel, like a smart aleck, for instance, that every qualification put in the path of our budding passions makes them all the keener instead of curbing them, and then, when it really happens to you, you're nothing but a scrap of sorrow and helplessness.

He had to muster all his strength of thought and will to enforce his decision to stop looking across the way. But suddenly he found himself at the window again, opening it and almost leaning out in order to see more clearly that he could not see what was going on over there. Turn back, away from the window, tell yourself you mustn't subject yourself any more to the disappointment that awaits you. And there he was at the window again, looking out. He realized it was foolish to ask the impossible of himself. He practiced lengthening the times between his trips to the window, hoping eventually not to have to go to the window at all. It suited him to require something of himself he could regard as requireable. The resolution NEVER AGAIN to go to the window was wrong. It was artificial, a resolution that was already a lie. That NEVER AGAIN makes you into a liar. But to remain seated a little longer each time was a program he could carry out with some prospect of success. After all, you were always interested in learning what was happening to you. Perhaps son August is right. He was rococo. Now, all of a sudden, it's in earnest. To extinguish yourself like a lamp. That would have been the thing. The miserable preparations that need to be made: pistol, poison, noose. To extinguish yourself like a lamp. Puff. Too late for the howl of derision to reach your ears: So, he finally managed to imitate his Werther after all. You could always be sure of the ridicule of those who hadn't experienced it, escaping into bushes, fishes, celestial unattainabilities. That will annoy them the most, that you have attained unattainability. Let it rain, Lord, even if it be fire. Let it rain on me.

Stadelmann was knocking. It must be five. Stadelmann had fetched water from the spring. He was in the habit of bringing it to his master's bedside. Goethe called to him to leave the glass by the door.

If she is a woman now, what does that mean? He became aware of a fairly keen mistrust of women, supposedly based on experience. You can see what you did wrong from the fellow without a given name. You know it, too. Women—you've got to make a conquest of them. They want you to possess them, do with them whatever you please. A woman's vulnerability is not submission, not a service to please you. It's her idea of pleasure. You've only experienced such lack of reserve once: with Christiane. She passed her lack of reserve on to you. You became a man as others are perhaps born to it. You needed a Christiane—nonono, not a Christiane: You needed *the* Christiane, the one and only. But when she danced and more than danced with the Frenchmen, it was not pain but a mobilization of melancholy that was just waiting to be awakened.

When he again had been compelled to go to the window—and by now he went there without taking it amiss that he did—Stadelmann announced from the other side of the door that breakfast was served. He had fetched it from the catering house. Almost peevishly and louder than necessary, he called to Stadelmann to take it all away. Eating, drinking, giving the day its due—no, he had to sit down and try not to think, try to think nothing. All he was doing now was standing at the window. He couldn't resist anymore. Actually, he had no desire to resist. He could feel he was in danger, but he didn't know how to escape. He would stand at the open window and stare at the Klebelsberg palais until they came to take him away, wherever they wanted.

Then he was startled by a cry from the street. He looked down. It was Julie, the Hohenzollern princess he still owed a dance from yesterday. Since she made a pantomime of pleading, he replied with an elegant, practiced gesture that meant, Please, come on up, I'm so happy to see you. He was surprised that he was able to produce it so automatically. She came up, bringing a woman named Lili with her.

The princess launched into a humorous complaint that he had predicted good weather last week and since he was said to be an expert on clouds and weather, she had trusted him. And what happened? She got wet, that's what.

Goethe said, "Last week I was still young, and hence cruel."

"I'm bringing you a young lady from Berlin who has greetings for you from . . . ?" She looked inquiringly at the pretty young thing who couldn't have been more than twenty-five.

"From Zelter, my voice teacher."

"That's it, Zelter," said the princess.

"Perhaps the only friend I've ever had," said Goethe.

"Zelter, Schubert—soon everybody will be singing only you," said the princess. "But you resist Schubert," she chattered on, "and I know why, too."

Goethe pantomimed his great curiosity to hear why.

"Because he wears spectacles, poor Franz, and such spectacles."

"Dear Princess," said Goethe, "you could wear ten spectacles and it would not bother me in the least."

"Thank you!" she cried, which she always preferred to speaking.

Goethe urged them to please sit down on the sofa or on the chairs at the round table. The young woman named Lili sat on the sofa on the very same spot where Ulrike had sat a few days ago. But she could not rest her hand on the yellow cushion with the pale pink fairy-tale birds; he'd fired it into the corner. He was about to sit on a chair when the Lili woman unceremoniously said he must sit next to her. And he gave his standard reply that he wouldn't dream of sitting anywhere else.

And obviously trying to stress that she hadn't come here as a voice student but as an admirer, she said, "My name is Lili, but I don't have a park."

"Just wait, you will," said Goethe, "just like in a pastoral play." It always did him good when someone alluded to something he'd written long ago like "Lili's Park."

"What good does a park full of admirers do me," she said, "if there's no Goethe among the lovesick crowd? Do you recall the last line of your poem about Lili's park?"

"Sometimes I think that the world and time have extinguished more than was ever there," said Goethe.

And Lili recited the line as only an enthusiastic fan who had studied voice could: "I feel it, I swear! I still have power!"

And Goethe: "Superb, Lili. Hearing you, I could believe I don't need to worry about my posthumous reputation."

"You're still alive, Herr Privy Councilor," she cried. "I can feel it through and through."

He said that Zelter was always writing about his beautiful voice students, and now he knew what he meant.

Lili turned to face him straight on and said, "You are much more handsome than one would gather from Rauch's bust of you."

"Oh my, oh my," Goethe said, sounding distressed.

"It's better than the other way around, though," said Lili.

"If you say so, you're right, even though it might not be true at all," he said.

"I think it's superb the way you talk just like you write," she said.

But he hadn't said anything, he protested.

"Yes you did," she said. "You said 'Last week I was still young, and hence cruel.' What a sentence, and the way you say it, it goes right through me."

It was a conversation, Goethe heard himself talking and saw that his visitors were charmed. When it emerged that he had been to Berlin only once, and for much too short a stay, he had to promise that he would come again soon. He said that his son August and daughter-in-law Ottilie now spent the winter months exclusively in Berlin and every year talked with more enthusiasm about driving through the Brandenburg Gate.

And what about him?

All right, as soon as he got the urge to travel this winter, he'd promise . . . and as he still hesitated, Lili turned to face him again, even took his hands in hers, and cried, "Forgive me, but you must come, for the sake of Zelter, for the sake of Berlin. For my sake." She had tears in her eyes and suddenly let go of his hands. Now she was abashed. How dare she have done that? All she could say, with a sob, was "Forgive me, please, please, please. She jumped up, struck a pose, and sang "Only the yearning know how much I suffer" to Zelter's melody. And sang it so that Zelter's simple setting expressed more feeling than Schubert's pretentious music.

He could not remain seated. Julie von Hohenzollern also

stood up. Standing, they listened. Then both embraced the singer. He bent to kiss her hand. As he straightened up, she drew him to her, kissed him on the mouth, gave an almost shrill laugh, and said, "Zelter told me to do it. As a greeting—*ein Gruss*—he said, and then give him what rhymes with it, by which he must have meant *einen Kuss*." She looked enquiringly back and forth from the princess to Goethe.

They both nodded. Goethe stepped closer to Lili and said as off-handedly as possible:

> Dear Lili, if I did not love you,
> How delightful would be your gaze!
> And yet, dear Lili, did I not love you,
> What misfortune would haunt my days.

Lili spun around in a sort of pirouette and cried, "A thousand thanks, Excellency."

Goethe, in his brightest tone, "That was 1775."

"It certainly was, the year you moved to Weimar," cried the princess.

Lili ran to the door, turned back and said, "Adieu, before I commit any more stupidities!" And very quietly, almost pleadingly, "Until Berlin." And then even added, "Give my best to Ulrike." And out the door.

The princess nodded and said, "That was Lili Parthey," and spelled her name. Then she said, "Life is not trivial."

"Ah yes," Goethe agreed.

"You're a success," said the princess. "All you need to say is 'Ah yes.'"

And Goethe, as if he were surprised, "Ah, yes!?"

And the princess, "Which proves the universal utility of Ah yes."

"Ah yes," he almost sighed.

The princess took her leave. He went to the window and waved to the pair who waved back up to him. Then they were gone and all he saw was the Klebelsbergs' palais. What a pleasant thunderstorm, that Lili, and so . . . ? And nothing. Conversation. Routine. Even when she was singing the song, he was thinking only of Ulrike. Was he lost? If he could get loose from her, he would be lost. Because he had lost her. To a fellow without a given name. Now in the daylight, the loss was much more bitterly painful than during the night. The night had been merciful with him. But now, the fullness of light, the surrounding heights, the allée down there that led to the Kreuz Spring, every tree along it a witness to how he strolled with Ulrike. If he now went down there, every tree would ask, What's wrong? Where is she? He would never walk along that allée again, never again go the Kreuz Spring. He did not want to have to bear the amused glances or malicious whispers of the promenaders. Awful things are only as awful as they are thanks to their surroundings. And still, he stood at the window.

Sure enough, over there on the Klebelsbergs' terrace, she appeared. Ulrike. He didn't move. She'd already seen him in any case. She looked over and up. Then she slowly raised her arms, effortlessly raised them as high as only she could raise them. Thanks to the independence of her limbs, she made it look like human arms were not meant to hang down right and left, but were in the position that Nature wanted only when lifted high in the air. Gravity didn't apply to those arms, that was it, it certainly was. Just as the entire creature was so light that one feared exposing it to any strong wind. And now at the end of her upraised arms, her hands were waving. That, too, looked involuntary. They were waving by themselves. Perhaps in a breeze. He now raised his arms, his hands, so slow, so heavy, as if it wasn't certain when his arms and hands would ever fall back again, but then forever. She pointed to herself with one hand and to him with the other. He understood and answered with a gesture: Please, come on up. And she came. She almost ran. He even heard her running up the stairs. And came in and said, "You just disappeared, Excellency. One loses sight of you for an instant, and you're gone."

"Oh yes," he said. "I didn't want to be a bother."

"To whom?" she said.

"To you," he said.

"Oh yes?" she said inquiringly.

"Yes," he said.

"A bother," she said. "Excellency, you've never learned how to be that."

Exactly, that's why he left. If he hadn't left, he would have been a bother. And mentioned the name right away. She'd just have to bear it.

"De Ror," she repeated. "A swift person, that Herr de Ror," she said. And she said the man without a given name was only nameless till midnight. Wherever he was at midnight, he divulged his first name.

"Interesting," said Goethe.

"Let's not think about that velocitanical fellow anymore," she said. She stressed "velocitanical" so that he would hear that she was using a word she learned from him. And she

77

added that she loved that word, loved it a lot, velocitanical. And please, she didn't love the man she called that, but only the word. She loved words that sounded like what they meant and you understood them right away. Words that still left something to the imagination.

He offered her a seat. She sat down on one of the chairs at the round table. Now he could really ask her where the fellow without a given name—which he must be again in the daylight—where he was.

"Gone," she said, "and good riddance."

Goethe gave her a look to let her know she had to explain.

Herr de Ror had wanted to take her with him, into his suite. First, he said, he was going to tell her his first name. Then he told her his first name. Then he said that telling her his first name put him entirely in her hands. He didn't know how he was going to survive the night without her. Let me out of here—she knew that much. Tore herself away, had freed herself from him, but he—surely without a second thought—cried out, Not so fast! Caught her, took hold of her, pulled her to him, against him, already had her head between his hands, pressed against her, his face on hers, his mouth. That gave her the strength she had lacked at her initial attempt to break free. She was gone, was in her room; locked the door, trembled, didn't know for how long. She was still standing at the door, listening to hear if he had followed her. She doesn't know how she made it into bed, and then couldn't fall asleep. She would like to ask Herr Privy Councilor something.

"Of course."

She had done all the wrong things. She treated de Ror like a madman or a savage. And that's what made him insane and savage. Ought she to have played along with him at first? "Rococo, Excellency? Rococo instead of Beethoven right away?"

Goethe said nothing. He tried out several kinds of facial expression and couldn't find one.

"Ex-cell-en-cy," she cried. "I'm still here."

In him the scene was being reenacted, word for word, emphasis for emphasis, exactly as she had described it. She had also expressed in gestures the fix she was in. Now he had to know if he was allowed to ask the given name of Herr Nameless till Midnight.

"That's just it," she said. "He made me promise not to tell anyone his first name. Not until I was his wife before all the world, only then was I allowed to tell the whole world his first name." And now she couldn't abuse the trust he had so tempestuously placed in her. She had the feeling she would be injuring him personally if she abused his trust. He'd made her feel that a breach of trust meant a personal and even physical injury. She should have immediately refused to be burdened with this trust. But she was unable to in the face of his extraordinary condition. "How can I rid myself of this nightmare now, Excellency? I have the feeling that I need you, Excellency."

He stood up, walked back and forth, hands clasped behind him. His right hand firmly held the wrist of his left hand. That's how he always walked when it was important to seem not the least bit stooped. That's how he walked when he needed the erect posture he was so famous for. Must she grasp, could she grasp, that right now he could not react any other way? He looked toward her. And was astonished. She was in a completely different mood than he.

Once again, she cried "Ex-cell-en-cy!" She mimicked calling to someone hard-of-hearing. She had stood up, too, and stepped into his path. They stood facing each other, and Goethe said, "Oh yes."

She said, "This morning, a note that he was on his way to Paris. And he wished me a happy life and a happy reencounter. *Et il-y-a quelque chose dans l'air. Entre nous.* De Ror. Without his first name, thank goodness."

Goethe said—and suddenly he felt combative—"How nice to see you, Ulrike."

"So I'm rescued," she said in pure jollity, almost mischievously. Adorably mischievous.

She reached for his hands. She lifted his hands. That brought him closer to her, which may not have been her intention. If he kissed her now, he would be imitating the other fellow, competing with him. He'd become comparable. With that man. He pulled her a little bit, which she didn't need to feel if she didn't want to, but she pulled him a little in return. Then they were so near each other that without letting go of his hands, she reached him with her mouth. Their mouths remained on each other an instant like two beings who don't yet know what language to speak to each other.

She still held his hands in hers as she said, "Ah, Excellency."

He was still able to say, "I'm supposed to give you regards from Lili Parthey."

"Oh," she said, "how sweet of her."

Then she was out the door, downstairs, across the street. He got to the window in time and waved back when she waved. He will never forget that when she left that morning he was at the window in time to wave, and she waved back. What are Egyptian pyramids by comparison! Then he sat and thought for a while. The most beautiful thing was that when their mouths approached and then touched each other, she had closed her eyes. He had never experienced an intimacy as intense as those closed eyes.

At this moment, he could allow nothing to interfere with those closed eyes. And yet he had to give in to a veritable howling storm of thoughts: himself as a kisser who'd never been pushed away. He had never pulled a woman or girl to himself, never pressed his mouth to hers, his into hers. He'd never kissed without initial shyness, true. There was reverence no matter what they'd been talking about beforehand. His mouth and her mouth grew toward each other, involuntarily, without a hint of drama. Herr Nameless plays the passionate lover. What was that like for Ulrike? What does she think about it now? What does she think about him now? Asking her is out of the question. He can only observe. Is she still the Ulrike she was before that scene? The first time he kissed Frau von Stein, she said, "You kiss brilliantly, dear sir." And Ulrike—the way Ulrike had closed her eyes as her mouth and his mouth brilliantly approached each other—that was the most profoundly beautiful response to Herr Nameless's theater of passion. Perhaps Ulrike and he would never have drawn so close without his brutal theater. He will play that scene over with Ulrike, and when their mouths smash violently together as in the play by de Ror, they will pull apart, look at each other, and laugh. A comedy by August Wilhelm Iffland, an imitation of the Paris boulevards. That's where he got it from. They will laugh. Together. This idea made him

happy. From now on, instead of Oh yes, he would say, Oh
Ulrike. And say it so that the whole world could hear. High
and bright and cheerful, a signal of never-ending bliss! Oh
Ulrike! The i in her name like a long-drawn-out cry.

Chapter Five

AND SO IT went. Once again he was inseparable from Ulrike, Ulrike inseparable from him. On the day of that first kiss, when he had watched her leave and she had waved and he had waved back, he sat down at his desk knowing that writing was the only answer to the storm of his emotions. At first, he simply let routine guide him, i.e., he started rhyming until the paper before him read . . .

> Long ago you captured me
> (New life astir is hard to miss).
> A lovely mouth's a friendly thing to see
> When it has given us a kiss.

He sent this routine outpouring right off to three recipients: to Lili who was still in town, to his daughter-in-law Ottilie in Weimar, and across the street to Ulrike. He explained the triple transmission to himself by treating it like nothing more than one of the hundreds or thousands of occasional poems that simply crop up and must be written—a social obligation. To be sure, the poem goes only to individuals who know why they're receiving it. Even between him and Ottilie there had been a kiss, during the maiden ride in his new coach, that miracle of lightness. That's what she was supposed to recall. Yes, he thought to himself, Metternich himself couldn't have arranged it more diplomatically.

He included a letter to Ottilie saying how amiable everyone was here. Stadelmann was out in the hills wielding his hammer. The King of Württemberg was giving one more ball and then the ball gowns would be packed away. Women were looking for a way to transport their hats undamaged, and then the curtain would come down on this fairy tale. He would stay until the twentieth; the solitude would help him catch up on several things he had neglected because of all the conviviality. He also wrote a harmlessly conventional letter to his son August: that he was enjoying watching from his window all the goings-on on the terrace across the street, that the grand duke was returning from a duck hunt, that the weather was very pleasant, that Count Sternberg had gone to Hungary for a few days but would be back soon, that John was keeping a record of atmospheric phenomena, and that he was always capitally fed from the six little tureens the catering house sent over. His dietary regimen was functioning, he had been able to protect himself from too many public appearances, otherwise one couldn't be one's own master. He hoped thus to lull to sleep any alarming reports and rumors that may have leaked out.

The fact that his mouth and Ulrike's mouth had been so close remained his secret. But he wasn't satisfied with his kissing poem. Inside him another scene was playing: She breaks away, he catches her, pulls her to him, crushes his mouth against hers, into hers, and only then she really breaks away. He could send his kissing poem to Lili and Ottilie, but not to Ulrike. Its harmlessly cheerful rhymes all but thrust her into that nocturnal scene with the passionate leading man.

He must write the Duke of Leuchtenberg, Prince of Eichstädt. It was his duty. He began a draft: His behavior toward the esteemed count at Rehbein's engagement must not continue to go without an apology. He cannot think of a single person who can have participated in so much history as the Duke of Leuchtenberg. His father guillotined, his mother Napoleon's consort. He'd been in every war with the emperor, then was Viceroy of Italy, married the daughter of Max I, King of Bavaria, was adopted by the emperor Napoleon who made him a gift of Italy. What had he not done to deserve that gift and what had he not salvaged for his stepfather in the midst of the Russian catastrophe and finally in Vienna, at the congress? And in the crush of the ballroom he, Goethe, had so much neglected a man with such a powerful history and capacious character that ever since, he turns red with shame whenever he thinks about it. Which is all too often. And hence this earnest request to see each other as soon as possible in order to discuss the count's thrilling vision of peace, the Rhine–Danube Canal, and reach some decisive conclusion.

It was all an attempt to not be constantly thinking of Ulrike. In anything that had nothing to do with her, he sensed malevolent meaninglessness and boredom. It was always painful to distract himself from her. But the fact that at the most, hours would have to pass before he saw her again made all his privations bearable. They were the seasoning for the meal of their next encounter.

The letters arriving from Weimar were letters from a world that he wished never to return to. That he had to return to. As unimaginable as it was, it would certainly come to pass. He refused to think it possible. Even when he returned, he would not be where he then is. He invented ambiguous temperaments in which those who sought him, would not be allowed to find him. His vision: to have escaped. Modes that would make him unlocatable. He must not admit anything and not deny anything. Either would be fatal. Besides that, Ulrike's presence would put an end to all reproachability. He had to enter Weimar with Ulrike and with a novel he would need to write—or at least begin—at once. A novel that no man or woman could contest. A novel that legitimized him and Ulrike. Not just in Weimar, but in the whole world. All at once, its title stood on the page:

A Man in Love.

It was a novel he could no more dictate to a secretary than he could have dictated *Werther*. But this was a novel that would have a happy end. For long enough he had couched life's difficult negativities in palatable language. At last, a tone without that tawdry tension pressing for resolution. A tone without discord or harmony. A tone made of nothing but itself. No borrowing from a chromaticism distorted by artifice and anguish. No program. A tone. There on the paper at its first outpouring:

A Man in Love.

Again he can believe what the summer is telling him. Again he can mingle with the butterflies and be mistaken for the glowing lupine. Fortunately, this day will never end. The era in which something was more important than something else is over. At long last the questions have fled to their negative continent. Ulrike's independence makes him rich. He still hears the prompts but he doesn't understand them. His willfulness is pure gold. Ulrike and he succeed at what was always meant to succeed. As soon as Ulrike is his, he will found world peace. Enmity—a dead language. Everything bad in this world comes only from his not yet having Ulrike. His entire life long, he was never bored for a second. Now he could go mad from boredom if he can't at least see her. Whoever wants to save the world must give him Ulrike. When he touches something, it blossoms, and doesn't stop blossoming. The days are of silk, the world a warm wind. The birds strut their resounding jewelry and sing only her name. I wish never again to be as devout as I am now. Because he lost beauty, Plato invented memory. I will lose memory because I have found beauty. If you are with me, the future and the past have no value. Privation, please, do not break out. Dream, safeguard me. To sit opposite her makes you as light as she is. Her gaze holds you. There is nothing as reliable as her gaze. I will not cry out anymore and will weep only from happiness. I shall surprise your mouth carefully, discover your breasts with devout hands. Your lightness will celebrate victories. When you extend both hands across the table to me before we begin to eat, my hands will receive you: saying grace in a new religion. There will be nothing we shall not want to learn from each other. If I am permitted to love you, I am immortal. Then and only then. Now I know why I was never able to hate anyone. My whole life long there was a love living within me that slept and dreamed and once or twice ran riot. Its name was such-and-such or so-and-so. It fled back and was really only waiting. That is what gave me the strength for everything. Now I know: My love was waiting for you. If you do not want it, it will destroy me. And I won't resist. My love does not know I'm over seventy. Neither do I.

He was aware of how he had written his way into the tone he desired.

The King of Württemberg's costume ball will be the public dress rehearsal for the Man in Love. Costumes from dark bygone ages down to the sunlit present is what the invitation said. Even before he had finished reading it, he knew what his costume would be: a light blue frock coat, a yellow vest, and boots. But that had to be kept secret from everyone. Only Stadelmann and Blastimir the tailor were in on it.

Stadelmann was delighted to again be allowed to be part of an adventure. And when Blastimir—who until now had only been asked to do alterations—had been told what the costume was to be, he cried, Werther! He was the right man for the job. Blue frock coat, yellow vest, boots of very pale leather.

When Ulrike asked who he would be at the ball, he told her he wouldn't say.

"All right then," she said. "I'm happy to join in this secretiveness." Her mother would appear as Madame de Pompadour and Count Klebelsberg as Louis XIV. Dr. Rehbein and Catty von Gravenegg were coming as Romeo and Juliet, the Duke of Leuchtenberg as Prometheus bringing mankind not fire, but the steam engine . . . Like Ulrike and Goethe, the Princess von Hohenzollern and the Count of

Saint-Leu weren't giving away who they would be, either. The ball would be held across the way in the palais.

As often as they continued to promenade before the evening of the ball—since he wouldn't say who he was going to be, she wouldn't reveal her costume either.

Was he allowed to guess?

He was, but she wouldn't tell him if he was right or wrong.

"The Maid of Orléans," he said. Since she gave him an almost instantaneous look of surprise, he thought he had guessed her costume at the first try and said it wasn't hard. After all, Schiller was her poet and female figures one would like to escort for an entire evening's ball were rather scarce in his work. You could eliminate Queen Elizabeth and Mary Queen of Scots because they're too political. No one would ever want to be Amalie from *The Robbers*. And so, and so, and so . . . the Maid. Now there's a figure with which you can dominate the ballroom. The natural boldness inherent in all of Ulrike's gestures always had something of the Maid of Orléans. She is smiling, he thought, as never before. He had guessed it.

"What about you?" she asked.

"Not a hero from Schiller," he said. He was glad she wasn't coming as Gretchen at the spinning wheel. She had everything necessary to be the Maid.

It was good that it was raining the day of the ball, because as their coaches drove up to the Klebelsbergs' portal, they emerged wrapped in overcoats and shawls. Since Goethe had only to cross the street, he walked to the ball in a coat and hat. His dark summer coat had a stand-up collar lined with red velvet. At the top, the collar was turned over the width of a finger to let the red velvet shine. Goethe looked himself over and was quite satisfied. He was glad the weather made it possible to hide his Werther costume beneath the light-weight summer coat. He bowed to Stadelmann like a courtier from the ancien régime and Stadelmann called out, "Excellency, *s'il vous plaît*," ran for the powder puff, and muted the white of his hair with a whiff of ocher powder. "It was too stark," he murmured, "much too stark."

Goethe said, "Ah, Stadelmann, many thanks," and gave another, even more effusive, bow, and left.

In the palais, the men and the women were supposed to wait in separate groups for a signal from the orchestra and then enter the ballroom through various doors, but simulta-neously. Then the gentlemen lined up against one wall and across the room, before the enormous windows with incised floral patterns, stood the ladies. He saw Ulrike. It was more than a bolt from the blue. She stood there in a simple white dress, pale red ribbons on the sleeves and at the rather austere neckline, austere in comparison to the neckline jamborees on display to the left and right of Lotte-Ulrike.

Directly the *maître de cérémonies* raised his golden staff, struck the floor three times, and the orchestra began to play. Couples walked toward each other and bowed. Arms encir-cled and hands took hold according to the roles that were to be acted out and danced. Ulrike-Lotte—pure Nature. Little white stockings, little flat, black, buckled shoes from bygone times. She had set her usually free-falling hair into tight curls as part of her costume. And today, the girl who wore new fashion statements from Vienna every day was wearing the simplest little white dress. It was a costume, or rather, she was Lotte. He could picture how Amalie and Bertha had laughed when Lotte appeared before them and asked, What do you think of me? A starker contrast was not possible than that between the mother, costumed as a splendid courtier and this daughter as an everlasting girl.

Abruptly, the orchestra fell silent. The *maître* announced that now each couple would have a dance to perform whom they were representing this evening. The jury, chaired by His Serene Highness Grand Duke Carl August would award the Golden Laurel Wreath of Terpsichore to the best couple. First Julie von Hohenzollern whirled into the center of the ball-room and the Count of Saint-Leu as Marat had no chance, so quickly did his Charlotte Corday pull out the flashing red dagger that dangled between her breasts and plunge it through his opened shirt into the pre-painted bloody spot. The Duke of Leuchtenberg's steamship *Prometheus* was divided in two halves between himself and his wife. When they joined in a dance, they made the whole ship. The *maître* helped out with humorous commentary.

Then came Werther and Lotte. There wasn't much to say. Everyone had recognized who they were. However, the *maître*'s commentary showed that he thought this pairing was Goethe's idea. Only he and Ulrike knew that Ulrike and he had chosen these roles independent of each other. That was their adventure: that they had chosen each other without previous agreement. That she had chosen Lotte on her own and he Werther on his own made them a happy couple now amid the ballroom splendor and the clamor of the music. Ulrike emerged from herself completely. She played Lotte.

Played the Lotte who at the boring provincial ball is immediately captivated when that passionate beanpole by the name of Werther whirls her around so that she loses all earthly weight. Enjoying her role completely, Ulrike told him so loudly that it was audible in the ballroom—shouted it rapturously into his ear: "When I was younger there was nothing I liked better than novels." And faithful to his text he shouted back, "I've never danced so easily before." And so it was. And never since they'd known each other had they been the same age, but now they were. He could feel it: She leaned back, he held her, they flew. They were demonstrating that nothing in the whole world could disturb two people in love. Clearly, they had left their personalities behind, had become roles, costumes, Lotte and Werther. And it was also because the music had immediately understood and assumed this mood. And oh, how they thanked each other for what they had just accomplished together!

Next came Romeo and Juliet—another display of ardent intimacy, but play with an eye to the tragic ending. Dr. Rehbein and Catty von Gravenegg, one half of each face florid, the other pale as death. He was florid on the right side, she on the left, and the sides turned away from each other were deathly pale. At first came a melancholic performance, but the florid side won out. Then Amalie von Levetzow as Madame de Pompadour in a dress (a billow of green-golden silk that made it hard to know how she kept it on) and earrings brushing her naked shoulders. Golden sandals held on her bare feet by almost invisibly thin straps. The towering mass of black hair was held up by a golden butterfly. Amalie von Levetzow! Without doubt the evening's most beautiful woman. The count as her Louis made an almost sober impression despite his magnificent black costume. Only his wig and the white lace emerging from his cuffs could claim to hold their own against his consort's glorious fleshiness. To be sure, his gestures and demeanor were genuinely sovereign. A bit labored, they smacked of lessons from a dancing master. But why not? He had to act out his need to conceal his appetite until Madame de Pompadour brought him to the point of admitting how pleasant it was to be conquered by her.

The couples rested while the jury conferred. Amalie von Levetzow said to Ulrike and Goethe, "That was a real conspiracy—Lotte and Werther!"

"Madame de Pompadour was already taken," said Ulrike.

And her mother: "But the Maid of Orléans was still free."

"Yes," cried Goethe. "That was my guess the whole time."

Ulrike: "I did not want to carry a weapon."

Her mother refused to believe the two of them had done this without consulting each other.

Ulrike said, "Nothing is as hard to believe as the truth."

Her mother: "If that's the truth, then . . ." and fell silent.

Goethe saw her looking at him as she had never looked before. He waved his hand through the air to dispel her gaze. It succeeded. With a shake of her head and a laugh, she relaxed an expression that had quickly turned severe. Even before Goethe lifted his hand to distract her gaze, Count Klebelsberg had called, "Where are we then, Amalie?" in his Viennese accent.

At some point Goethe asked Ulrike if they shouldn't fetch themselves a little something from the caterer in the buffet room. He looked at her in such a way that she had to see this was only a pretext. She went along. Those taking advantage of the buffet table had the choice of sitting or standing. Ulrike took some of her favorite pralines—the ones with cognac filling—and he had a waffle. But they had barely sat down at a little table when they were joined by others. When Romeo and Juliet came up but found all the seats at this table taken, Goethe said, "Please, take my seat." He said it to the big, blonde, half deathly pale, half wildly florid Catty. Catty, who was carrying several little plates of delicacies, sat down gratefully and remarked loudly that chivalry was not dead yet. Goethe looked at Ulrike, gestured with his head and also pointed his thumb in the same direction. Ulrike understood and without further disturbance, they went out. On the uphill side of the palais was a sloping meadow. The path was lit intermittently by hurricane lanterns. Goethe led the way, then allowed Ulrike to catch up with him. They stood facing each other in the half-light. He knew he mustn't do anything that would bring them closer together. It was all as beautiful as it wasn't. The path grew steeper and led to an old grove of trees.

He said that in the first version of his Werther novel, Lotte had worn a single flesh-colored bow instead of pale red ribbons.

"Flesh-colored instead of pale red," said Ulrike, "I would have liked that."

He wouldn't have, he said. Pale red was not an ingratiating word, but flesh-colored even less so. And besides, she had applauded as a vegetarian.

She said she wasn't one and would never be. Oh, she didn't know what she would be or wouldn't be.

"Ulrike," he said, "come, let us return to humanity."

He was expecting her to say, Not yet, let's tarry another minute in the rain-fresh air. Because she said nothing, he had to go and he walked faster than intended and tripped over a branch. His hands and arms flailed wildly, trying to keep his balance. He didn't succeed. He fell. He threw his right hand forward, stretched out his right knee, both too late. At the last second, he tried to turn his face to the side, and was only half successful, landing on his forehead and nose, between the middle of his forehead and his right temple and on the right side of his nose. Ulrike screamed. Then she stood looking down at him, crying and repeating "No, no, no, no." He was at once overcome by the fear that always lay in wait. Anything but a fall. Often enough in the Weimar winters, he would hear news about who had fallen and how bad it was—a fractured femur, a dislocated hip. The resolution he had drummed into himself was: Never fall! Now he had fallen. And he had fallen because he was with Ulrike in the semidarkness and hadn't been watching the path. He had given in to an emotion made necessary by their conversation. He rolled onto his back. He must seem to Ulrike like a fish out of water. He fingered the places on his forehead and nose where he had fallen. He felt the blood running over his face. It was difficult to stand up. Ulrike wanted to get help. "No, please no," he said and painfully got up on one knee and then even more painfully back up on his feet. Now he asked Ulrike to go back to the palais after all and ask Dr. Rehbein to come out without attracting attention. "And bring bandages," he called after her. Dr. Rehbein came and was horrified, wanted to help support Goethe back into the palais, where there was more light, but Goethe wouldn't allow it. It was nothing, only two places that Dr. Rehbein should please look after and stop the bleeding. The doctor cleaned the wounds, dabbed at them, brushed them with ointment, and observed the effect. Then he said, "We're lucky, it's not bleeding anymore." Goethe refused the bandage he wanted to apply. The doctor gave in. "Herr Privy Councilor, I am so sorry you had need of me, but it makes me equally happy." He would have another look at the wound tomorrow. Now back to the ballroom for the award ceremony. And he was gone. Goethe and Ulrike stood facing each other. Ulrike was still looking up at the wound. Driven out of Paradise, he thought. Fallen from Paradise. Ulrike was speechless. She obviously didn't know what to do or say. It had probably been an awful sight when he tried to stand up. She would never forget his arms and hands flailing just before he fell.

He said he wouldn't return to the ballroom.

"What about the Wreath of Terpsichore?" she suddenly asked in a different tone, "the Golden Laurel Wreath of Terpsichore? Please come! A stupid branch, a wet path, half-darkness—it could have happened to anyone." She was lying now. She knew very well that it could only happen to him, and only to him because he was seventy-four.

So now he said resolutely, "I am seventy-four."

Her vehement reply: "You're exaggerating again, Excellency—seventy-three."

"No," he said, "On January first of every year I'm always as old as I will turn on August twenty-eighth."

"But for me, you're seventy-three. Believe it or not, seventy-three is a wonderful number. Numbers can also be beautiful or less than beautiful. Seventy-three is such a beautiful number you want to kiss it." And she laid her hands on his shoulders and approached her mouth to his until they touched and then a little farther. And that's where she left her mouth. He laid his hands on her shoulders, pulled her a little closer, but really only a little bit. They stood thus for an immeasurably long time.

"Come, Excellency," she said.

Inside, the *maître* was just about to announce the winners of the Golden Laurel Wreath of Terpsichore, and he asked His Royal Highness to officiate. Up on the podium, the Grand Duke (Ulrike had remarked that with the immensely broad white vest that always emerged from his open coats, he looked like a master baker) announced that the five-man jury unanimously awarded the Golden Laurel Wreath of Terpsichore to the couple Lotte and Werther. The applause showed that that was the opinion not just of the jury, but of the audience, too. Goethe walked forward with Ulrike, Ulrike taking his arm. The pain had to be accepted. They mounted the podium and the duke first placed the Golden Laurel Wreath on Ulrike's head. Then he went to crown Goethe as well, but his hands paused halfway up, and he cried, "Worthy friends, illustrious co-celebrants, the president of your jury was on the point of overlooking what makes this couple particularly deserving of the prize. When they moved us all so deeply with their fervent dancing, the dim lighting made me miss the high point of the Werther-poet's Werther costume. Now at the last second and from close up, I see—and perhaps one or two of my fellow ball-goers have noticed, too—only now do I see what makes

Werther Werther: right where the forehead becomes the temple, the bullet hole! Bravo, dear friend, esteemed poet, bravissimo!" Everyone applauded. Then as the duke finished placing the wreath on Goethe's head, he said, "What should we celebrate if not our wounds! I congratulate you and I also congratulate you, lovely lady, without whom there can be no Werther." Thunderous applause. Ulrike pressed even more firmly against her friend. The orchestra struck up a spirited accompaniment. Ulrike and Goethe bowed and returned to their table. Ulrike informed her mother and Count Klebelsberg of his fall. Both were horrified, but Goethe said in an almost jaunty tone, "Merely a kiss from Mother Earth."

The ball continued. Julie von Hohenzollern came to fetch Goethe for a contra dance but he pointed to the bullet hole. She said it was obvious that any excuse would do to avoid dancing with her.

The night was uncomfortable. His forehead and nose were hurting. Stadelmann was happy to be more important than ever. He had to apply cold compresses to his master's head. Goethe couldn't sleep. He asked Stadelmann to wake up his secretary John. John came, ready to serve but not without resentment. It wasn't the first time that the privy councilor wanted to dictate his nocturnal ideas.

"Your Majesty, Royal Highness," he began and continued dictating, without hesitation, that he was venturing to entreat his friend and most gracious sovereign for an unprecedented demonstration of his friendly attachment. Namely: as his representative and suitor to ask Frau von Levetzow for the hand of her daughter Ulrike in marriage. It was much to ask, but should it not be in accordance with His Majesty's views, he could eschew it entirely. By leaving it completely up to the discretion of his Most Gracious Sovereign whether to grant his servant—whom he often had the goodness to call his friend—this service not anticipated in the list of official duties, the undersigned conceded that he left it wholly to the wisdom of his Most Gracious Sovereign to decide whether what he was asking was or was not feasible. "With the expression of deepest attachment, Your Goethe."

Then he said, "A clean copy as soon as possible tomorrow morning, dear John, so that it will arrive over there by noon."

If the kiss had been one of sympathy, then he had embarrassed himself with this letter. As if it mattered. The Wreath of Terpsichore, Ulrike-Lotte, the kiss, the gentle pressure she had lent it! The fall is trying to destroy all of that. Darkness, rain, a branch, the end. Seventy-three, a lovely number. But she participated. It was not sympathy at all. Her shock, her consternation, and the way she gradually recovered from it, then—and this was what allowed him to continue living now—then she forbade him to flee. She wanted to return to the ballroom with him. She knew, he knew, that the Terpsichore Wreath could only land on her head, on his. And when they danced their dance, the Lotte-Werther dance, they were the same age, and that decided everything.

Beneath this torrent of words ran an accompanying stream that negated all that was happening within him. He had to see to it that that negation had no chance. It was nothing new. All his life he had banished this accompanying, negating text back to where it came from, to the district of defeat.

The pain radiating from his forehead and nose became a helmet of pain sitting firmly on his head, the guarantee that all night long, the pathos would not leave him.

Part Two

Part Two

Chapter One

HE HAD TO persuade himself that he was doing his work as always. But he wondered why he had to persuade himself he was doing his work as always when he knew it wasn't so. Why couldn't he admit it? Five times an hour he jumped up from his desk and ran to the window, always hoping Ulrike would appear on the terrace over there and wave so he could wave back and let her know she could come right over if she wanted. He found it dangerous to admit that to himself. It's in the nature of weaknesses to gain even more influence over you the more you think about them and admit they exist.

Two days after the costume ball, and he had still not seen Ulrike. Dr. Rehbein had taken good care of his injuries.

The grand duke had replied at once, saying he would press his friend's suit before leaving for maneuvers in Berlin. He wrote that he was optimistic. And because he was a man of action, he added an explanation of how he would supplement the suit: with a house in Weimar for Ulrike's mother. Ulrike would be the first lady of the Weimar court. And in any case, a widow's pension for Ulrike of 10,000 thaler a year. That was an embarrassment for Goethe, but if that's how Carl August saw the matter, it couldn't be completely wrong. The duke wrote that he had sent word to the Levetzows that he would be calling on them. After all, he was staying in their palais only one floor above them.

Then the news that changed everything: The Levetzows were packing to leave Marienbad and travel to Karlsbad day after tomorrow. Goethe read and reread the lavender-blue note Ulrike had slipped into Stadelmann's hand. Ulrike wrote that, as frequently happened—actually, as always happened—her mother wished to end the summer in Karlsbad. It was true. Last year Goethe, too, had ended the summer in Karlsbad. With the Levetzows. In the much older, much more dignified Karlsbad, where he had passed twelve happy summers cultivating society and his health. And he felt it would never be the same again. Once more in his mind's eye he saw what had transpired in Frau von Levetzow's face when she heard—and could no longer doubt what she heard—that her daughter and Goethe had dressed as Lotte and Werther without consulting each other. Goethe had read what happened in her face. First, that she saw in the couple's spontaneous commonality the sign of a spiritual kinship she had not reckoned with, and second, that she had to separate the two of them as quickly as possible.

Then Ulrike herself arrived. Her first concern was for his forehead. She wanted to touch it. One could see that. She was wholly an impulse held in check. She pointed to it and asked if it still hurt.

He shook his head. Had the grand duke's letter of proposal arrived at the Levetzows? Or had his most gracious sovereign perhaps delivered it in person? He had not told Goethe how he planned to execute his mission. But if Ulrike knew of the proposal, she would have entered in a different way. But how?

Now she repeated what she had already written: The Levetzows were leaving for Karlsbad soon, before the twentieth. She said it casually, in a way that made it sound harmless. He remarked her effort at harmlessness. And the girl to whom he had recommended more energy and animation when reading aloud—as he had recently been reminded—was now making quite clear by the way she repeated her assignment that what she was saying was not her decision but her mother's. It was a performance of saying nothing herself but only repeating what had been said to her.

He was thrilled. He laid both hands on her shoulders but avoided the slightest hint of drawing her toward him. The very idea that this enormous proposal would land on the Levetzows' doorstep without a word having being said by the proposer himself! He had to hope that the Levetzows still knew nothing of it. If the proposal had reached her ears, Ulrike would not have been able to walk in here as she did. That was clear enough.

So, Ulrike, he has to tell you, and high time: Perhaps at this very moment His Majesty has had himself announced to your mother. Perhaps he has already been admitted and at this very moment is saying that as the representative of Herr von Goethe, he is asking for your hand in marriage.

He got that out at any rate. And in his best, firmest voice, uncontaminated by the least doubt. Yes, his heart wanted to remind him what a tremendous moment it was. And now, the power of Ulrike's eyes, those eyes that could conceal nothing. Perhaps not everyone who looked at her would say that. For him, they were eyes that told stories. Her gaze now told him in no uncertain terms, I am surprised. You can see my astonishment. I will not conceal that what you say enters my soul as a joyful message. But I don't know what the message is. I'm much too surprised. I'm happy and don't know why. Perhaps I'm dreaming, too. You don't always have to know what you're doing when you do something. Now I know I'm dreaming. But, a pretty dream, Excellency.

Because she said nothing but gazed so tellingly, he said, "Luckily we're both people without tragic inclinations."

"That's true," she said. She sounded relieved. Her face—it could be her kind of happiness. And she looked intrepid as well. She always liked to look up, which was appropriate now.

Suddenly he needed to say that the gracious sovereign, who in his letters had often enough addressed him as friend, had insisted on furnishing his proposal to her mother with realities that he—the proposer—would never have been able to enumerate in such a loud and sober voice. And in general, she should please take it as his position that this entire proposal was an excursion into unseemliness that suited her just as little as it did him. He knows that marriage is a way to make the impossible possible and as such, is worthy of all respect, but if one is serious, one has no need of it. If both parties are serious, nothing is as superfluous as marriage. You see that not even in this highly precarious moment—rendered completely untragic by the look in your eyes—not even now can he completely forgo a ruminating undertone. Marriage is only necessary when one of the couple is not as serious as the other. That was it, dear Ulrike. Now the look in your eye is perhaps the same look as that of the first person to hear it proved long ago that the earth is not a disk but a sphere.

He withdrew his hands from her shoulders. She looked up at him. I'm not even six feet, he thought. She sent her mouth as an avant-garde, approached her face to his, and made sure that their two mouths again touched. For an immeasurably long time. But her eyes were closed as he felt her mouth on his mouth.

Then she was gone. And he hadn't prevented it! She was no longer here, if you please! As long as she is standing there before him, visible, reachable, it's impossible to say or feel what it will be like when she will have gone, will be outside, no longer visible, no longer reachable. If one could feel this condition in advance, one wouldn't allow her to go, one would—ah, what would one do then . . .

But she is still nearby. You'll see her again soon . . . He walked back and forth, thinking. That ridiculous proposal, the most helpless way of expressing his earnestness. But perhaps a mother needs such assistance. She is only fifteen or sixteen years younger than Count Klebelsberg and the two of them don't seem to need to get married. Granted, the proposal was a sort of relapse into the unnecessary, inappropriate, inopportune . . .

That same evening, the letter from his sovereign and friend arrived: a most amicable reception of his proposal by the Levetzow family. Frau von Levetzow, herself having been damaged by marriage, will never force a daughter into marriage. A long conversation between Ulrike and her mother, the result communicated to him: If Ulrike can be useful to

Herr von Goethe, she is absolutely willing. A reservation: His family in Weimar. His son, daughter-in-law, and two grandsons could feel themselves shortchanged, and that throws everything into question.

Goethe read it more than once. Of course, only such a formal answer could follow such a formal approach. The only word that resonated within him was "useful." If women who had read *Wilhelm Meister's Journeyman Years* used that word in such a fatefully exaggerated situation, they knew that it contained the phrase "from usefulness through truth to beauty." It was all he wanted. And Ulrike had surely already informed them over there that he had in the meantime talked the whole marriage business out of Ulrike's and his own life's plan. This entire answer smacked of the mother's style when she was playing the role of mother. It was not Amalie von Levetzow, the splendid courtier who dominated every room she entered. Any more than it was Ulrike's style. That's how he carefully restored his feelings, his perspectives, his situation.

The farewell was scheduled for the early afternoon of August 18, 1823. The carriage was ready and waiting, mother and daughter already in their traveling clothes. It's certain, agreed, irrevocable that they will see each other again. The scene was animated by the mother's sparkling cordiality. The embraces, more than routine. He did not abuse the hug with Ulrike with any sort of passionate pressure. Amalie was the only one who even mentioned the reduced size of the sticking plasters on his forehead and nose: "If you had walked up to the grove with me, that wouldn't have happened. Ulrike always walks as if her limbs would fly away." And Bertha felt compelled to add, "All the best, Herr Privy Councilor, until next time."

Since it all transpired outside on the terrace, kissing her hand was out of the question. They had almost reached the carriage when Ulrike turned around, came back to the edge of the terrace, and said, "N-C-O-L-W-N."

Some instinct told him he ought to understand that. But he just couldn't think that fast. Ulrike had obviously counted on him knowing what N-C-O-L-W-N stood for or signified. When she saw that he didn't, she said as though reminding him of something he knew, "It's our abbreviation language." She called out to her family, "Please translate N-C-O-L-W-N for Herr Privy Councilor."

And Amalie and Bertha answered in chorus, "No change of location without notification."

She said to him—said it softly, almost fervently—"Understood, Excellency?"

"Understood." Into that single word he injected all his happiness.

Parodying routine, she said, "*Au revoir.*"

Waving hands from the carriage windows. The last to be withdrawn was Ulrike's. When he was back in his room looking down at the terrace, it struck him as devastated. He would spend his remaining days here behind drawn curtains. It was an order he gave himself. His heart responded (he needed to steady himself on the window frame). His heart against the wall of his chest, throbbing at his throat. His heart behaved like a prisoner banging on his cell door to be released from an unjust incarceration. He tried to conciliate his heart with movements and cautious breaths. In vain. If this increased, it would be over soon—breathing, everything. He called Stadelmann, who came.

"Dr. Heidler," he said. Stadelmann saw, understood, and ran down the stairs and out into the street. Goethe was still standing at the window. Two steps to the sofa, then he was sitting. He could not lie down. His breathing was short and shallow. The spa doctor arrived. There was no need for Goethe to explain anything, but he must go lie down in the next room.

Dr. Heidler auscultated him and said, "A convulsion. A bloodletting would help," and performed one on the spot. Goethe fell asleep at once. When he awoke, Stadelmann was sitting on a chair at his bedside. Goethe thanked him and said he could go.

Back to the farewell scene. It was ridiculous to think he could imagine anything. Once something is there, you feel you couldn't have imagined it at all. She is gone. Only now. And now that scene was there again, the abbreviation language of the Levetzow daughters—he'd witnessed it often enough, God knew. The first time when they read Scott together, two years ago. Bertha had begun too far into the book and Amalie had at once cried out "W-A-N-T-F-Y." Which they translated for him. W-A-N-T-F-Y meant, We are not that far yet. It was their abbreviation language. Indeed, they were children of the nineteenth century. Soon everyone would communicate only in abbreviations. Amalie and Bertha had babbled it out, but this apparently serious explanation came from Ulrike, quite calmly and with no proselytizing fervor. She was apparently the inventor of this language.

He would leave on the twentieth. On the twentieth, he did. There was nothing more for him to do here. And without activity, he was at the mercy of thoughts he could not resist. A sort of involuntary decision was made within him. He could not imagine leaving here tomorrow in the knowledge that he was going to Weimar. It was clear that tomorrow, he was only going to Eger. On his way from Weimar to the Bohemian spas and back he always stopped in Eger to visit Police Superintendent Grüner. That's what he would do tomorrow. The police superintendent was a discoverer and collector of the past. And an admirer, but not in the worshipful way that could make you doubt yourself. Both of them had passions in common. He and Grüner had always gone on excursions together, excursions into the history of the landscape. Grüner could read the landscape: the stones, the trees, the brooks, the walls. He was a student of everything that existed: languages, people, furniture, wind, and weather. And when the need arose, he made poems he gave Goethe to read. He knew that they were only poems to fix momentary impressions or rhymed documentation of extralinguistic events. The police superintendent radiated a modesty that for Goethe—who was usually surrounded by fairly egotistical people—was like fresh spring water. In his thoughts, which were still under attack from the farewell on the terrace, Goethe had determined that at the moment, he was completely incapable of looking beyond Eger—beyond traveling to Eger to visit Grüner, who had been given advance notice. He could not bear any further direction.

But the day before his departure he found another activity, or rather, the activity found him: he wrote. In the evening, there was his day's work on the best paper Stadelmann was able to scare up. He not only read it, he studied it. And here is what he studied:

For your profound involvement with my songs,
in thanks and fond remembrance
of pleasurable hours.

Duet on the Pangs of Love
Immediately after Parting

He:
I thought that I would feel no pain
And yet my heart was sore somehow,
A hollow feeling in my brain,
A tightened knot around my brow—
Until at last, tear after tear
Flowed in farewell to one so dear.
Her farewell—a cheerful, calm adieu.
But now she's crying, just like you.

She:
Yes, he has left, it had to be!
My dear ones, do not mourn for me.
I may seem strange to you,
Yet it will not last long.
But now that he is gone,
I am weeping too.

He was happy. This kind of day was the kind for him:
surrendered to a still unexpressed feeling which, however,
unmistakably guided him in his search for words. Whatever
did not correspond to the feeling did not remain on the
paper. That was the most beautiful thing about writing,

especially poems: utter confidence that they would come into being. No matter what anyone said about the results, for him the decisive happiness was that what he had written corresponded completely to the feeling that had guided him while he wrote. The utterly clear-cut progress of his feeling, as if the text already existed before he wrote it down and all he had to do was find it. And when he had found it, this experience of perfection. Not a single word could be changed or be placed somewhere else. Of course, experience taught that tomorrow or in a week, you can see or feel it differently, but today you are one with the perfect poem that is written there. The completeness of the text is enhanced by what needs to be expressed. At first, the feeling that guided him was a pain, an unspecified ache, a nasty imposition, a miserable feeling of abandonment, a lurid impossibility. That this degrading prostration found its way into a feeling that could lead you from word to word until the end—that was the miraculous happiness of writing. Listen to me, Ulrike! Can you hear me? If you could hear me now, you would be very close to me. An understanding would bind us together, an understanding whose name is inseparability. Ulrike.

Silently and out loud he read what he had written and was happier than happy because he knew from many visits that when Police Superintendent Grüner had read and unraveled this text he would participate in the feeling it expressed. It was unthinkable to have written these lines yet know of no one who would read them at once and sympathize with them. He wished he could leave for Eger on the spot. He knew this about himself, that for poems he needed the company of others sooner than for other kinds of writing. Poems were express mail. Express mail of the soul. It was a happy day to have handled his despair so that it would have to concede that as expressed despair, it was more beautiful than in its natural state. And he would see to it (he didn't yet know how) that Ulrike would get to read what he had written today in exactly the same way as the police superintendent. He foresees not being able to survive a single day on which he doesn't see Ulrike if he can't apprehend that unreasonable demand in a poem. Today he had succeeded. Today—for today—he was saved.

And as if that weren't enough already, in midafternoon came the news that Count Sternberg had returned and would be pleased to at least see his great friend. Isn't one happiness enough? Apparently not. Ah, these weeks of emotional storms had drowned the fact that as the count was departing for Hungary, he had called out, "I shall be back soon, very soon I hope." And then he entered, smiling. Goethe wanted to embrace this man in a thought-provoking way. Indeed, he wanted him to be touched. You can count on one hand the people anywhere in the world who are as well-disposed to you as he is. That feeling that permeates you: You can let yourself go. You don't have to hold your breath and be prepared for whatever might come. And then you can tell that he feels exactly the same way. You haven't seen much of each other. You've exchanged letters with a feeling of agreement in so-called scientific matters, but there was even more agreement in the tone than in the details. On July 11, on the promenade, the Levetzows. You recognized their group silhouette and, not wanting to interrupt the discussion of your beloved stones, you steered yourself and the count toward the squadron of Levetzows. Greetings, a meal together, and then the count, the only one who sensed it (how many others had remained seated on evenings last year and the year before, stupid and deaf, hadn't noticed how their continued presence was destroying the mood)—the count with his fine manners had graciously taken his leave because he'd sensed that you needed the Levetzows all to yourself. Without embarrassment he could explain to the count the sticking plaster, the only one still on his forehead, and add an amusing account of Carl August's quick-witted response to his injury. He couldn't think of anything he would not talk about with Sternberg. That fact alone—that it doesn't matter what you talk about— shows an alignment of your lives which all by itself can make you cheerful. And then the news that the count was also traveling to Eger.

The count, a patron of the arts and sciences who sees to it that Bohemia with all its treasures continues to live in the museums and university faculties of Prague, is of course also acquainted with Police Superintendent Grüner. The fact that they both love him equally is another indication of how close they are.

It was raining—no, pouring—as they departed. Along their route, large holes filled with water whose depth you couldn't estimate because they were full of water. Goethe noticed how his friend leaned forward anxiously, watching Stadelmann. The count was not just a patron of museums and clubs devoted to preservation, he also made sure that the instruction in engineering skills in the secondary schools and universities was up to European standards. So Goethe began to praise his own carriage, which he considered the most well-designed and constructed conveyance in Saxony and Thuringia, if not beyond. There isn't another in his country with comparable suspension and yet complete stability. No carriage is as light, fast, and safe as his. Goethe made every effort to assure his mobility since otherwise, he wouldn't be able to stand it in Weimar. Whenever he wants to, he can quickly be in Frankfurt, Dresden, or any other town. To be sure, he admits that most of the time he doesn't want to go far away, but he does at least want to get around the little duchy quickly.

The count said he was seeing a new side of Goethe.

And Goethe, almost boisterously, had to tell him about his maiden drive. He and Ottilie. She had insisted on being the only one sitting next to him on this maiden drive. Her husband, his son August, had to stay home. And in fact, that rushing, rocking, at times even risky-feeling drive had brought him and his daughter-in-law almost too close to each other. When they had returned to Weimar and rolled up the drive from the Frauenplan, he had handed Ottilie down from the carriage and said, "That was velocitanical." And that's how the word, which in the meantime had become known as one of his words, was born. He didn't have to translate it for the count, but he did for Ottilie: velocity and satanical. Then she understood.

"A lovely word," said the count, "which expresses what's already happening. Has to happen." But as long as he's sitting in the very carriage, he said, he wouldn't demonize it.

Goethe said that lacking a driver like Stadelmann, he wouldn't want to be traveling in this featherlight four-wheeler. "You can see how he steers: directly through every puddle, even into the biggest depressions, so the carriage can never be tipped over?" Once he had told Stadelmann that if he'd wanted to do Napoleon a favor he would have given him Stadelmann as his personal coachman. And Stadelmann replied that he would rather string himself up from the nearest tree than be parted from Goethe.

And so they came to Eger. The weather improved, rooms had been reserved at the Sign of the Sun. Police Superintendent Grüner joined them there and they enjoyed a grief-free evening. As Grüner was leaving, Goethe gave him an envelope with the "Duet on the Pangs of Love" and said that the superintendent was so much a fellow poet that when he read it, he would not be overcome by pity but—he hoped—by the art.

The following morning, the police superintendent's rather restrained embrace conveyed thanks for being admitted into Goethe's innermost feelings. And since he could express it so simply, Goethe announced that his summer had blossomed in Eger, too.

Then for three days, they roamed the countryside. Goethe was all alert engagement, as if there was nothing but limestone quarries, marl, gneiss, granite, idocrase (around here they called it *egran*), smoky topaz, wulfenite with visible crystals, and amethyst, all in the neighborhood. And as a precaution, Goethe ordered some of Grüner's duplicate pieces for his collection in Weimar and promised to give him in exchange a big piece of granulite from Siberia, of which he had three. As they were driving along, Goethe suddenly asked to stop. He got down and went over to men who were mowing a field of grain and pausing to sharpen their scythes. He asked where they got their whetstones. All they knew was that you could buy them on the market square in Eger. When Goethe said they could use some like that in the fields around Weimar, the superintendent promised to have some sent.

Goethe was exaggerating his interest in everything. He needed to prove to himself that he could go for hours without thinking of Ulrike. Or, if not for hours, then for a few minutes at least.

As they sat together on the third evening, praising Eger's beer and outdoing one another in telling all sorts of stories in the most congenial way, the police superintendent announced that, with his well-known insatiable nature—or rather, it had just become insatiable when he realized that no matter where you touch the world, it teems with stories, and, inspired not least by the beer, he declared that the world was a veritable story-teller—in his insatiable style, then, he was grafting a new branch of research onto his life's green tree: folk songs. And at present, he was asking anyone interested to help him. No one could do it alone. Example: there's a folk song, and he even has the melody in his head, but he only knows the beginning of the words.

"Let's hear how it starts," said Goethe, "and Count Sternberg and your humble servant will take care of the rest."

The superintendent half hummed and half recited, "On the redoubt in Strasbourg, that's where my heart grew sore . . ."

Goethe suddenly pressed his right hand against his left eye as if to protect it. When he realized Grüner was looking at him, he turned his head toward the count while still holding his left eye.

The count said, "Of course, it's familiar" and also hummed

the melody. "Yes," he said, "that must be the song of the Swiss soldier in the service of a foreign army." And he continued to sing, "Hark! Did I hear an alphorn playing. . . ?" And both tried to remember more text.

Since the weather today was again quite raw and an east wind had occasionally really hissed in their faces, Goethe could now announce that defying the laws of symmetry, his left eye had taken a notion to be more sensitive than the right one; it must be inflamed and he found it necessary to excuse himself rather abruptly. And he left the room, still holding his right hand over his eye.

He knew his own mind pretty well and knew that tonight he would not be able to make any demands on himself. Especially no directional demands. Anything but toward Weimar. He couldn't think further than that. All night long he was at the end of his tether. A night at the end of one's tether is a long night. His head on the pillow was so heavy it felt like he was pressing it into the pillow with all his might. But his head was heavy all on its own. On the redoubt in Strasbourg, that's where my heart grew sore . . .

He was calm when he came down to breakfast. Count Sternberg said he was going to continue on today, too. But Goethe had not yet said that he was leaving. Sternberg, however, was able to read his friend's face. Grüner appeared, handed Goethe an envelope, and said it contained a copy of the duet in case His Excellency could use one. Grüner took his leave with the parting words, "To a joyful reunion!" When the count asked when the next coach left for Karlsbad, Goethe said, "In an hour," without giving it a moment's thought. "Stadelmann and I will expect you."

In the carriage, Goethe at first covered his left eye with a cloth. The eye was inflamed. A bit inflamed; he had checked in the mirror. They left Eger at 1:00 and it was not yet 4:00 when they reached Karlsbad. As they pulled up in front of the Golden Ostrich, the eye was no longer inflamed. Goethe congratulated Stadelmann. Stadelmann laughed.

During the ride, the count had let Goethe know without saying so directly that the Levetzows had been informed of his—the count's—arrival. He had mentioned it in a way that suggested he knew they were not informed of Goethe's arrival. Goethe was in no mood to treat himself with as much discretion as the count did. He simply said how things stood. He did not say it in a way that would make the count feel obliged to be sympathetic and consoling. That was exactly what he sought to forestall by his cool account. He did not feel the least bit in need of sympathy. It was a miraculous and most beautiful dispensation that his dear friend Count Sternberg was traveling to Karlsbad with him, proof that he, Goethe, was a darling of fate. Unimaginable how it would be if he had to travel alone today from Eger to Karlsbad. It would have happened. He would have gone. Alone. He had to free Ulrike from the prison of her family. His life and Ulrike's must not be sacrificed to maternal narrow-mindedness, however noble it might be. Ulrike expected it of him.

Since he arrived with the count, his arrival was a social matter. A surprise, of course. But in these circles and with an impulsive Goethe, completely understandable. It absolved him almost more than necessary. To arrive alone would be a lightning bolt of passion on a summer day with no warning of thunderstorms. He would have enjoyed serving that up to them. Them? Whom? All of them. The entire, ever-prying world.

In the Golden Ostrich in the Alte Wiesen Strasse they were both familiar guests. There were rooms for both and both were treated as if they had reserved the rooms. Goethe learned without asking that his rooms were where they had been last year: one floor above the rooms of the Levetzow family. Was that not touching! A hotelier treating you in a way that ought to teach the whole world how to treat a traveler! Travelers are always suffering from an injury. The hotelier knows. The hotelier is the emergency doctor of the soul. How awful it would be if you had to tell him, This is how things stand. Please give me a room on such and such a floor. Not in the Golden Ostrich, which couldn't be more aptly named. And they were announced to the Levetzows and were admitted. Both halted at the door, each bidding the other enter first. The count sensed that his appearance here was more harmless than Goethe's and he walked toward the family, who stood arrayed in front of armchairs and side tables, ready to be greeted. The count did so in perfect form. From his trip to Hungary, he brought back greetings from one or two castles and one or two cousins. His greetings were answered in high-pitched voices. Then the count stood beside the family as if he were one of the people Goethe needed to greet.

Because they stood there like that, Goethe began with the smallest one. First, after taking two steps toward the group and then halting once more, he said, "I have been yearning to see you again."

Amalie responded at once, "Us or Ulrike?"

"All the Levetzows," he said quite seriously. He feared that it sounded too solemn, so he said in a clearly more jocular tone and only to Amalie, "All of you."

Amalie was unrelenting. "And how have you missed me?" she asked.

Goethe looked straight at her and her alone and said, "Like a rare stone longs to be picked up and examined by a girl because it knows that only this girl understands it, understands the language of stones."

For the moment that seemed enough for her to chew on. But of course, now Bertha had to ask, "And how have you missed me?"

"Like a stag dying of thirst," he said, "longs for the spring that will save his life."

Bertha was speechless with astonishment. Now it was the mother's turn. She said, "We won't insist on knowing how the Privy Councilor has missed me."

"That's a shame," said Goethe.

"Well then?" she said.

And Goethe said, "I have longed to be able to beg your pardon for an action born out of panic whose awkwardness is exceeded only by its ridiculousness."

"Bravo," said the baroness, went up to Goethe, and cried, "Napoleon was right: *Voilà un homme!*"

Now they all surrounded him. There were handshakes and embraces, but Ulrike had not budged. When everyone noticed that and turned toward her, Goethe walked over to her. She turned away and said, "I need to hear why Excellency missed me."

No one moved or spoke.

Goethe said, "Because I love you."

She extended her hand before he could extend his. Perhaps he could not have spoken as he did had Count Sternberg not been there. What he said in the presence of this man felt like a deed. The count pressed his hand.

Goethe said "Thank you" and left the way you leave when you know everyone is watching you.

Chapter Two

IT WAS IMPOSSIBLE to misunderstand how Frau von Levetzow was going to manage his presence. He was welcome to take breakfast with the family. It began at seven and could extend to nine. So he was at the spring by six every day, where he had taken the water and permitted a Polish poetess to speak to him; in Karlsbad every September for years, she had waited to press her latest poems into his hand. Three days later, she would approach him again to learn whether she had made any progress. Or, she was already lying in wait by the second day to see if he was perhaps burning to say something about her poems. Nothing had changed. Many years ago, he had not been able to decline to read her poems, and if you read someone's poems you cannot later pretend you haven't read them. Luckily, by six there was already a lot of activity at the spring, so he never had to comment on her poems without being interrupted. And every time he said something about one of her lines, she would recite the line in Polish and say the translation was only a pale shadow of the original.

Count Sternberg was always at the spring by five-thirty. If Goethe was simply unable to end a conversation, he could give the count a signal and the count would come and liberate him in the politest possible way from the verbal snares of the person speaking to him. Julie von Hohenzollern, who always ended her season in Karlsbad, also seemed only to wait for his signal. In Karlsbad's steeply notched valley there was no broad oval of meadow. You passed one another at closer range and so were more vulnerable to being addressed. But once Julie von Hohenzollern hastened to his rescue, nothing conversational could happen to him anymore.

Only in the evenings, after supper, did the count take part in whatever togetherness Frau von Levetzow permitted.

Goethe told her daughters they had to realize that in the count, they had a paleobotanist famous throughout Europe. Pa-le-o-botanist. Amalie and Bertha snapped at the word like fish after bait. He knew they would.

The count was happy to participate. He said that the workers in his coal mine had just stumbled upon an upright, carbonized tree trunk. His workers were trained to report such a discovery to him at once. He had the trunk carefully excavated and would soon examine it. Why didn't this trunk turn into coal and how long ago was that? That's what interested him. A paleobotanist is a historian interested not in kings and battlefields, but in how plants had been doing all that time.

Goethe always sat down next to the mother and across from Ulrike. He needed to be able to see Ulrike without having to turn his head. He needed to seek her glance. As soon as their eyes met, he heard only from afar what was being said. Ulrike saw to it that her eyes and his eyes left each other punctually. She displayed a remarkable interest when the count talked about progress in the engineering disciplines.

He said that since his holdings included a factory or two, he did what he could to promote knowledge of engineering.

Ulrike asked if she could visit one of his factories, preferably one where spinning or weaving was going on, where women and girls were working, perhaps even at the machines.

The count was delighted by the prospect of giving her a guided tour of his factories.

Ulrike pointed to the skirt she was wearing, red with wide green stripes that crossed one another in a checkered pattern. "Scottish," she said. "Just feel this cloth, it's heavenly. We could have such sheep, too, and the rest is learnable."

The count turned to Goethe and said, "I see that you're surprised. More than we imagine is always possible. Perhaps it would interest this circle to know that I hear reports from England that Ada Byron, the daughter of the poet, is handed around London as a prodigy. Not just in mathematics, but also in physics. She talks about programmable machines that can be taught numbers that then guide their operation. That is her dream."

Ulrike was positively electrified by this bit of news.

The count promised to keep her informed of everything he learned about Ada Byron, who, by the way, grew up separated from her father.

Goethe felt like he was sinking into an abyss. On so many pages of his journeyman novel he had celebrated manual labor—spinning, weaving—with all the workaday words no writer had ever used before him. Now he knows no one after him will ever use them, either. He had not suppressed the drive toward mechanization, but his fictional figures fear the approach of machines. They see the wasteland expanding as people flee their valleys because their work has been taken over by machines. His world of work was a museum. Ada Byron is the name of the future! Ulrike and the count, the two dearest people he knew, were the future. Now he felt not the least desire to defend what he had written. He loved Ulrike, he loved the count. He wanted to belong with them and was prepared to betray any of his principles. Life—the two of them were life. He sat there, feeling that way, and that made it possible not to defend what he had written.

When Goethe and the count were alone, the latter fetched from his room the blowpipe the Swedish chemist Berzelius had given him. He wanted to show Goethe how easy it was to identify titanium in rocks with this device. He knew that finding traces of titanium was Goethe's favorite topic of conversation this summer. He was all the more surprised when Goethe asked him to show Ulrike how to use it instead of him. The count hesitated at this strange suggestion. Goethe simply shook his head.

The next day, he was able to tell the count without beating around the bush that he was now entirely preoccupied with Fräulein von Levetzow. None of the diverse interests he used to cultivate had survived. Only his interest for Ulrike von Levetzow remained. He could tell this to the count since he already knew it anyway.

The count pressed his hand and said, "What interests us invigorates us. And the more it interests us, the more invigorated we are." Whatever someone was interested in, the important thing was, how much.

"You talk to me about myself," said Goethe, "the way I usually talk to others about others."

The count laughed and said, "Now I have to tell Your Poetical Princely Highness that you are too good to an industrious engineer who never in his life has been able to rhyme one word with another."

That was practically an invitation to tell the count that that could change at any moment. And he could not resist telling him what had happened when he gave Ulrike the "Duet on the Pangs of Love." It was the copy; he had made sure it was identical to the original. And he recited the entire duet to her. But what was the machine-mad Ulrike's reaction? In her jolliest tone she had said, "Although She got two lines less than He, She feels herself well expressed." But she needed to lay claim to the two lines withheld from her. And for the first time in her life, she composed poetry and then read the two lines:

> In a wolfsbane blossom I'll send him my tears
> To remind him of us in the coming years.

"You'll make us all into poets," said the count.

Goethe said, "Because everyone is a poet."

Frau von Levetzow was happy. The count was an entertainer who fulfilled every wish a mother could have. Evening after evening she could oversee everything. Even when they were sitting outside at tea and a waning moon rose over Mount Dreikreuz, no feelings unacceptable to a mother had a chance to be stirred up since the count explained the waning but rising moon not as mood lighting for lovers but as a fascinating theater of heavenly physics.

Goethe had the clear, sharp sense that he was part of a production against which he had no defenses. As if requesting the postponement of an execution, he asked to be allowed to go for a walk with Ulrike in the meadow along the Tepl on the other side of the road. In broad daylight. And Frau von Levetzow, who in Marienbad up to a certain moment had been the splendid courtier Madame de Pompadour, made him pay for the walk in the meadow by agreeing to listen to Count Wallenski that evening, who would tell him terrible things about the sufferings of the Polish people, in the hope that the world-famous poet would at once lift his world-renowned voice so that international aid could ease or even end the sufferings of the Poles. The Ulrike-mother had often enjoyed playing this role in Marienbad, arranging a meeting between people from her circle and Goethe. And because of Ulrike, not once had he said no.

Now during this tightly controlled walk, he had to tell Ulrike that the day was upon them when he would have to exchange the lovely number 73 for the insultingly angular 74. And it was his unpleasant duty to plan the day's events. If he could spend tomorrow uninterruptedly in her vicinity, then even that coffin nail of a date would perhaps be bearable for an entire day. But she would have to be constantly in sight. His proposal: 7:00 a.m., departure for Elnbogen. Stadelmann and John would be there already, and the family and he would arrive at 9:00. Breakfast would await them at the White Horse, then a long walk along the right bank of the Eger on the newly tunneled path through the cliffs. It was narrow and winding with sharp curves so that not even a Frau von Levetzow could keep all of them in the bondage of observability every instant, but they would never be invisible to her for more than nineteen seconds. Then a tour of the Enchanted Prince, a meteor that had fallen from the heavens—or as the count would say, from the universe— right into the castle well of Elnbogen. Then they would eat and drive back (provided that the Levetzows would be his guests tomorrow, Ulrike would promise to always be in his sight, and third, that the word "birthday" as well as the number that might be associated with that word would never occur).

"Ah yes," said Ulrike, clearly imitating, parodying him.

"Promise?" he asked and held out his hand.

"Promise," she said.

As he released her hand, he said, "When we go back, you must at once explain to your mother, who is surely watching us, that that handshake served only to seal a promise that will not survive beyond tomorrow."

The day went off as planned. Except that on the lunch table up in Elnbogen there was a crystal drinking glass. It was Bertha who presented it to Goethe. The names of the three sisters encircled the glass in a wreath of ivy. Goethe read the names and looked at each one in turn as he read her name. First Bertha. Then Amalie. Then Ulrike. Then he read the date: August 28, 1823. And the place: Elnbogen. Then he looked at the mother and said as cheerfully as he could that all they needed now was a rhyme.

"Yes," cried Bertha. "Something to rhyme with Elnbogen."

Goethe said, "May devotion be your slogan."

"Bravo," cried Bertha.

Amalie said, "I'd rather be ruled by a shogun."

And Ulrike: "Instead of being shot with a blowgun."

And the mother: "I'm speechless."

And Ulrike: "At last, something to celebrate!"

They drove over the Hammer River and back to Karlsbad, singing as they went. Even before they alighted from the coach, they could see a crowd in front of the Golden Ostrich. A brass band struck up a tune. Cheers, cheers that seemed they would never end. Frau von Levetzow quickly disappeared into the crowd with her daughters. Almost instinctively, Goethe had reached for Ulrike and managed to grasp her left hand; his hand came away holding a lavender silk glove. He put it into his pocket at once. He could not run after them. He must not even show that he wanted to. He had to stay where he was. And suddenly—it was an unmistakable feeling—suddenly it pleased him to stay. His arms and hands lifted themselves into the air. Since he simply could not remain silent, he cried out words, sentences into the friendly noise of animated band music and cheers. He felt swept up, carried along, and himself shouted "Hurrah, hurrah, hurrah." And that spurred on the crowd. The band intoned a tune they all knew. It played only the opening bars and then the melody was taken up by five natural horns played by tanned twenty-year-old angels, and what they were playing so silky soft and heartfelt was "Spied a lad a little rose." People fell silent. The five horns celebrated the song and the setting sun did the rest. Everyone was crying, including Goethe. He didn't try to hide it. With his lace-bordered handkerchief he wiped the tears from his eyes. More than once. And the people wept with him, including the men. Because words came to him in reaction to everything, a word came to him now: popularity. He felt popular. For the first time in his life. Popular. And the feeling filled him to the point of invulnerability. At this moment he knew that everything would turn out. "Bertha, Amalie, Ulrike," he said—he shouted. But the brass band saw to it that besides itself, anything audible was no longer necessary. The band leader had given the downbeat and the band set off in the direction of the spa, playing the newest march from Vienna. People stepped aside. What a great man that band leader is, thought Goethe. He leaves the square with a jolly march where just a moment ago he had brought people to tears. That's music for you, he thought. He avoided shaking his head.

Two waiters from the inn ushered Goethe the short distance to the front steps. At the door Goethe turned once more, cordially accepted a last chorus of hearty cheers, and went inside.

In his room he asked himself, couldn't one live from such popularity? By now, this talking to himself had become a routine, an interrogation of everything that happened to see whether or not it could make his longing for Ulrike more bearable. What had happened out there on the square in front of the Golden Ostrich: he wanted to—needed to—experience it with Ulrike. Only then could he be completely absorbed by such a friendly storm. Without Ulrike it was a play without a heroine.

He pulled out the lavender silk glove that had ended up

in his hand. He was not about to return it. To ensure that, he wrote—inscribed—on the back of the glove

Karlsbad, on August 28, 1823

Only then did he notice a wrapped package on his table. He unwrapped a pale red bow from her simple, white Lotte-dress. And a card on which was written

Like her beloved predecessor, it would please the successor to be present at your birthday with a pale red bow. Ulrike.

That's right, Lotte gave Werther the bow on his birthday, the pale red one. Ah, Ulrike! How can he express to her now that Lotte didn't exist. That he was Lotte, just as he was Werther. That it was a love story with himself. The story of an illness. Ulrike, you are so much above everything that ever was and could have been. Ulrike. He kissed the bow. Then he emptied out a box lined in black velvet that contained buckles, brooches, and stickpins and carefully laid in it the glove and the bow. This box could be locked with a tiny key, and he did so. But where to put the key so he wouldn't lose it and would immediately know where to find it when needed? That was a new tribulation: that he put things he especially wanted to keep safe in such a safe place that he could no longer find them, or it took a long time to do so. He called Stadelmann and assigned him to go up into town at once and fetch from Count Taufkirchen's shop the thinnest gold chain they had. It had to go round his neck twice and then hang down on his chest. It was just the sort of assignment Stadelmann loved.

Two hours later the little gold key was hanging from Goethe's neck by the thinnest of gold chains.

The next morning the crystal glass with the names in an oval of ivy and the date and place stood on the breakfast table. "Ah yes," he said to Frau von Levetzow, "thank you for letting me spend that painful day with you and for not mentioning it. Let us call it the Day of the Open Secret. Thanks, many thanks for this glass."

"It is meant to bear witness that we were there with you," said Frau von Levetzow, "and you with us. Ivy is for remembrance. We don't want to be forgotten."

In a quiet voice Goethe said, "Nor do I," and gave her what he hoped was a combative look and would have looked at her longer, if Ulrike had not said, "Nor do I."

So he looked at Ulrike.

Once again, Frau von Levetzow had arranged the program for the day. A young English aristocrat needed to speak to Goethe about Verona, where England had pushed through the decision that Europe would not support the Greeks' struggle against Turkish occupation. He wanted Goethe and Walter Scott to address a petition to the king.

Because he was aware of the way Ulrike was looking at him, he agreed. "This evening, after dinner. Although I know, Ulrike, how useless such gestures are."

Ulrike said, "The English are the most modern nation and have the most old-fashioned government."

"I'm sure she got that from Count Sternberg," said Amalie.

"Bad luck, tattletale," said Ulrike in here sweetest voice, "Herr Privy Councilor was present when the count said it."

Their mother forbade any more arguing. "We'll see one another again at five, for the farewell concert in Saxony Hall."

Anna Paulina Milder: his friend Zelter had praised her wonderful voice. All Berlin is at her feet, just as Vienna was earlier. And because one thing always leads to another, that bubbly Lili Parthey—who takes Frau Milder as her model—has brought with her to Bohemia Frau Milder's wish to be permitted to sing for Goethe and has delivered it to the right address: Count Klebelsberg. He is bringing her over from Marienbad to Karlsbad. An unalloyed treat, not open to the general public, a farewell concert dedicated to Goethe.

Saxony Hall was sectioned off with folding screens to create an intimate space for forty or fifty guests. They sat in a semi-circle around the artist and her accompanist. Ulrike sat on the far end of the semicircle as if she had known that Goethe, who had to sit in the middle, would be able to look at her almost without turning his head. That gave the event a purpose.

He knew a brief speech was expected of him after the concert. When something was dedicated to him, a speech was required. Even before he could really listen to it, he heard that this was a voice that stopped at nothing. At first, he sought some keyword for his little speech. Then he saw Ulrike, sitting straight and almost leaning forward a bit, saw her in the spell of that voice. She had left her hair freer than ever before. A dark blue dress with glistening black stripes. Her neck and head emerged from a large, black roll collar. Repeatedly he had to look away from her, had to look up at the artist singing in her penetrating voice, but he sensed that he heard more when he looked at Ulrike than when he watched the singer singing.

He began his little speech with the sage sentences that could be expected of him on such occasions. He said that Count Klebelsberg had told him how much this artist exceeded all expectations once one had seen and heard her for oneself. Count Klebelsberg had said it, and now he, Goethe, was repeating it. Eleven years ago, he had sat in this very hall and heard Beethoven play his first, great piano sonata. It was absolute music. Beethoven was a grateful admirer of Anna Milder because for him and for the world, she had become the model of his Leonore in *Fidelio*, and that fact makes us into an illustrious company, the privileged auditors of an absolute art. When Anna Milder performed for Napoleon in Schönbrunn, the only thing he could say was, *Voilà une voix.*

There were several knowing laughs, and he turned toward them and said, "An emperor can be terse, but the likes of us can't escape verbosity."

Why does reality always outstrip our expectations? He was thinking about that as he spoke. Then suddenly he sensed that he was talking without being present, and without a transition he freed himself from his routine. He knew, he confessed, that on such occasions, people expected reflections of this kind from him, simply because one can't be overwhelmed every time, but can be clever every other time. And all of a sudden, he experienced the same thing he had just experienced when he experienced Ulrike as an auditor. And now he allowed that experience to be his prompter. He counted on reality—even when it seemed almost scandalous—to be the only thing worth talking about. So, during this concert, his gaze had rested for a while on Fräulein von

Levetzow, and then he had looked away again, as was proper, and looked up to this lovely and gifted artist. Then the surprising thing: when he looked back at Fräulein von Levetzow, he heard the music more purely—so to speak—than when he watched it being produced. For as an auditor, Fräulein von Levetzow gave the impression—in case the eyes of other auditors, or even all other eyes were upon her—that she was moved to listen exactly as one was supposed to listen. Surely without intending to, she had become the model listener. She did not distract a single bit from our great artist, but rather drew one toward her and her art. He could not and would not separate the effect of that voice from Ulrike's exemplary listening. The fact of her exemplary listening was the effect of the music, which through her listening became its real effect for him. Nothing can be more direct than that which, thanks to the power and glory and daring of such a voice, becomes visible through such a listener. He had always been against losing himself in impressions and events. He had felt that Schubert sung by Klebelsberg had an effect that wasn't justified by its cause. This time, the voice took possession of you without the music dissolving you into helpless surrender to its tones. Without losing yourself. And that came from this auditor, who was by no means lost, but a model of self-possession and even full of curiosity. Frau Milder has awakened in a nineteen-year-old a continent of feeling, a continent unexplored by her. And he ventured to prophesy that when this auditor comes to know the yearning (expressed here in song) in the nonmusical world, where yearning exercises its real power with the text, "You cannot live there where you are and you will not reach where you yearn to be," then she will flee to this continent of music in order to demonstrate to so-called reality its downfall in beauty. That was what he had experienced: as long as the yearning is in this music, it cannot destroy us. We do not simply withstand it, we celebrate it. For a few moments, we are indestructible. Reality has no chance against beauty.

And he went to the singer and reached up to shake her hand as well as the count's. Toward Ulrike he bowed gently. People applauded and he directed their applause to the two performers. Then he motioned to Julie von Hohenzollern as he always did when he needed her help. She was by his side in a flash and led him out while he acted more in need of help than he was. When he had bowed toward Ulrike, his shoulders had involuntarily performed a kind of shrug while his hands signaled helplessness or even begged for forgiveness. Ulrike had immediately understood and moved her head atop the roll collar back and forth, but really only the slightest bit, a gesture of complete agreement. It meant, Not the least reason to apologize. The whole thing superhumanly lovely, heartfelt, relaxed. A second of harmony on which the world would draw for a thousand years. In that mood, he left the hall.

Meanwhile, Julie von Hohenzollern said, "If I know the Privy Councilor, he'll be wanting a lager from Eger right now." And she led her charge with the flair she displayed under all circumstances into the Prince's Taproom.

When he had taken his first, deep draught he said, "Princess, how many times will you continue to rescue me?"

And she: "Rescuing Goethe—that would be my favorite occupation."

And he: "I fear you have your work cut out for you. Cheers." And he drained his glass.

In the evening, after dinner, Amalie wanted to know why Herr Privy Councilor had not looked at her.

"Or me," Bertha chimed in.

"Or me," added Frau von Levetzow.

Before Goethe could answer, Ulrike said, "You were sitting right next to him but I was way out at the end of the semicircle. Imagine how he would have had to turn his head to look at you—impossible. So only I remained. And seriously, ladies, I'm not sure if what he said about me would have occurred to him about you. Through his description, I could really imagine how I had been listening."

"Oh of course," said Amalie. "Don't pretend you didn't notice that he kept looking at you. Then you just provided him with the face he needed."

Count Sternberg begged to differ. In fact, no matter where one sat, one had to notice that for the Privy Councilor, Ulrike was as important as Frau Milder. He, for example, had followed the Privy Councilor's gaze. Looking over quickly now and then at the figure sitting way out on the left flank, he understood why the Privy Councilor kept looking over there. If he might express it, he would say that Ulrike's objectivity in listening was the controlling factor.

"But it was also a bit embarrassing," said Amalie, "that staring at Ulrike."

"Not for me," said Ulrike merrily. "I've learned how to be stared at this summer."

"And enjoyed it," said Amalie.

"T-O-Y," cried Bertha.

Ulrike quickly whispered to him, "Typical of you."

"That's enough," commanded Frau von Levetzow, and without even attempting a transition, said that she'd always considered the most plausible distinction to be that hardened men like Napoleon loved soft, melancholy music and gentle men like perhaps our dear Goethe were more for lively, cheerful tones.

"If that was true," said the count, "then beginning today it isn't true anymore."

"Correct," said Ulrike.

Goethe's favorite conversations were those that got along without him. In his room, he sat down at the desk and wrote:

A Man in Love

Women are the objective sex. A man experiences everything only as a mood. As his mood. The woman always experiences the thing. The thing itself. Then she deals with the thing, about which she has an opinion. The opinion is determined more by the thing than by her. This constitutes her objectivity. The man judges according to what he's feeling at the moment. His opinion has less to do with the thing than with himself. If the world is to be administered more in harmony with itself, it must be administered by women. When will that be? Men belong in the sandboxes and the ivory towers, women at the helm.

Since he is a man, this statement says more about him than about its object. Wanting to maintain a bit of accountability, he has to add that.

A woman is more transparent than a man. Ulrike

almost said it: the more she reads by him, the less she knows who he is. Only someone sure of herself can talk that way. High-flown tall tales is what she called his writing. But who is he? she asked quite objectively. He will ask Ulrike before they part—i.e., tomorrow—he will ask her if he still seems as ambiguous as he did in his works, if he is still only who he is in any given situation.

One isn't responsible for oneself. Know thyself: an agreeable illusion. Or an invitation to invent yourself. Then it's not you, but an invention. Only others can know you. The more they love you, the more precisely they know you.

He is clearer to himself now than ever before. Through Ulrike. All vagueness ends with her. The way she reacts to him shows him how he is, who he is, what he is. He will become freer toward her. Involuntarily. She will know him as the person he is through her. That's who he will be. Through his love for her.

Already, in anticipation, he senses how the world will be then: peaceful, because those who need each other have each other. Then they will need nothing else. The world is no longer a globe with nerves. It is a benevolent event when those who love each other are together. If that succeeds a single time, Ulrike, the world will be changed forever. Not a leaf or bloom, not a jailor or president will remain untouched by it. All the ills of the world have arisen through lack of love. Ulrike and he will redeem the world of all evil because they are sufficient unto themselves.

Even he can see his own grandiosity, Ulrike. His tone sounds exaggerated because humanity is trained to suppress, denigrate, and silence. To belittle.

The explosiveness of his words comes from something that was missing his whole life long: love. And now it's here. So it exists. That is not just playing with words. It is the greatest precision possible. It is the most vivid possible presence and fills you to the brim. The greatest possible certainty.

He gives himself over to Ulrike's objectivity. He has no defense against it. The result is that he can forgo everything in the world except her. He is defined by his love for her. He is his love for her. A declaration of love, whenever hats occur: whenever he sees women wearing ambitious hats, he imagines them on Ulrike. Every last one of those hats, even the most outrageous, becomes beautiful only when Ulrike wears it.

There he stopped writing. He sat and experienced the feeling that when she was not there in person, he had to write. As long as he was writing, she was there. As soon as he stopped, she was gone. But since she was missing only until breakfast, her absence was bearable. If he always knew when he would see her again, there would be no suffering. This had been rehearsed all summer long. In the pauses, everything increased that would burst out in an excess of feeling when he saw her again.

Chapter Three

FROM KARLSBAD TO Diana's Hut.

At breakfast, Ulrike had given him a look that let him know her mother had agreed to allow them that afternoon a last walk up to Diana's Hut without the family.

Frau von Levetzow could not resist including in the way she formulated her farewell to the two of them the information that it was she who had permitted this walk and that they should please not violate her trust. That was the stuffy gist of what she said. But the manner in which she couched her moral rules and regulations and the rhetorical and oratorical flourishes with which she expressed them, came straight out of the best French farces. That is, nothing was said that couldn't be said amusingly. Madame de Pompadour, the splendid courtier in her motherly role.

Both the cautioner and the cautioned could always act as if it were just a game. They would soon discover it was unmistakably serious if they thought the playful tone was only a playful tone. Goethe liked playing along. He acted the virtuoso of rococo, outdoing Madame de Pompadour in half-playacting. It pleased him that the family accepted his frightful seriousness as a farce. And so they would part for four hours—the excursion to Diana's Hut should not be, must not be, was not permitted to last longer—the perfect closing scene for the third act of the five-act farce entitled "The Uncle as Nephew."

As soon as they were really alone, Goethe thanked Ulrike for the pale red bow with which she had reminded him of Werther's birthday on his birthday. And he begged her pardon that he had snatched her lavender-blue silk glove half by accident, half on purpose. Before he could say he would like to keep it, she said "But it belongs to you" in a serious tone that was rare for her.

Goethe said, "When you express too much thanks for something, you suggest that you haven't earned what you're thanking someone for."

"Shall I turn that assertion around?" she asked.

"You may do anything," he said.

Well then, for the next four hours she wanted to address him with the familiar *du*. Keep the Excellency, but use *du*. It would please her to be on familiar footing with an Excellency.

He would like to be on a familiar footing with the Contresse Levetzow, he said.

"For how long?" she asked.

"For . . ." he pretended to think about it, calculate it, and then said in the simplest tone in the world, as if there was nothing as sensible, predictable, and unsensational as what he was now saying with such utter nonchalance, "Forever."

She said, "W-H-G-T-Y."

And to prove he had learned their abbreviation language, he said, "We haven't gotten there yet," and added "B-S."

She: "What does that mean?"

He: "But soon."

"Ah, Excellency," she said and involuntarily began walking faster.

If she weren't walking with him, she would go faster and faster. On the promenade in Marienbad he first of all had to teach her how slowly one needed to walk on a promenade among so many famous persons. She then took his arm and more or less let him guide her, but even then she kept applying forward pressure. It did him good to put the brakes on her will to accelerate with the same energy she used to apply it. On the way back from the promenade to the Klebelsberg palais, however, she fell into her pace and he had to keep up. It was something of a climb. When he drove out into the country around Weimar in his carriage, he liked to walk much of the way back home. And in his house he would walk back and forth for hours through a suite of six rooms and write standing up. There was no question of sitting in an armchair or on a sofa unless he was receiving visitors. When she could walk the way nature intended, Ulrike was another person. Her walk had nothing to do with hurry. She was so light, her limbs flew on ahead of her all by themselves. It was glorious to watch her walking, but he had trouble keeping up. He was a heavier person than she.

Now, on the steep path to Diana's Hut, as she raced off without meaning to and without noticing and despite the steep path, he pretended it was the right tempo for him, too. If she was going to go as quickly and lightly as she wanted, he was not about to lag even a bit behind. It was unimaginable to fall behind or call to her to please moderate the tempo. On the contrary, he not only caught up but forged a half-step ahead at her pace. She noticed, looked over and, since he was a head taller, up. They were as united and attuned to each other as they had been in Marienbad, dancing. As they raced up the mountain, they were the same age. If she had begun to sing it wouldn't have surprised him. But she didn't sing; she began to recite a text he recognized. She recited by heart a passage from his Werther novel. Without getting stuck or hesitating or any other sign of uncertainty, she recited an entire Werther-episode. It didn't slow her uphill progress at all, on the contrary, the text seemed to just make her lighter. Now it was unthinkable that he fall behind or ask for a more leisurely pace. And this is what she said:

On September 15

It's enough to drive one mad, Wilhelm, that there are people without sense or feeling for the few things on earth that still have value. You know the honest parson's walnut trees beneath which I sat . . . with Lotte, those marvelous trees that, God knows, always filled my soul with the greatest pleasure! How intimate they made the yard of the parsonage, how cool! And how marvelous their branches were! And the recollection going back to the honest clergymen who had planted them so many years ago. The schoolmaster often mentioned one name in particular that he had heard from his grandfather, and he was said to be such a virtuous

man, and the thought of him was always sacred to me
as I sat beneath those trees. Believe me, the schoolmaster's eyes were filled with tears yesterday when we
spoke about their being chopped down—Chopped
down! I shall go mad. I could murder the dog who
made the first cut. I who could die of sorrow if a few
such trees stood in my yard and one were to die of old
age, I had to stand by and watch. Dear friend, there is
one good thing about it! What are human feelings! The
whole village is grumbling and I hope the pastor's wife
will notice from the eggs and butter and other dona-
tions she will not receive what a wound she has struck.
For it is she, the wife of the new pastor (our old one
has died), a gaunt, sickly creature who has good reason
not to care about the world, for no one cares about her.
A foolish woman who pretends to be learned, meddles
in discussions of the canon, labors away at the new-fan-
gled moral-critical reforms of Christianity and shrugs
her shoulders at Lavater's enthusiasms, has ruined her
health and therefore takes no joy in God's earth. Only
such a creature could have chopped down my walnut
trees. As you see, I can't get over it! Just imagine, the
falling leaves are making her yard dirty and dank, the
trees are blocking the sunlight, and when the nuts are
ripe, boys throw stones at them and that gets on her
nerves, disturbs the profound contemplation she
devotes to comparing Kennicott, Semler, and Michaelis.
Since I saw how dissatisfied the villagers were, especially the old ones, I said, Why did you allow it?—
Around here, they said, if the mayor is for it what can

we do? But one good thing happened. The mayor and the pastor (who wanted to get some profit from his wife's foolishness, since it wasn't making his soup any thicker) intended to sell the wood and share the returns. But the village treasurer's office found out about it and said, Step right in here! For it had old claims to the part of the parsonage yard where the trees stood, and they sold the wood to the highest bidder. They have been felled! Oh, if I was the prince! What I would do to the parson's wife, the mayor, and the treasurer—prince!—If I was the prince, what would I care about the trees in my country?

When she stopped there and declared the *Werther* recitation over, she had no intention of standing still—for instance, to hear what the author of *Werther* had to say about this passage or even about her recitation. Soon after they had first met one another, all the Levetzows had read something aloud and requested and received from him wise advice for improving their recitations, and now she had recited *Werther* in a way that had never been discussed in the long evenings spent talking about how to read aloud, because no one had ever done it like this—neither he nor any of the other readers in the family. In July while they were still in Marienbad, the outspoken Bertha had taken pleasure in repeating that two years ago, he had criticized Ulrike more than anyone else. She needed to work on developing more energy and a livelier presentation. And dispassionate Ulrike had answered calmly that she had no desire to be another Tieck.

Now he understood why Ulrike had mustered neither

energy nor a livelier presentation as a reciter of Scott's novels. Her nature refused to produce anything that didn't come from within. She was against all artificiality, even if it was art. She was the soul of unbending objectivity. She had allowed the sentences to form unpretentiously, as if they came of their own accord, without any attempt at expressiveness on her part, but with unconcealed interest for these sentences. He could definitely sense enthusiasm. But it wasn't her enthusiasm; it was the enthusiasm of the sentences. An enthusiasm that pressed inward without the need for external support.

Without speaking further, they came through the mature forest to the hut. Only when there was he able to tell her, "Ulrike, how lucky it is that at your suggestion we've used the intimate form this afternoon, otherwise I probably wouldn't be able to say that that passage can never have been read like that before. And the fact that you chose that passage—"

"Learned it by heart, you must say," she interrupted.

". . . learned it by heart, makes me happy without knowing why."

She replied quite carelessly, "When you know why you're happy, you aren't happy anymore."

"Well then, now I'm very happy," he said.

"I've infected you, Excellency," she said.

"I've infected you," he said.

"We've infected each other," she said.

He whispered, "The fact that you always have to have the last word makes me happiest."

"However," she whispered in return, "since you can't let anything go without comment, you've had the last word."

He pantomimed that now she'd had the last word after all.

On their way back down the mountain, Ulrike said that before they found themselves back in the terrain of formal address she had to tell him why she'd had to learn the passage with the walnut trees by heart. In those sentences, Goethe had become clearer to her than in anything else of his she had read. He had once suggested that he was Lotte just as much as he was Werther. That produced the ambiguity that made it hard for her to pin him down. But not in this passage. If someone is mourning another person, we are not as sad as the mourner because we don't know the other person. But we know the walnut trees! They are as close to us as they are to Werther. We don't mourn with him, but like him. Whenever in this world nut trees—or trees in general—are chopped down, we will recall Werther mourning for his nut trees and we will feel him more intensely than any other literary hero. And now she finally feels Goethe completely. The question, Who is he? has vanished from the world.

As they emerged from the last bit of forest into the evening light framed by clouds, heat lightning flickered across the western sky. They had to stop and watch the excited and exciting display.

Ulrike stepped up to him, took his hands, raised them, and said, "N-C-O-L-W-N."

And he replied, "W-A-T-F."

Then their mouths approached each other, came closer than they ever had, and stayed there until, with a shrill cry, a magpie shattered eternity.

"Ah, Excellency," she said.

"Ah, Ulrike," he answered.

When they saw below them the crowded ranks of Karlsbad's buildings stretching along the river, she said that as long as they were still in the *du* zone, she had a confession to make.

He said he looked forward to whatever it was, but it was a drier announcement than he had expected.

She could only tell him if he promised that no punishment or disciplinary action would ensue.

He promised.

She assumed that he knew that down there in town, his wonderful Stadelmann was selling the hair he regularly harvested from Excellency's head.

Goethe nodded in concern. He said he had put a stop to that in Weimar but he didn't know that the business had relocated to Bohemia.

So she had ordered hairs from Stadelmann, at least three, and had gotten seven in a little decorative tin. She was very happy to possess those seven lovely long hairs of his. She needed to tell him, and as promised, no punishment?

Goethe: "As promised."

As they passed the spring and the Golden Ostrich came into view, she said, "Here ends the *du* zone. Ah, Excellency."

And he replied, "Ah, Ulrike."

"But," she brightly cried, "it was the most beautiful afternoon of the summer."

"Agreed," he said.

An exchange of glances and they walked the last few yards as if they were both equally cheerful.

And because in his room he still felt cheerful, he had to write to Frau Isolde Berlepsch at last—in a quatrain, of course:

But I'm ashamed of having rested.
To suffer with you is my gain.
Because the anguish you have tasted
Makes you greater than I am.

"Herr John, you have the twenty letters from Frau Berlepsch. Please send her this reply."

You could never tell what his secretary Herr John thought about a task he'd been assigned.

Chapter Four

WHEN HE REPORTED back—not without irony—to Frau Head
Warden, Amalie and Bertha took over the job of evaluating
the report. They had been waiting for the pair of walkers.
The plan had been to pay a visit to Count Taufkirchen's
shop, for they'd done almost no shopping yet this year. So
off they went to town to see Count von Taufkirchen, whose
shop had everything you didn't need but were all the more
eager to buy. Goethe came along and bought earrings of
Bohemian garnet for Amalie, a bracelet of enameled lozenges
for Bertha, and a tiny golden ginkgo leaf on a slender chain
for Ulrike. She bought a silver ivy leaf on ditto for him. The
sets of wooden and stone building blocks reminded him that
he hadn't yet purchased anything for his grandchildren in
Weimar. But he couldn't bring himself to play the grandfather now, in the midst of the Levetzows and with Ulrike's
eyes upon him. The family bought glassware, cups, coffee-
pots, a Chinese tea service, black wooden teacups with lac-
quered gold interiors, a Persian blanket with Persian letters,

blouses, scarves, skirts and stockings, and sandals (also Persian). Goethe looked on and rendered an opinion when asked.

Count Taufkirchen delivered it all to their rooms in the Golden Ostrich and unfortunately stayed all evening. Since he encountered customers from all over the world here, he had much to tell. Goethe sought Ulrike's eyes, but he realized she was engrossed in the conversation this evening, as if there were a hundred such evenings still to come. He also managed not to have anyone ask him if he wasn't feeling well.

And today, the last breakfast together. Then the real farewell. He had told Stadelmann to have the fully packed carriage ready at nine o'clock near the spring in front of the Golden Lion. Goethe did not want to be remembered as a hand waving from a carriage window. On the other hand, it was unthinkable that he would walk away from the Golden Ostrich alone as the family watched him go. But none of that planning was necessary. When the breakfast had become the last breakfast, Count Sternberg was the first to rise from the table and say with utter nonchalance, "I'll be waiting downstairs" and to the family, "We'll see one another again. Adieu."

Now the farewell embraces, nothing but comic theater, the Uncle as Nephew, with a good deal of commotion permitted and the most incredible phrases uttered. The two younger girls played along, probably without perceiving the ambiguity of this scripted farce. Frau von Levetzow welcomed the jolly tumult. Not until the very end, as Goethe was raising his head from kissing her hand and their eyes met, did she become serious. Although she imitated the abbreviation language of her daughters and said "N-C-O-L-W-N," it sounded more pleading than playful. Equally earnest, Goethe repeated "N-C-O-L-W-N." He kissed the younger two. He extended his hand to Ulrike and said, "Well then." She said it, too, "Well then," but her Well then was not an echo of his Well then. Then you turn away and marvel that you're able to. From the door, a final comedic wave.

The count was waiting downstairs. He takes Goethe—there's no other way to say it—under his wing. The count is at least as tall as the fellow without a given name. Goethe could not fend off that thought, which suddenly befell him. Both have a moustache, but what the count has is no sneering pencil line but a delicate, well-disciplined shrub. Even when they strolled the promenade together over in Marienbad, Goethe had always felt that he was in something like the armpit custody of the count. Now in Karlsbad on the sunny morning of September 5, 1823, he would not have been able to walk from the Golden Ostrich to the Golden Lion without the count. Not that he clung miserably to that big, handsome man, but he lent him his left arm to link with his right arm; they walked along in balance. He could feel it. And there was no need to chat to protect themselves from passersby. Goethe felt it and knew that the count felt it, too: they could not be disturbed. Goethe even felt that watching them from the window, the family had to be watching their exit without commentary. And before he climbed into his elegant convey-ance, he told the count, "You are always welcome at my house." And added, "To the very end." A mutual nod. No hand-waving.

The weather couldn't be better. Stadelmann took to the

road for all it was worth and maybe even a little more. And since it had been so dry for days, the dust billowed up, reddish-brown in the sun, and then sank back down behind them.

Which thoughts should he allow to enter his mind now, which should he keep out? As if that were something you could decide. But you have to act like you can, otherwise you're a team of horses racing along and ignoring all commands. And you know how that ends.

As soon as the town was out of sight, he returned to the final scene. More than once he replayed it in his mind, and each time only to get to Ulrike's "Well then." Ulrike's Well then had been brighter than his Well then. Braver. With more trust in the future. More challenging. More adorable. He was ashamed of his broken-wing Well then. How much future rang in Ulrike's Well then! Every time he got to this Well then, he heard that it was a Well then that challenged him to create the future. Which meant writing. And he began to write—in the coach, in his rocking carriage with the fabulous springs, he wrote in pencil in his travel diary in which each date filled only half a page. The decision to make it an elegy had already been reached before he wrote the first line.

Marienbad Elegy. That was what it would be called.

By the time he climbed out in front of Grüner's house in Eger, the first six lines were written down in his diary. He did not show his friend Grüner the six lines. The Marienbad Elegy grew from those six lines, from one stop to the next. From Eger to Jena via Gefell, Schleiz, Kahla, and Pössneck. The elegy was no express letter from his soul. It was an exercise in visualization so that as long as he was writing, Ulrike would be less absent, or not absent at all.

The following morning when they parted—Goethe was already in his coach—Grüner called up to him, "I'll venture to hope for a reunion next year. We still have to make our excursion to the menilites." At that point, waving was called for, by both of them. But when Goethe waved, he could never help but feel that waving minimized the farewell. But perhaps that's the point of waving.

Grüner remained in his thoughts a while. Goethe reproached himself for getting impatient the previous day when they were in Grüner's mineral collection and he was expected to stop and look at some newly acquired fossils in bituminous coal from England. "That will interest Count von Sternberg," he had said somewhat nervously. Even worse, when Grüner noticed that he couldn't interest his friend in minerals today, he had begun to describe the terrible famine in the Erzgebirge range. Goethe forced himself to look sympathetic. What's that, how's that? The world is cruel? Yes, of course, but what's the point of participating?

And now in Zwotau, he got the news of a catastrophic fire in Hof—Hof, entirely consumed. At once he told Stadelmann to detour around Hof. Stay as far away as possible. Bad enough that the baggage cart he'd sent on ahead with five crates full of minerals and six cases of Kreuz Spring water must be in Hof this very minute, perhaps tipped over in the panic, crates of minerals and Kreuz Spring bottles lost. He drew the curtains. The elegy was calling.

Since they stayed in Gefell that night where they had never stayed before, Stadelmann first checked the bedroom doors in the inn to make sure the hinges were oiled. If not, he always had some oil along and didn't summon his master until the doors swung silently. Next day to Schleiz, where people knew this visitor and his coachman. However, Goethe was awakened toward five in the morning by the cooing of doves and then had to listen because he'd never been so close to cooing doves or heard them for so long. He drew a staff and entered what he heard.

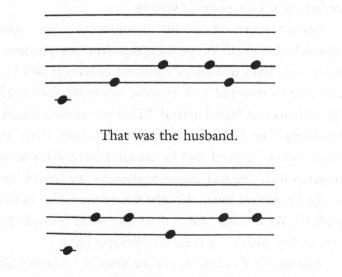

That was the husband.

That was the wife.

The husband was in one of the trees fairly close to the window, the wife more distant. They went on for an hour. Then the wife came nearer. The husband flew to meet her. Energetic beating of, probably, four wings. Then quiet, but for only a quarter hour at most. Then the cooing began again. He nearby, she farther off. Goethe closed the window. The cooing was now muted, but unmistakably cooing. If he could write Ulrike a letter now, tell her what was happening here in the treetops outside his window, then everything would be good! But no! The elegy was waiting.

Through Pössneck to Kahla, with Jena already looming. He had to secure the elegy as if it were a bastion that could protect him and Ulrike from Jena and from what must follow Jena. Jena was the mundane business even now deployed against him, against Ulrike and him. On this last day before Jena, as he was writing in the swaying coach as always, he had the feeling that he was on his knees, writing. And as soon as he stopped writing even for a moment, he again heard himself uttering brief little cries. They were pitched much too high. They were ridiculous little cries. But he needed them.

Stadelmann called to him that they were in Kahla. He pulled back the curtain, climbed out, let himself be led to his room, sat down at the table, and worked on revising today's strophe. Stadelmann was able to report that the baggage cart had passed through Hof unharmed, had arrived here yesterday already, and had left early this morning for Weimar.

They reached Jena the following day. By the botanical garden that he had designed, in the inspector's house where he had an apartment furnished for his visits to Jena, his son August was waiting for him. Goethe was dismayed. He did not recall his son being this fat. He would have liked to begin the conversation by recommending the Hahnemann diet he himself followed. But he knew his son took pride in the fact that everything tasted good to him. He held epicureans in contempt and thought special diets were a malicious invention of greedy doctors. One of his favorite sayings was "Everything complicated is foreign to me; Napoleon wasn't complicated, either." August was an admirer of Napoleon.

He had gotten himself and his father invited to dinner by Goethe's dear friend Knebel. That pleased his father. Besides Zelter, Knebel was the only person he addressed with the intimate *du*. It was almost fifty years ago that Knebel, the court tutor of Duke Carl August, had brought him together with Goethe in Frankfurt. Knebel and Goethe had become and had remained fast friends. To be sure, Goethe had not been able to prevent his friend from falling into negativity and becoming more and more of a critic and condemner of everything. They set off for Knebel's house. For the length of one evening, it was always superb. But if on the following evening Knebel was the slightest bit negative, Goethe would give up on him again for a while. But this time, Knebel greeted him with, "What have they done to you?"

Goethe: "They've made me happy."

Knebel: "You've been to the valet for rejuvenation you employed in 'The Man of Fifty.'"

Goethe: "People who love me notice."

Knebel: "It sounds better the other way around: Whoever doesn't notice doesn't love you."

Goethe: "Agreed."

Knebel: "Goethe agrees with me? What an evening it's going to be!"

Then the topic for this evening: the students had staged protest marches against Goethe because they'd heard from somewhere that he was coming to Jena for a few days. *Pereat* Goethe! and Down with Goethe! all evening long. August reported that an investigation of the ringleaders was already underway.

Knebel said it was what came from being liberal and constantly giving in. Expel all the marchers from the duchy immediately!

Goethe asked what they were protesting.

August had already found that out. They were softheaded nationalists who hated and scorned Goethe ever since his meeting with Napoleon.

"Idiocy never dies," said Knebel.

Then it could have turned into a congenial evening except that August came out with the news that Dr. Rehbein had left for his home town of Eger at five this morning to fetch his bride and they were to be married almost immediately.

That was a blow for Goethe. He praised the bride in the most glowing tones but called the rushed marriage a stupid trick. An extempore engagement was all well and good, but a wedding on the spur of the moment? Horrors. Love always arises instantaneously. But marriage is a synthesis of the impossible. It needs some thought first.

Goethe was furious. He was eager to leave. Afterward he sat with August for a bit in the inspector's house. It was impossible to overlook the fact that August would have liked to talk further about the topic of weddings. Goethe sensed that August was waiting for him to say something about Ulrike von Levetzow.

August said how much they had heard all through the summer. And how it had pained Ottilie. That shouldn't surprise his father, given the special relationship between him and her.

For his part, Goethe felt it impossible at this time to tell his son the news that August could then send to Weimar by courier this very night. When August realized that his father would not mention the name Levetzow, he dropped any further trick questions.

Then he announced his plans for the next three days. Goethe was scheduled to visit everything he had founded: museums, libraries, the school of veterinary medicine, the botanical garden, the observatory, the new building for the veterinary hospital. Then August handed him the letter he had been charged to deliver from the grand duke, wishing Goethe a happy return. The letter ended with the sovereign's urgent wish that Goethe at once be named trustee of the University of Jena. He hoped Goethe would not deny his friend this wish. Especially in light of recent student unrest, it was obvious how important it had become to have Goethe as a trustee in Jena.

Goethe folded the letter and said he was genuinely exhausted. Until tomorrow, dear August.

August still wanted to hear: yes or no?

Goethe said nothing, but shook his head more energetically than usual.

In the study, which contained only the bare necessities, he sat down at the desk. He could not go to bed yet. He dreaded the very sight of his bed. Not because it was as plain as a soldier's cot, but because it was a bed. He had to write. It was too late for further work on the elegy. He was too tired. And so, since he couldn't address Ulrike directly in the poem, he wrote to Frau von Levetzow. She had stage-managed the days and nights in Karlsbad so that he had walked around and sat around like a man in chains. But if he was going to write, he had to thank her. Any other register was out of the question.

Whatever he wrote, he was always sure to write that he was writing. The writer shouldn't act as if what he is writing gets committed to paper all by itself. Especially when he wasn't dictating but writing with his own hand, the writer also had to talk about his writing. Whenever the necessity to write was as unmistakable as it was in Jena on the night of September 13th to 14th, 1823, the writer felt secure in that necessity. The condition he was in can be called innocence or lack of hesitation or freedom.

From the outset, he openly confessed to the Ulrike-mother how much he had to say and how little he was able to say. How much he had to thank her for this summer and especially for the last few days. He couldn't enumerate it all, but he knew she would know what he meant. And he wrote to the mother what he wrote to the daughter but was not allowed to write to her. He was in the same state with the daughter as with the mother. The daughter knew the state he was in, knew his state of mind by heart, so that if he occurs in her thoughts from time to time, she can tell herself everything better than he can in his present condition.

". . . in my present condition . . ." That's exactly what he wrote. And because that said more than he wanted, he switched to a frivolous tone. Her daughter would know that it's a pleasant business, being loved, even if her friend sometimes breaks his stride. Everywhere he goes he hears how good and healthy he looks and how cheery he is. They both knew what elixir he'd been taking.

He mentioned Bertha and Amalie in a way they would find satisfactory if the letter was to be read aloud. Given what Frau von Levetzow had told him about her life—for instance, about her contact with Madame de Staël in Geneva—he felt closer than ever to the family. And she should please tell her daughter that the more he got to know her, the more he liked her. He would like to personally prove to her that he knows what pleases her and what displeases her. And so he is hopeful. At the end as in the beginning.

"Your faithful and devoted servant G."

Then he realized he was unable to stop. Writing to Ulrike's mother was now his only chance to talk to Ulrike, so on a new page he admitted at once that he now saw he couldn't stop writing to her.

The only thing that immediately occurred to him was to send greetings to Count Klebelsberg and thank him for the surprising variety of provisions for their journey he had carefully packed and delivered to Stadelmann. And then he stopped. And then he couldn't stop. He started in again. He had not taken leave of the Broesigke grandparents in Marienbad. She should please convey his best wishes and tell them that if his luck held, he would like to be their guest again next year. By which he hinted that he would like to stay in their palais again. He stopped. He started again. There was one more important thing, he wrote. He implored her to let him know in case the Levetzows relocated, and to where. To emphasize this point again after all that N-C-O-L-W-N nonsense was superfluous. But now they had it in writing.

Now there were already four postscripts, each one signed as if it was the last.

And he began again: the glass with the three names wreathed in ivy was standing on the table in front of him. That beautiful day of open secrets. He made his meaning clearer: the sight of the glass makes him happy but it doesn't console him.

Bed was still impossible. He couldn't write anymore. This was going to be a constant problem. As long as he wrote, if only to the mother, he was with Ulrike. If he was too tired to write, where was he then? Every day in the coach he had continued to work on the elegy, always as early in the morning as possible, as soon as they had set off. Now he took out his travel diary and read what he had written but not yet found a place for in the elegy.

> And hear a word, the loveliest to bind you
> As you have left me, just so you will find me.

> And is surprised to find out that the sun
> Does not stand still for her.

> And even after the last kiss she ran
> To press yet one more kiss upon my lips—

> What we had, where has it gone?
> And what we have now, what is that?

Tomorrow, he thought, as soon as he was in Weimar, he would write the elegy down and revise it so that he had it. He would not show it to anyone. To Ulrike of course, at once. But since he cannot send her anything her mother will not see, he cannot send the elegy to her, its sole addressee. And so what now begins within him will never come out. And he will cheat the world out of what is happening within him now.

Whenever his thoughts behaved like this, he always submitted them, complete, to Ulrike. He always needed to know what Ulrike thought of what he had just had to think. Fortunately, she was so present within him that when he confided in her, he never went unanswered.

Part Three

Chapter One

Weimar, October 7, 1823

Dear Ulrike,

When I asked you if I was permitted to write you when I couldn't stand not to, you said, "But of course."

When you say yes, you say YES. If I didn't sense that so keenly, I could not write to you. It helps that I don't know if I'll be able to send what I write immediately. Partly because I also fear that Ottilie has persuaded or enchanted or bribed or threatened our postman not to let anything of mine leave Weimar without showing it to her first. She would immediately confiscate a letter from me to you. Ever since I returned from Bohemia, she has been ill. Obviously, more than we could have imagined had been reported from Marienbad. It seemed that she and I had barely greeted each other properly when she took to her bed. I was not allowed to visit her, said Little August, since I was the malady she was suffering from. My Dr. Rehbein added that there was a promising new therapy that prescribed treating a malady with the same malady and so curing it. He managed to get me visiting privileges. How long it had been since I was last in the mansard apartment that is her realm! Even Son August sometimes jokes that he's only a transient up there (in the mansard). It was ghastly how she lay there, staring at the ceiling. Her face, always inclined to tense up, was tense to the breaking point. Her nose, always too prominent for her rather small face, now dominated it brutally because that little face had practically disappeared. Her lips, never substantial, were gone. Her arms lay feebly at her sides but the hands were clenched into fists. She granted me not a glance from her black eyes. Fortunately. I've become accustomed to other eyes. We remained silent a long time. There was nothing I could say. I tried once to lay my hand on her fist and she screamed, a scream of pain, a scream of resistance, a leave-me-be scream. But then suddenly, the tirade poured forth. Aimed at you, Ulrike. What names she called you, you and all Levetzows. A gang of social climbers, occupying the spas and on the lookout for the juiciest morsels (an image that doesn't fit me). I cannot repeat the images she dragged in to describe you. Not yet. Perhaps we can have a correspondence that allows me to say more than is allowed. All Europe knows that you, Ulrike, are an ambitious whore. Just so you know what I have to put up with here. I've visited her every day since then. Dr. Rehbein says that before I visited her she lay there, didn't utter a peep, and ate nothing at all. I don't believe the latter. Making all that known is part of the war she's waging against me. And no war has ever been caused by one person. For a war you need at least two. My war guilt: for all these years, I put up with, participated in, and was responsible for Ottilie feeling as if she were married to me. Between us, Little August was part of a game she had to play to get to me. Of course, all this was always couched in a humorous vein, but the banter only served as the disguise required by propriety for an improper feeling, which for its part grew stronger the more it had to be disguised. It didn't bother Little August, for it legitimized his own erotic excursions.

That's the situation I always left to come to Bohemia. Then there was you and your sisters and your mother, a family that encountered the world effort-lessly. You will have noticed I'm not a laugh-out-loud person, but nowhere have I laughed more than in your circle. I will confess that without you, I'm unimag-inable in any cheery family. Wieland, the poet and sage (you've heard of him) had an ever-ready good mood he called humor. Smart as a whip he was, and he regaled me splendidly for hours on end with lectures concerning humor. That's how I know I'm not funny. Everyone who is funny . . . I just don't believe that anyone can be funny: everyone who would be funny is pretending. A funny person is cheating life of its seri-ousness. Its terrible seriousness. Little August said Goethe was rococo. The truth is that my entire life before I was allowed to meet you was rococo. The seriousness that entered my life through you, the laughing one, makes everything before that seem like rococo. If Wieland were still alive (he died because when he paid me a visit one winter, he waded home on foot through snow and ice from Weimar to Ossmannstedt, against my urgent advice, shod only in little patent-leather shoes and silk stockings and wearing velvet pants and a thin little coat: pneumonia, gone), if he were still alive I could offer him a lecture on why humor is a greater fraud than that which made history under the name rococo. Rococo was always a fraud that knew it was fraudulent. Rococo never took itself seriously. Humor takes itself seriously, but it's not serious, so it's the real fraud. My pedagogical vein is running strong again. Forgive me. I just meant to say that you have brought a previously unknown seriousness into my life. Rococo was no match for you.

That's what I publicly announced in Bohemia. The fact that my love for you was then passed on and arrived here, untempered and even distorted by the most malicious tones, made Ottilie into the fury that she is. Everyone's a fury under the right circumstances, and they're certainly the right ones here. It may be a universal law that if person A is happy, it makes person B just as unhappy as A is happy. It keeps the world in balance. At Dr. Rehbein's insistence I must visit her bedside regularly and let her scream at me and call me a dirty old man, a sycophant, a groper, a pedophile, and

worse. Now I am a monster, too. I present the world
with a noble façade, but in reality, I am crueler to those
nearest me than Nero was to his enemies. Ottilie's suffering is great. So is mine, I could say. But when I am
with her, I have nothing to say. Nothing at all. I cannot
say (and it's only this that I would like to say, that I
would have to say), I cannot say that I love Ulrike and
how I love her and that there is nothing, nothing,
nothing I can do about it. I have to dissemble. I have
to say: Marienbad, Karlsbad—nothing but summer
flings. That's the kind of nonsense I have to dose her
with. I have to be interested in getting her on her feet
again. I am a business enterprise, among other things.
Do you have any idea how many coworkers I have?
Stadelmann, John, Meyer, Riemer, Kräuter, Eckermann.
And almost every day, my bosom confidant Chancellor
von Müller, who will be the executor of my estate. I
have the greatest trust in his kindness. I consider him
loyal. Weimar—and that means the world—has access
to me through my staff. And that's how people find
out what goes on here. Then the unending procession
of persons and personalities highly eligible to call on
me. Should I be indifferent to the fact, dear Ulrike,
that I now appear as a dirty old man—the foul name
that gores me the most—and a monster? Or am I one
in fact? Please, please, please tell me. Permit me the
non-exaggeration that I have infinite confidence in
your ability to see and judge. If even a whisper within
you is for calling me so, please do it. The appalling

thing is, if you would call me that, were compelled to call me that, it would not touch me at all, would not insult, vex, or even upset me. And I'm easily upset, as you saw in Bohemia. Please, give it a try. Call me names as seriously as you can.

You gave me permission to write to you. As soon as I arrived in Weimar, I began to struggle with this letter-writing permit. Every day for twenty-four hours— for even in my dreams I struggled—I did everything to not have to write you. I survived more than one sudden letter-writing attack and, however wounded I was, I controlled myself, i.e., forced myself to accept what had to be: no letter. A letter to you, what can it be besides continual deception? I am not reaching you at all, only prolonging the pain of stretching out my hands in your direction. Will I have the courage to send you what I must write? How can I? Ottilie has certainly long since made a conquest of Postmaster Leser as well as Postal Secretary Steffany in the Alexanderhof. I could assign Stadelmann the task of mailing the letter from Kranichfeld or Blankenhain or Buttelstedt, assuming Ottilie hasn't already corrupted all the postal officials in the vicinity. I'm justified in feeling persecuted even if the post office is not yet prejudiced against me, persecuted by supervision from a thousand quarters. Every sort of custom, morality, habit, propriety, and orderliness has been bundled into a unified supervision to tell me in every way that I am impossible. Because I love you, Ulrike. I've taken to calling this conspiracy of all legitimate society against me "dramaturgy." It is an organization in which no one need consult anyone else, yet all conspire in a single goal. The goal is me, or more exactly, the demonstration of my impossibility. Which I know better than my dramaturges. The distinction, the absolutely decisive difference between the supervision I call "dramaturgy" and myself: those spontaneously united in my supervision oppose my impossibility by all means, cultural and societal, while I commit myself to my impossibility. They will do everything they can against my impossibility. I do nothing against my impossibility, but do everything for it. Everything I can. One could call it a life-and-death struggle, if one wanted to be completely theatrical.

Dear Ulrike—and I say this to you, only to you, and I can only say it to you because I don't know if I will ever send you what I say in this letter—I am sick. Lovesick. For you. And can only tell you in a letter I shall never mail! What a world! After how many millennia of cultural practice in becoming humane! But I do have practice in this: although I won't very soon see you again, although I certainly cannot send you this letter tomorrow, although I probably will never send you this letter, writing to you is still something. As long as I write, I'm talking to you. I see you. You listen to me. I tell myself that I know how you will react to this sentence or that. And I incorporate your reactions into my letter. I read in your listening face a heartfelt, yes, even a sympathetic approval of my letter-writing. You remember that my *Werther* is a novel in letters. I cannot commit suicide. I still overestimate the value of the world, that is, the people around me. I begrudge them the derision they would unleash in their papers if they could report, What a pity, he's finally killed himself. Headline: The Sufferings of Old Werther. Perhaps my impossibility will increase so much that these people will soon be indifferent to me. Then I'll do it, Ulrike. And now the most serious thing must be said. I can only do it if you agree. Don't rush to say, Never! Wait and see if I can make my impossible life so comprehensible to you that you say—for my sake, for the sake of ending my suffering—Yes, do it. That would be the moment to return to the *du*-zone. I'll draw you quickly into the greatest inner proximity. Did we not talk about this once in Marienbad? That to leave the end of every life to so-called nature is to remain mired in barbarism? Nature doesn't care how much we suffer. We care. In a precarious case, we have the right to decide not to allow some cultural veneer to make the unacceptable seem acceptable. Period.

If my love for you would establish itself in me as hopelessness, something I am now resisting day and night, I would have to cease to exist. And not even a Napoleon would be able to nitpick about mixed motives weakening the plot. Even though Herr XY has earned much more money with his parody of my *Journeyman Years* than I have with the original, not even a Napoleon could discover in my suicide, if it were to happen, a trace of professional grievance. It would happen out of love and nothing but love. I admit it: that amounts to saying I still have hope. But I know it's hopeless. But I don't believe it's hopeless. I have to confess that I still have an obligation to finish the second part of *Faust* and revise the *Journeyman Years*. But what is an obligation compared to a hopeless love! Fortunately, hopelessness is a goddess one can appeal to. I negotiate with her day and night. She is cunning and I am not without ideas myself. In any given moment, I'm not thinking everything I could be thinking. One must not do hopelessness that favor. Dear Ulrike, I am only just beginning but already coming to realize I shouldn't make any demands on myself. For now. Everything could be wrong. If one sentence should be considered more important than another, then always the sentence that says the least. For now: one rises above adversity by acknowledging its necessity, but that's all. For now. You once said admiringly that Napoleon had an unconditional character. Ah, if only you thought I had one, too!

I am only just beginning. Julie von Egloffstein, the painter, her sister Linchen, the singer, Adele Schopenhauer—as smart as she is beautiful—and Ottilie's sister Ulrike von Pogwisch (she is always tripping on things from pure hunger for life and whenever she forces herself into my thoughts I refer to her only as the Pogwisch woman)—they all hang around wanting to comfort me. There's been far too much talk about a dismayingly beautiful girl who must have been the privy councilor's most eager listener, most witty interlocutor, and most devoted escort. They were inseparable, day and night. . . . Yes, yes, YES, the chatter is still going on. Chancellor von Müller, my bosom confidant, goes the furthest. He prefers sitting with me to playing the chancellor over at court. Chancellor von Müller leaned over to me so I told him things that could be taken as a confession and used against me. But nothing can turn the chancellor against me. Ottilie and Little August can turn all the rest into traitors. Only the men, of course. Not all the men, but all the men who make poems. And all the men around me make poems. To anyone who writes poems, his poems are the most sacred thing. Everything else is negotiable. However, even here the exception proves the rule. Chancellor von Müller, who naturally also makes poems, will never betray me, not to anyone. Riemer, John, Stadelmann, Eckermann, and Kräuter are a different story. If Ottilie takes pity on the poems of these men, she can do with them what she will. She cannot do anything with Meyer, my Johann Heinrich Meyer, a non-poetry-maker par excellence and thus incorruptible. Ah, Ulrike, there would be a friend for you if you came. Won't you come? Privy Councilor Meyer, known as Art-Meyer, shared a bed with me in Rome. I lured him over to Weimar, a painter, Ulrike, who doesn't paint, a Swiss painter in Weimar—hence inconsolable. You MUST

know that I divide my friends into hopers and despair-
ers. Hoper Number One is Chancellor von Müller,
Despairer Number One is Meyer. I don't need to say
a word to him and he knows everything. I shall draw
sustenance from him.

The Countesses von Egloffstein and Adele
Schopenhauer are as loyal to me as I am to them. To
all three I've issued a standing invitation. Every day
from five o'clock on they can come and stay as long as
they want. And a small miracle: I keep them marvel-
ously entertained. I was always a pretty good entertainer for young ladies. Now I am unsurpassable. And
since my other clients are always in attendance, I can
see how well my program works. Within me, the small
miracle looks like this: since September 17th I have
learned that whether sincere or malicious, expressions
of sympathy are a disaster. I must make myself invulnerable. I cannot display an inscrutable demeanor from
one moment to the next. But I have learned. I am fairly
good vis-à-vis women and girls. Here is the inner secret
of the small miracle (and I had to inflict this introduc-
tion on you only to tell you this), the inner secret is
that the power and richness of my demeanor come
from you and you alone. That is why it works so well
on women and girls. And at the end of half an hour,
even one of the Carolines, should she appear before me
today, would think I was the pattern of an amiable
admirer. And I'm capable of it because it is you I see
and feel and thus admire in every girl, in every woman.

Since taking you up within me, I've known that till now, every feeling, every word I projected onto girls and women was simply routine, lines from a play. Now for the first time I am myself the one who feels and speaks.

Is my hand allowed to hurt? Never since Werther's days have I written so much by hand. Good night, Ulrike.

Weimar, October 10, 1823

Dear Ulrike,

Yesterday after *Der Freischütz* they arrived in a swarm and were served. I carved the roast myself. Ottilie, resurrected from her gloomy paralysis, stood next to me and watched my carving hands as if to make sure I was doing everything right. Indeed, she even praised me out loud, and much too loudly. She simply has no sense of propriety. Even my son August took offense. "Father is not a servant," he said severely. "If you love me you must not judge me," said Adele Schopenhauer, quoting me to put an ambiguous end to the episode. By the way, here's another tactical accomplishment in my conduct of the war: if I'm invited to the opera, I always happily accept and then at the last minute, I don't feel well. If I were to decline right away, I'd have to beat around the bush and conceal the fact that without Ulrike, I can't stand to listen to music anymore.

Thus my tactic of declining in stages. In the meantime, I have brought the young women (to everyone's amusement I've taken to calling them my little foot soldiers) to the point where their eyes no longer search mine for traces of Ulrike. Except for Ottilie, of course. So we sat down to supper. One of the party was the young Nicolovius, a fine fellow who deserves support. And what do you know, the young ladies turned toward that fabulous young man like sunflowers. I was left with their backs. And there, too, it was Ottilie who did everything to keep young Nicolovius at the center of attention. I sensed her need to demonstrate how uninteresting I am when a young man shows up. That spoiled the evening for me, dear Ulrike. On one hand, I could be proud of the fact that no one noticed, but on the other, no one looked at me anymore because under Ottilie's direction, the magnificently young Nicolovius really deserved everyone's attention. So the host slunk off and hid in his room. Stadelmann came and lit five wax candles so I could read. Stadelmann knows what vice his master falls into when he makes himself scarce. He reads, but he reads the elegy. He reads it not once or twice, but exactly innumerable times. Dear Ulrike, please allow me to say HE. It is HE whom I need to be ME. What I write you is different than what HE writes you. I never hesitate whether to write as ME or as HE. Since Werther's nut trees you've known who I am. HE is a façade one hopes will grow inward. ME is the admission that no façade can succeed. From September 17th to September 27th, he made a fair copy of the elegy on the best paper that John could obtain and it was unthinkable even for a second that John would be allowed to copy the elegy. And another thing: the elegy was still undisplayable and is so to this day. Of course, he seemed to himself a little immature as he read the elegy in his room, knowing that he should not have indulged himself. And luckily felt spirited enough to tell himself, Why should you deny yourself something that does you so much good. Gradually he came to know the elegy almost by heart, but that by no means led him to skim over the text. He read every line not just with his eyes, but with his soul. With his heart and soul. And now, Ulrike, it's ME who's come back. Now I have a confession: how many things I've put out into the world about the reasons I write. Whole schools seek their salvation in my avowals that writing can overcome everything that would kill you if you didn't write. From Werther on. And now, dear Ulrike, I've written the elegy! For the first time, it doesn't help to have written. Only writing helps. But what would I be without the elegy! It spells out my longing. It is proud, proud of itself. I would like to learn that pride from it. I would like to be like the elegy. So composed. It is your elegy. Our elegy. Before you have gotten it and read it, no one will read it. It doesn't exist, the elegy. Just as you don't exist. And thus I don't exist. Listen to how one can grind one's soul just like grinding one's teeth. Now I'm going to write the elegy down and send this letter off! Even if Stadelmann has to transport it to Kahla or Pössneck first. Here it is, Ulrike, the Marienbad Elegy.

1.

Was soll ich nun vom Wiedersehen hoffen,
Von dieses Tages noch geschlossner Blüte?
Das Paradies, die Hölle steht dir offen;
Wie wankelsinnig regt sich's im Gemüte!—
Kein Zweifeln mehr! Sie tritt ans Himmelstor,
Zu ihren Armen hebt sie dich empor.

2.

So warst du denn im Paradies empfangen,
Als wärst du wert des ewig schönen Lebens;
Dir blieb kein Wunsch, kein Hoffen, kein Verlangen,
Hier war das Ziel des innigsten Bestrebens,
Und in dem Anschaun dieses einzig Schönen
Versiegte gleich der Quell sehnsüchtiger Tränen.

3.

Wie regte nicht der Tag die raschen Flügel,
Schien die Minuten vor sich her zu treiben!
Der Abendkuss, ein treu verbindlich Siegel:
So wird es auch der nächsten Sonne bleiben.
Die Stunden glichen sich in zartem Wandern
Wie Schwestern zwar, doch keine ganz den andern.

4.

Der Kuss, der letzte, grausam süß, zerschneidend
Ein herrliches Geflecht verschlungner Minnen
Nun eilt, nun stockt der Fuß, die Schwelle meidend,
Als trieb' ein Cherub flammend ihn von hinnen;
Das Auge starrt auf düstrem Pfad verdrossen,
Es blickt zurück, die Pforte steht verschlossen.

A MAN IN LOVE

1.

What have I now to hope from the reunion,
The still unopened blossom of this day?
The gates of Paradise and hell stand open,
How changeable, unsteady is my mind!
But doubts, begone! She comes to heaven's gate,
And opens wide her arms to raise you up

2.

And thus you were received in Paradise,
As if deserving of eternal life,
With nothing left to wish, to hope, to long for.
Here was the goal of all your inner strife,
And contemplating her unequalled beauty,
The source of yearning tears had quite dried up.

3.

And how the day did beat its hasty pinions
And seemed to drive the minutes rushing on!
The kiss at evening was a seal, a promise
That it will still be thus at the next sunrise.
The hours ran their smooth and gentle course
Like sisters, yes, but each a little different.

4.

A kiss—the last one. Cruelly sweet, it severs
A glorious web of intertwining loves.
My feet, now keen now loath to leave that threshold,
As if a flaming cherub drove them off;
I stare morosely down the gloomy path,
And looking back, I see the gate is locked.

5.

Und nun verschlossen in sich selbst, als hätte
Dies Herz sich nie geöffnet, selige Stunden
Mit jedem Stern des Himmels um die Wette
An ihrer Seite leuchtend nicht empfunden;
Und Missmut, Reue, Vorwurf, Sorgenschwere
Belasten's nun in schwüler Atmosphäre.

6.

Ist denn die Welt nicht übrig? Felsenwände,
Sind sie nicht mehr gekrönt von heiligen Schatten?
Die Ernte, reift sie nicht? Ein grün Gelände,
Zieht sich's nicht hin am Fluss durch Busch und Matten?
Und wölbt sich nicht das überweltlich Große,
Gestaltenreiche, bald Gestaltenlose?

7.

Wie leicht und zierlich, klar und zart gewoben
Schwebt seraphgleich aus ernster Wolken Chor,
Als glich' es ihr, am blauen Äther droben
Ein schlank Gebild aus lichtem Duft empor;
So sahst du sie in frohem Tanze walten,
Die lieblichste der lieblichsten Gestalten.

8.

Doch nur Momente darfst dich unterwinden,
Ein Luftgebild statt ihrer festzuhalten;
Ins Herz zurück! dort wirst du's besser finden,
Dort regt sie sich in wechselnden Gestalten;
Zu vielen bildet eine sich hinüber,
So tausendfach, und immer, immer lieber.

5.

And now this heart, locked up within itself,
As if it never opened, never felt
Those blissful, luminous hours at her side,
Shining as bright as every star in heaven;
Now discontent, regret, recriminations,
Weigh upon it like a muggy day.

6.

But have I not the world? Do not the cliffs
Still wear a crown of blessed shadow, fields
Still ripen in the sun? Is there not green
And open land, a meadow by the river?
Does not the sky unfold unearthly greatness,
So full of figures, shifting, disappearing?

7.

How light and dainty, clear and finely spun,
A slender image, luminous and hazy,
Floats up, angelic, from the clouds' stern choir
On high, in the blue ether, so like her.
You saw her thus, the sovereign of the dance,
The loveliest of all the loveliest dancers.

8.

But only for a moment do you dare
Embrace an airy image in her place;
Look in your heart! There you will better find it,
There where she appears in shifting guises;
In your heart the one becomes the many,
A thousand shapes, each dearer than the last.

9.

Wie zum Empfang sie an den Pforten weilte
Und mich von dannauf stufenweis beglückte,
Selbst nach dem letzten Kuss mich noch ereilte,
Den letztesten mir auf die Lippen drückte:
So klar beweglich bleibt das Bild der Lieben
Mit Flammenschrift ins treue Herz geschrieben.

10.

Ins Herz, das fest wie zinnenhohe Mauer
Sich ihr bewahrt und sie in sich bewahret,
Für sie sich freut an seiner eignen Dauer,
Nur weiß von sich, wenn sie sich offenbaret,
Sich freier fühlt in so geliebten Schranken
Und nur noch schlägt, für alles ihr zu danken.

11.

War Fähigkeit zu lieben, war Bedürfen
Von Gegenliebe weggelöscht, verschwunden,
Ist Hoffnungslust zu freudigen Entwürfen,
Entschlüssen, rascher Tat sogleich gefunden!
Wenn Liebe je den Liebenden begeistet,
Ward es an mir aufs lieblichste geleistet;

12.

Und zwar durch sie!—Wie lag ein innres Bangen
Auf Geist und Körper, unwillkommner Schwere:
Von Schauerbildern rings der Blick umfangen
Im wüsten Raum beklommner Herzensleere;
Nun dämmert Hoffnung von bekannter Schwelle,
Sie selbst erscheint in milder Sonnenhelle.

9.

The way she waited for me at the gate
And cheered me as we mounted, step by step,
And even after the last kiss she ran
To press yet one more kiss upon my lips:
So clear and vivid is her image now,
Inscribed upon my heart in flaming letters.

10.

My heart, which like a lofty battlement
Defends itself and keeps her safe within,
And for her sake is glad to be alive,
Not knowing itself save in her revelation,
And feels more free in such beloved strictures,
And only beats in gratitude to her.

11.

Was ever readiness to love, or ever
The need for love snuffed out or disappeared,
At once hope reappears, makes joyful plans,
Puts resolutions quickly into action.
If ever love gave lover inspiration,
Then I am he, and in the loveliest fashion;

12.

It was through her!—How heavy lay an inner,
Unwelcome fear upon my mind and body,
My gaze enwrapped by images of terror,
My heart a bleak and empty desolation;
Now hope is dawning at a well-known threshold,
Where she herself appears in the mild sunlight.

13.

Dem Frieden Gottes, welcher euch hienieden
Mehr als Vernunft beseliget—wir lesen's—,
Vergleich ich wohl der Liebe heitern Frieden
In Gegenwart des allgeliebten Wesens;
Da ruht das Herz, und nichts vermag zu stören
Den tiefsten Sinn, den Sinn, ihr zu gehören.

14.

In unsers Busens Reine wogt ein Streben,
Sich einem Höhern, Reinern, Unbekannten
Aus Dankbarkeit freiwillig hinzugeben,
Enträtselnd sich den ewig Ungenannten;
Wir heißen's: fromm sein!—Solcher seligen Höhe
Fühl ich mich teilhaft, wenn ich vor ihr stehe.

15.

Vor ihrem Blick, wie vor der Sonne Walten,
Vor ihrem Atem, wie vor Frühlingslüften,
Zerschmilzt, so längst sich eisig starr gehalten,
Der Selbstsinn tief in winterlichen Grüften;
Kein Eigennutz, kein Eigenwille dauert,
Vor ihrem Kommen sind sie weggeschauert.

16.

Es ist, als wenn sie sagte: "Stund um Stunde
Wird uns das Leben freundlich dargeboten,
Das Gestrige ließ uns geringe Kunde,
Das Morgende, zu wissen ist's verboten;
Und wenn ich je mich vor dem Abend scheute,
Die Sonne sank und sah noch, was mich freute.

13.

The peace of God that grants more bliss on earth
Than even reason can—as we have read—
For me is like the peace of love serene
In the presence of the being I love best.
The heart's at rest and nothing can disturb
The deepest sense that I belong to her.

14.

In our pure breasts there surges aspiration
To give ourselves in voluntary thanks
To something higher, purer, yet unknown,
Decipher what remains forever nameless;
We call it piety!—And in her presence
I feel a part of such a lofty bliss.

15.

Her gaze is like the working of the sun,
Her breath is like the gentle airs of spring.
They melt away the icey self-absorption
That long has lingered deep in wintry crevices.
No selfishness, no willfulness remains,
For at her coming, both evaporate.

16.

It is as if she said, "Hour by hour
Life is offered in pure benevolence,
Little remains of what was yesterday
And what tomorrow brings we cannot know.
If ever I felt dread at the coming evening,
The sun still sank, and looked on something joyful.

17.

Drum tu wie ich und schaue, froh verständig,
Dem Augenblick ins Auge! Kein Verschieben!
Begegn' ihm schnell, wohlwollend wie lebendig,
Im Handeln sei's, zur Freude, sei's dem Lieben!
Nur wo du bist, sei alles, immer kindlich,
So bist du alles, bist unüberwindlich."

18.

Du hast gut reden, dacht ich: zum Geleite
Gab dir ein Gott die Gunst des Augenblickes,
Und jeder fühlt an deiner holden Seite
Sich augenblicks den Günstling des Geschickes;
Mich schreckt der Wink, von dir mich zu entfernen—
Was hilft es mir, so hohe Weisheit lernen!

19.

Nun bin ich fern! Der jetzigen Minute,
Was ziemt denn der? Ich wüsst es nicht zu sagen;
Sie bietet mir zum Schönen manches Gute,
Das lastet nur, ich muss mich ihm entschlagen.
Mich treibt umher ein unbezwinglich Sehnen,
Da bleibt kein Rat als grenzenlose Tränen.

20.

So quellt denn fort und fließet unaufhaltsam,
Doch nie geläng's, die inn're Glut zu dämpfen!
Schon rast's und reißt in meiner Brust gewaltsam,
Wo Tod und Leben grausend sich bekämpfen.
Wohl Kräuter gäb's, des Körpers Qual zu stillen;
Allein dem Geist fehlt's am Entschluss und Willen,

17.

So do as I do, in cheerful understanding
Look the moment in the eye! No hesitation!
Meet it head-on, lively, and with good will.
Whether in action, at play, or loving someone.
Where'er you be, be all, and always childlike,
And thus, in fact, you're all, invincible."

18.

Easy for you to say, I thought. Some god
Bestowed on you the favor of the moment.
Whoever stands at your fair side, at once
Feels himself the favorite of fate.
I'm daunted by the sign it's time to leave you—
What have I gained by learning such great wisdom!

19.

Now we're far apart! So what befits the
Present moment? I don't know what to say;
It offers much that's beautiful and good—
But that's a burden, one I must cast off.
Driven by unconquerable yearning,
The only thing that's left is endless tears.

20.

So let them rise and flow on without ceasing,
But never will they quench the inner fire
Already roaring, raging in my breast!
Where death and life contend in fearful struggle.
There may be herbs that still the body's pain;
The spirit lacks decisiveness and will,

21.

Fehlt's am Begriff: wie sollt' er sie vermissen?
Er wiederholt ihr Bild zu tausend Malen.
Das zaudert bald, bald wird es weggerissen,
Undeutlich jetzt und jetzt im reinsten Strahlen;
Wie könnte dies geringstem Troste frommen,
Die Ebb' und Flut, das Gehen wie das Kommen?

22.

Verlasst mich hier, getreue Weggenossen!
Lasst mich allein am Fels, in Moor und Moos;
Nur immer zu! euch ist die Welt erschlossen,
Die Erde weit, der Himmel hehr und groß;
Betrachtet, forscht, die Einzelheiten sammelt,
Naturgeheimnis werde nachgestammelt.

23.

Mir ist das All, ich bin mir selbst verloren,
Der ich noch erst den Göttern Liebling war;
Sie prüften mich, verliehen mir Pandoren,
So reich an Gütern, reicher an Gefahr;
Sie drängten mich zum gabeseligen Munde,
Sie trennen mich—und richten mich zugrunde.

21.
Lacks any sense of how to do without her.
A thousand times it conjures up her image.
Sometimes it wavers, then it's snatched away.
One time it's vague, another: radiant, pure.
This ebb and flow, this constant fluctuation,
How could it bring the slightest consolation?

22.
So leave me here, companions on my journey!
Leave me alone on rocks, in moss and moor.
Go on without me! The world stands open, waiting.
The earth's unbounded, the sky is huge, sublime;
Observe, investigate, collect your samples,
And stammer out the secrets Nature holds.

23.
The universe I've lost, I've lost myself,
I who was once the favorite of the gods.
They put me to the test, gave me Pandora,
So rich in treasure, richer still in danger;
They urged me toward that mouth so blest, so giving,
They part us now and send me to my ruin.

Chapter Two

Weimar, October 15, 1823

Dear Ulrike,

The elegy has left the house. There are three things you cannot keep to yourself: fire, love, and verses. I've played the reserved privy councilor for too long. Now I've bribed Stadelmann and told him it was a bribe. The amount rendered him speechless and he started bowing like an acrobat. He suggested Bad Berka. And so the elegy is out into the world. The strength for that feat of strength came from a sudden feeling of faintness that drove me out of the Blue Room in the evening, day before yesterday. Ah, Ulrike, they shouldn't call rooms by such names anymore. That's what the salon is called because its walls are blue. And right next door is the Yellow Salon. Yellow as wolfsbane, Ulrike. It was Art-Meyer from Lake Zurich who painted it that color, my Despairer Number One. He renovated the house for me thirty years ago. If you ever climb the slowest, most protracted stairs in the world—namely, the flight of stairs I designed when I knew nothing about you, but which now always remind me of the way you walk, the way you move, so loose-limbed (even when you're on flat ground you're moving upward)—these stairs don't lead you vulgarly into the house from the square outside. No, they don't begin until you're already inside, at the entrance into the courtyard—so when you reach the top step with your upward-gliding gait, you will read on the threshold, inlaid into its light wood, the world SALVE. I'm telling you that ahead of time because I know that you never stare vacantly, never look down at the ground, but always upward, toward your goal. Then if you stepped inside, you would be surprised and probably turn down your over-active, ready-for-anything mouth when you see the much too large head of Juno and then all the other busts: Schiller (your favorite), Herder, Winckelmann. But since one of the rooms—the most beautiful—is blue, lavender blue, it would perhaps reconcile you to the artificiality of this dwelling, and the second most beautiful, dearest Ulrike, is yellow, yellow like wolfsbane.

But about day before yesterday: The host quietly excuses himself. Then they could start whispering again: Marienbad, the aging Werther . . . Shameful! And now I'm going to lay down the law to the man of the house; that must not happen again. He should write the following down. He promises he will make some lists. List number one: Rules to Avoid Any Possibility of Speculation.

1. No declining in stages. Attend every musical event. Ottilie and August naturally wanted to present him to the public from the balcony loge. Look here! He's back again! We've captured him! He ought to have appeared, exuding left and right the mood "They have won." Not even music, the deranger par excellence, can touch me.

2. In any gathering under the spell of a young man, be the most captivated. Drown the young man in compliments. Take the lead in making compliments. To anything he can say, make sure you think of a response even more brilliant than those of your foot soldiers in silk, Chancellor von Müller, Professor Riemer, Director of Buildings Coudray, and cohorts. It didn't bother him that those people in there made fun of him after he left. The loving man is invulnerable except toward her whom he loves. He lives beneath a different sky, is only apparently in attendance. When they are talking about Kant and the weather, within him reigns the sacred confusion of love.

The young Nicolovius: a trail that led to de Ror. So I thought I would feel better if I acknowledged the necessity of trains of thought that were not to be avoided. I had to baptize the fellow without a given name, so I baptized him Velocifer. Dearest Ulrike, you would not tell me the first name of the fellow without one. He took you into his confidence and you allowed yourself to be taken and are now in it. Excellency is left to wonder where he fits in. So Velocifer rushes off to Paris to present the French queen with a diamond, *gives* her the biggest diamond now in existence *as a gift*. A few days later—you and your sisters had gone out to pick flowers—your mother told me what she had learned about the fellow without a given name from Count Klebelsberg. The word "sell" was not in his vocabulary. Because every piece is so much more valuable than what he's asking for it, he calls every sale a gift.

Can you still see his gaze in your mind's eye? I can. There is nothing I see more clearly than his eyes. Pupils almost black, but encircled by light gray. I've only seen such a thing in birds before. And no matter how many loving and beautiful things you can say about birds, their gaze is deemed to be piercing and cold. Now I'm talking about him the way people talk about Napoleon. Not to denigrate the birds, I should have said that one sees that encircling gray only in Saturn, and it is the planet of threats. Without my having asked, your mother told me he was six feet two, and that he was almost constantly on the go between Paris and Vienna. And so it is not saturnine of me to think that he must sometimes stop off in Strasbourg and will know how to find that French boarding school. His Napoleonically short, very thick and dark hair gives him a handsome, military appearance. If it weren't for his violet frock coat . . .

Ah, I'll stop now, dearest Ulrike. His love was ignited by you. He is highly velocitanical. If I had to compete with him, I would not stand the slightest chance of winning. I wouldn't even be able to wish for it. For your sake. He doesn't just have a future, he is the future. I extract myself from this hopelessness of mine with a cruel wish: if only one could blind the soul as one can blind the eyes. So that you would be utterly unable to think of him ever again. If you answer me soon (I cannot shake off that delusion), say one more sentence about the last sentence he uttered as he bade you so presumptuously and possessively farewell. In my rooms in the Golden Grape in Marienbad, you quoted him in a very jolly and somehow insouciant way: *Il-y-a quelque chose dans l'air.* Did he say, *Je sais qu'il-y-a . . .* or *Je pense qu'il-y-a . . .* or *Je sens qu'il-y-a . . .?"* And if I remember your report correctly, he at any rate added, *Entre nous il-y-a . . .* Or in the end, *Il-y-a quelque chose dans l'air entre nous?* Or was the whole thing formulated, *Je sens, qu'entre nous il-y-a quelque chose dans l'air?* I would be very grateful if you took the trouble to tell me his parting words exactly. I think what you—what we—have to reckon with depends on that. When you let me know that you have been able to read the elegy, I will send you what I had to write you this evening. I cannot remain so negative. Our game of quotations, my favorite game, will help me now.

To the postrevolutionary, boarding-school young lady:

And so it but remains for Your faithful servant to express a modest request. Should Your Highness deign to continue to favor me with Your benevolence and grace, think of me generously in the circle of Your dear dependents and have the goodness to grant me in the near future the privilege and opportunity of diverse communications.

P.S. I'm a pedant, I know. But I would feel very neglectful if I did not tell you what occurs to me when I think about that fellow, now no longer without a first name. This past June, not long before departing for blessed Bohemia, my gracious sovereign summoned me, the expert on rocks, to have a look at some diamonds. Monsieur Soret, court tutor for the prince and a natural scientist to whom I am deeply attached for his anti-Newtonian views, had invited to Weimar a chemist, physicist, and engineer from his native city of Geneva. With the duke, myself, Chancellor von Müller, and Director of Buildings Coudray in attendance, this man opened a mahogany case and before our eyes, the most magnificent diamonds of every size and shape lay arranged on dark velvet. We were asked to examine them and choose some, and if we recommended it, our most gracious lord would buy them. The rather reserved Genevan gave us time. Each of us recommended two or three pieces we found attractive. Then the Genevan told us that none of the diamonds was genuine. He had produced them all himself and proceeded to point out imperfections he had in the meantime learned how to correct. Since the stones cost less than half as much as they would if they were real, our gracious lord bought the whole lot. The Genevan promised to return with even better-made pieces soon.

I had to tell you this story, didn't I? It could have a bearing on the brilliant future of our diamond-bestower, couldn't it? In any event, I tell it not for his sake, but for yours. Good night.

Perhaps I WON'T send these letters, something I cannot imagine at the moment. In any case, I could send them to you only as long as you are in Strasbourg. I live from the knowledge that you will read what I write. However, if you do not read them—to take the most impossible case—or read them only after I die and because some people here monitor and perhaps record how I conduct my life, if you then read what I did on a certain day or evening on which I wrote you a letter consisting of nothing but loneliness or abandonment (this is how it feels, if you will), then please do not believe what you read *about* me, believe my letter. Once more, good night. By the way, yesterday, an announcement printed on a most festive piece of paper: my friend Knebel, five years older than I, is getting married, married again. He is wedding a woman forty-three years younger than himself. I shall congratulate him, of course, I certainly will. I'm seething with congratulations and envy.

Weimar, October 16, 1823

Dear Ulrike,
Again and again, the moments when I was not good enough recur. I consider myself lucky that I can still

amend what I neglected to do. Do you recall this: You look handsome. That's what you said. It brought me up short, and you added, "Today!" So it was a joke. By TODAY you meant to say, Don't act so comically surprised, as if you didn't know how often you look good; I'll take it down a notch and say TODAY: fear not, just today. I, however, heard the sentence the wrong way. My answer should have been (and I'm writing now only to let you know the response I neglected to make), So do you! That's what I should have shouted out in the same high spirits. So do you! So do you! So do you! I should have told you that in my head, I'm constantly addressing you. Should have told you how exhausting it is to constantly have to suppress what constantly wants to get out. Constantly, I could—ah yes—rejoice. Dearest Ulrike, the lack of objectivity with which you talk about yourself now and then is impressive and grotesque. Let me summarize what you remarked in forty-nine summer days about your appearance: ears too big, hair too thin, color of eyes ambiguous, crooked nose, mouth too small. Now, what I observed and studied for forty-nine summer days. Ears: two petals of the most precious flower. Mouth: constantly in the service of an inexhaustible vivacity, it can never be too big or too small since it is never self-conscious, but is the embodiment of the most magically tender, entwining power. You should thank your nose for not wanting to be a ruler. But your hair, my dear, is completely independent of you. It doesn't need you, but you need this hair, for in its gentle fall it covers the head of a girl who broadcasts judgments that have the permanence of constellations. Your eyes—ah, Ulrike, you already know from me that your eyes are pure conquest. What makes you irresistible, dearest Ulrike, is your gaze. No one can withstand it. Like the sea, your eyes always have the color of the sky, but unlike the sea, they have in addition the powerful color of your inner sky. Enough! I hear you saying. A little bit less wouldn't have hurt your credibility, you say, because you like to rein in my natural lack of restraint. Good night, my lovely little intruder. Please take a seat wherever you like. Ah, you would like to dance. Alone? Aha, for me! I could not wish for anything better. You came into the world a dancer, fully formed by nature. Your every gesture succeeds. Your limbs dangle and swing with equal daring and precision. Your neck takes your head for a walk from one shoulder to the other and your hands suddenly discover themselves above your head. The music cannot hold still any longer. A beautiful white bird is directing a feathered orchestra with his wings. And you stride as if wading through a sweet swamp. And now you strut as if no piece of this earth were fit to be touched by your resounding little feet. You are a serious parodist of every possible movement of beasts and men. You fall and climb, but climb higher than you fall. Effortlessly you arrive at the top of the invisible stairs, which resound in their turn. Then you make of your little feet tender drumsticks that vibrate on something one cannot see, but that begins to ring under your vibrations.

The orchestra of birds—mostly strings—sinks down in high, sighing tones that end in the highest height. Their wings are folded, but the conductor and all the other birds remain where they are. The avian conductor turns to you and says, We don't want to go home. That is answered enthusiastically by an audience one has not noticed before. No one wants to go home anymore. An enormous chorus, a hundred voices, begins to sing a single sentence: No one wants to go home anymore. Then the custodian extinguishes the lights and shouts merrily into the hall, Tomorrow is another day! Good night, dear Ulrike. It would be quite a disappointment if I had to assume that you definitely would never read what I am writing to you and you alone.

P.S. More next time about *du* and *Sie*. Forgive me, Ulrike. I cannot go to bed. Ever since I met you, there's nothing harder than falling asleep. Always the vain wish never to have to sleep anymore. Am I a child again? Why don't little children want to go to sleep, Ulrike? Why do we have to entice them out of their insatiable, brilliant wakefulness with all kinds of stories and songs? Now I know the answer. In every second they receive a thousand pieces of information. For them, the world is one great attraction they follow with their senses, and then they feed on that receptivity their whole lives long. And then they're supposed to go to sleep, sleep that is merely silent and colorless. No! they cry, and struggle desperately against having to go to sleep, but are defeated at last by the practiced stratagems of adults. Am I a child?

Please answer that question tomorrow. I wanted to at least suggest why falling asleep and sleeping are now so unacceptable. Now I hear myself uttering the little screams that first happened to me after the appearance of the fellow without a given name. It's really something to be alone some night and then hear these short little screams emerge from oneself. If I often say, That's really something, and then am unable to say what it is, it's because I'm trying to avoid betraying a larger feeling with smaller words. My head is a battlefield where I am defeated day and night. The fact that I allow myself to survive under all circumstances is the reason for my defeat, once and for all. The reason for every defeat is irremediable dependency. Now it's becoming more serious, Ulrike. And if I had not earlier switched from *Sie* to *du* like a hussar, it would be impossible to recite such serious things to you. You are less dependent on me than I am on you. If you were as dependent on me as I am on you, you would borrow two bedsheets from two of your boarding-school classmates, knot them to your own sheet, and fasten them to the transom of your window—you mentioned more than once that you would never want to have a profession that tended to the theoretical. You would only consider something practical. You said your hands would need something to do—so you would make the sheets you have tied together at their diagonal corners into a sort of cloth rope (or cloth sausage), then use it to let yourself down, and then, to the envious well-wishes of your comrades, you would take to your heels. You have enough cash to get you to Weimar. And why not descend from the conveyance here at the posthouse and come over to Frauenplan square, less than a five-minute walk, and throw some pebbles at my window and I—sitting here sleepless, waiting for nothing but those pebbles—would be at the window in a flash, see you down there, be down in the blink of an eye, embrace you, kiss you, and lead you up to be with me forever. Dearest Ulrike, why doesn't that happen, exactly that? A banner runs incessantly through my head bearing the words, At any moment she can be on the way from Strasbourg to Dresden. There are reasons aplenty to suddenly need to be with your family. And from Strasbourg to Dresden, one passes quite near Weimar and even, if one isn't watching carefully, through Weimar. You can even change horses here, have a layover of at least an hour. If she were to set foot in Weimar, freshen up at the posthouse, and then continue on without wanting to see . . . It's unimaginable. I don't even need to think about it. But what if she was traveling from Strasbourg to Dresden for some family emergency and was capable of doing just that? What follows is not a reproach, but simply states a law of nature, a societally approved, thousand-year-old principle: you are less dependent on me than I am on you. When you read this letter—very soon, I hope—then recall when and how often and how long you thought of me from the evening of October 16th until, let's say, three o'clock in the morning on October 17th. The nature of your thinking of me is unimportant. It could have occurred to you that you quietly pointed out to me in the Grand Salon during Dr. Rehbein's engagement party that out of nervousness, I always roll up my handkerchief and then grasp that roll (or sausage) with my left hand and then pull it out with my right hand and then pull it back with my left hand, but never so far that it leaves the right hand completely. What am I trying to say? It would help me to hear how often I occur to you and what goes on inside of you when I occur to you. It really is three o'clock in the morning again. I'm going to lie down, leave the light burning by my desk, stare at the ceiling, and think of you. Tomorrow I'm going to make a list of all the things that can be dangerous for me, both inside my head and in my immediate vicinity. A list of what I should avoid. Good night, dearest.

P.S. It would suffice if you would write: My mother, who thinks of everything, writes you now and then, Excellency. She will write that you should not write to me. She has a policy. Then write me in secret, girl.

Weimar, October 17, 1823

List of Precautions and Things to Avoid.
Which Situations Are Dangerous and Likely to Provoke Attacks and Ambushes?
    Every look out the window conjures up the windows of the Golden Grape. Every glass in your hand

calls up the promenade. Every mention of Napoleon. Every mention of poetry translations. Every mention of the words "given name" as well as the words "palais," "spring," "Kreuz," and "chocolate." No more saying that all carriage rides are boring now and thereby letting people know that a certain person with whom they would not be boring is absent.

Know in advance when the church bells will ring, so that the shock of yearning doesn't again bring on a trembling fit. Always at about six, back from the promenade and still on the terrace, suddenly the church bells would start ringing, and we looked at each other in silence as long as they rang.

During sudden rainfalls, do not immediately recall that in Marienbad, on the path from the Kreuz Spring up to the Klebelsberg palais, you twice got soaked to the skin.

If the conversation turns to dancing, no angry, suppressed denigration of all the dances on offer here because Ulrike danced better than all the women in Weimar.

Caution: no commentary on the color BLUE.

Never begin a sentence to Julie v. E. with the words, If you were my daughter . . .

Great caution when someone mentions who is laying over in Weimar on their way from Dresden to Paris, like the composer Lecerf recently.

Great caution when the conversation turns to music and whether music heals wounds of the heart or makes them worse. Big mistake day before yesterday to thank

Madame Szymanowska for the healing power of her magnificent piano concerto. The looks Ottilie exchanged with August.

Biggest mistake yesterday, when at dinner, the Egloffstein mother raised a harmless, innocent toast to recollection. Then my angry outburst against that word, against re-collection, as if that were necessary when everything is already collected within us, and how! A foolish word, re-collection! My outburst betrayed everything I've been carefully concealing. Exchange of glances around the table.

Greatest restraint on the topic of jewelry. Neither pro nor con.

A dangerous moment recently. The young poet Platen quoted a passage from the *Journeyman Years*: the traveler with a borrowed name. He liked it, although such a thing would surely never occur. I could not suppress the fellow without a given name, who certainly had nothing to do with the topic. Chancellor von Müller: the only one who perhaps suspected something. All the others puzzled.

As soon as someone starts in about engravings, I'm no longer present because Ulrike's mother once clearly said that she found it most lovely when Ulrike and I would sit next to each other and look at engravings from the days of Raphael.

Riemer yesterday: It's too much to ask that we know something for certain and behave accordingly. That was aimed at me. And Ottilie at once tried to get me involved. I dodged the issue: we weren't that simply put together. Knowledge guides us less than faith. Ottilie pursed her—in any case—nonexistent lips.

Dangerous: when fog hangs over the woodlands as in Marienbad after a night of rain. How can I not recall saying to Ulrike, It looks like the tops of the fir trees are swilling in a sea of fog. Ulrike had never heard the word "swill" before. Which I had anticipated. I have to be cautious when there's fog after a night of rain.

Caution: don't let your loathing of couples get the upper hand.

As soon as the word "cushion" is mentioned, use all your strength to blur the memory of that afternoon that will thrust itself upon you: how she sat down on the sofa and then, with an unnecessarily wide sweep that ended with a gentle landing, laid her left arm on the large yellow cushion.

Caution! Your mouth! Whenever I pass a mirror, I see that my lips are pursed, the left corner of my mouth contorted. Move your lips in a regular way. Relax every part of your mouth. Nothing so poorly befits a pose of noble renunciation as that mouth twisted down to the left.

Be careful when news arrives that has something to do with getting married! Make trebly sure that you don't repeat that embarrassment with Knebel! It wasn't Knebel, your senior by five years, who was getting married. It was his son!!!

Weimar, October 19, 1823

Dear Ulrike,

A Man in Love.

When we were allowed to say *du* to each other in the forest glade, I picked you a lupine that had been waiting there for us. From among the blue and red lupines, I picked that one, a red one. I love that dark, glowing lupine red. Before I could give it to you, you walked out into the glade. When you walk through the grass, you don't trample anything down. I watched you bend down, saw how lightly you bent to pick your favorite flowers. And you came back with a bouquet of wolfsbane and opened up that dense, yellow bouquet for my lupine, whose dark red was drowned in your torrent of yellow. We laughed. Not loudly, but we bore the faces of laughers as we marched back into the world called Karlsbad.

What can I do except say how it was? Listen, you cannot know, so I have to tell you what the abbé, my pedagogical pigeonhole number one in *Wilhelm Meister's Apprenticeship*, says: "Everything is relative." You will see that after all the absolutist, dogmatic, nationalistic, and humanistic blather, a few cool heads will recall that sentence. The sentence is incomplete; that doesn't make it any less useful, however. But whoever experiences its incompleteness should say so. Otherwise the sentence is more valid than it ought to be. Everything is relative except for love, that is my experience. My experience through you. You will have to accept my telling you so. You are unique, and with your uniqueness, you have control over me, day and night. Are there not a thousand girls, a thousand women, of such and such a height, smiling thus and so, walking, dancing, looking—yes looking, too. Are there not miracles of girlish gazing, women's eyes, deep fairy-tale lakes waiting for the storm that will bring their riches to the world? Perhaps, perhaps, it may be so. For me, none of them is unique. Perhaps I am the only one who sees your uniqueness. I can't imagine that but I like to think it's so. If I'm the only one who recognizes your uniqueness, then you must be mine. That is the most beautiful, Platonic, fairy-tale idea: each person is unique, but only for a single, unique other person. And that is what you are for me. I do not need to specify what a characteristic is, or hair color. If I am the only one for whom you are unique, then it only remains to ask if I am unique for you. I am not. Or you would have been here long since, would have broken in, climbed through the window amid rain and wind, without regard for any kind of opposing orderliness. Nevertheless, you are unique for me, and this asymmetry is the calipers that measure my misfortune. But that is how I know what love is. I was too hasty in describing the admittance to Paradise in the *West-Eastern Divan*. Life had blinkered me: I boasted pretentiously:

> No lesser man it is you're choosing!
> Take my hand, that day by day,
> On your gentle fingers musing,
> Count eternities I may.

Now that flirtatious certainty has been shattered. I curse such cultural daydreaming. But cannot a utopia accomplish anything? Whenever it becomes abundantly clear that you are absent, I end up with the *New Héloïse* or something similar and whisper to myself, "And sitting at the feet of his beloved, he will break hemp today, tomorrow, the next day, and indeed, for the rest of his life."

Will he do that? Tell him. Soon.

Paradise exists: two for each other. Hell exists: one is missing.

Dearest Ulrike, I expect of you what I cannot expect of the poor people of my acquaintance here, numbed as they are by unnatural traditions. On the promenade in Karlsbad, where people passed one another in closer proximity, a fellow who saw us strolling arm in arm joked as he passed: "You must be rehearsing your immortality." That's cultured prattle. You think and never mimic, so I can tell you what I know because I've observed it. Some experience a repeated puberty, while others are young only once. It's not a privilege of artists or a gift of nature. It has to be earned through hard work. And the work is free of morality, like musculature, vision, hearing, voice, or heartbeat. Hufeland calls it life capacity. Thus ends the epistle about what is real.

Chapter Three

A letter from Ulrike.

Ulrike's letter fell from his hands. He had not been able to read it to the end, and now it lay before him on the floor. A letter on glossy blue paper with a border. He must not bend over. Stadelmann. He came at once. Goethe pointed to the letter. Stadelmann picked up the letter and left the room with obvious deference. He had brought Goethe the lavender blue letter with the rest of the day's mail. In Marienbad and Karlsbad, he had often had lavender blue letters to deliver. Goethe saw that his hands were shaking. His heart was pounding. He needed air. His breath did come on its own, but not until it was too late. Then he gasped for air. Again, nothing more until it was too late. He tried to breathe before he had to gasp again. He could only do so very shallowly. Walk up and down, yes, he walked up and down, fairly quickly, in fact. He hurried. He had to decide if he was able to finish reading Ulrike's letter.

He had read up to a sentence that contained the news that Herr de Ror was expected to be in Strasbourg on October 31st. In Ulrike's style, short and sweet and without embellishment. This piece of information had been preceded by an explanation of how it came to this visit. Count Klebelsberg and Ulrike's mother had seen to maintaining contact with Herr de Ror and now de Ror had announced either directly to her mother or again via the Herr Finance Minister that he wanted to show them a sensational collection from Brazil. Gems of a kind never before seen in Europe. He could bring them to Paris, Vienna, Dresden, or—why not?—to Strasbourg. And her mother or Count Klebelsberg or both—probably both—say: Strasbourg. And report it to Ulrike as already decided. Surely she can't have anything against them seeing one another again. And what cordial greetings Herr de Ror sent everyone, especially to the beauty named Ulrike. He still hoped to awaken in Ulrike a positive feeling for jewelry. It was a sin to neglect her aphrodisiacal neck and plump earlobes . . .

That was when the letter fell from his hands. Stadelmann had picked it up, waited for a second to see if he should return the letter to his master's hands or put it on the table, and had quickly decided to put it on the table. Where it now lay. The brisk walking up and down had helped. His breathing had returned to normal. He modified its speed. As he read the letter he had still thought, despite its contents, isn't that just like Ulrike. Like the notes she had written him in Marienbad: an unadorned language. And that brought

him back to her neck and her earlobes. Her aphrodisiacal neck. He found that even more vacuous than the
plump earlobes. Naturally, the eyes of a jewelry sales-
man would discover what wasn't there. But that Ulrike
harbored an anti-jewelry-affect because her mother
always ran around like a jewelers' trade fair on two
legs—that was something a Herr Velocifer wouldn't
understand.

He needed to walk up and down. He needed to
increase the tempo again. He needed to go fast enough
that his attention was taken up by catching his breath.
And when he trotted up and down like this, he also
knew why his heart was pounding against his chest wall
and throbbing in his throat. His heart, a caged animal;
he, the prison guard. With what clock could he count
the seconds between today and October 31st? Today,
October 24th. He would not finish reading the letter
today. He went to his desk where the third volume of
Adelung's *Dictionary of the High German Dialect* lay.
Reflexively he reached for the thick, heavy book and
laid it on top of the letter. Could he breathe more easily? Yes. He heaved a sigh. Laughable, but one lived
from such notions. It almost did him good to think of
the letter lying under that big, heavy book. In a way, it
felt like revenge. The only important thing was that
lavender blue was gone from the room, from the
world. And he remarked what a stupid thought that
was. The big, heavy Adelung was a monument to the
letter lying beneath it. The presence of that letter in
this room could not be demonstrated with any more

clarity than by this gigantic book. But although Adelung might remind him of nothing but the lavender blue letter, it is not the lavender blue letter. No matter what reminds him of what: if he doesn't see the lavender blue letter, it will be easier to not finish reading it. There was no reason to finish reading it. If he were to pick it up again and find the place where he had stopped reading, he would have to reread more than one of those terrible sentences, or would at least encounter words while skimming the contents: the plump earlobes, the aphrodisiacal neck, the beauty named Ulrike.

Before he could even touch the letter, he had to understand how it had been possible for Ulrike to write him such a letter. The letter begins harmlessly, even fondly. Enchantingly is how it begins. His heart had at once begun to beat faster as he read how Ulrike depicted her experience of the elegy. It was the heartbeat of revival, of an immediately perceptible increase in life. He had become lighter than he'd ever been as he read how she had read the elegy! Read it, reread it, read it until she knew it by heart. She writes that she read the elegy not just with her eyes but with her whole body. With body and soul she had read it. Reading that, he had felt happier than he had ever been in his life. Never had he been so light, so alive, so destined for every height, so capable of every height. She writes that she had walked up and down the elegy's verses, that this poem cannot be read, it must be walked, celebrated as one celebrates a holiday. There could not be another poem, another piece of language that so touched the heart and contained an entire destiny. Difficult as what happened in and through this poem was, the poem made it beautiful. And becoming beautiful is obviously the highest thing that can happen to pain. She loved every line, the dark and the bright ones, all the same. She confessed that she was proud to feel a bit like the poem was addressed to her. And proud because she knew that no one in a thousand years would understand this poem as intensely as she did. It was her poem. Her life. Her destiny. Her poem.

So how could his heart not have beaten faster! How could these Ulrike-sentences not have allowed him to fly to any height! Then the turn, the fall. Her mother is already in Strasbourg, the count is supposed to arrive the following day, and on October 31, Herr de Ror. On account of gems from Brazil . . .

If only he could read the first pages of the letter without the following ones. Ask Stadelmann. No, that won't work. Whatever you do now can be the wrong thing. Must be the wrong thing. Just run back and forth so fast you can barely still do it. That you can do. Or go outside, let them hitch up the horses. Have Stadelmann drive off faster than ever. Get away from this house where the letter is lying, from this house where they apparently expect him to accept everything that can happen to him in this house. Ran to the table, lifted off the book, took the letter, ran into his bedroom, felt right away that this was the right decision, called for Stadelmann: not to be disturbed! Then he collapsed into the wingback chair Countess Egloffstein had given him, almost forgetting to feel the little protest at the designation "grandpapa-chair" that he almost always had to brush aside whenever he sought refuge in this chair. Since she had given him the chair to celebrate the birth of his grandson Walther, the name he didn't like had remained. Ottilie had probably made sure it persisted. Ah yes, and October 31, Herr de Ror's day, is Ottilie's birthday. Twenty-eight. What dramaturgy! It's going to be a day that looks interesting as long as it remains unimaginable.

He took the letter, skimmed the beautiful and the terrible pages. He found the passage: on Friday, October 31. Then he read to the end and put the letter on his bed. His heart had begun to hammer again. The soul is an organ. He knew that now. You can die from the soul. His head was spinning with Ulrike's news. The impassioned jewelry-man wants to sell. Her mother is quite wild about the stones from abroad. This time, Ulrike will ask him if she can tell her friend Goethe his first name. She won't be coming along to his hotel room. Gems simply don't interest her, but of course, she doesn't want to insult the stormy fellow, either. She'll never be a customer, however. Her mother has seen to that. Perhaps de Ror has forgotten that night in the summer, he must always be so impulsive that he might have. If she goes along with them she has to be back at the boarding school by nine. Her mother wants special permission, but she doesn't, why should she? Although if she went along and if one passed the midnight deadline a second time with him, it would be interesting to see if he revealed the same first name. If she were allowed to tell Goethe the first name, he would understand at once what she means. In one midnight one way, in the next, another. That would explain everything about the lack of a first name. And if he then marries someone, the first name he gave himself in the first midnight with her would remain. It was all a game. Just like a jewelry dealer, for whom everything is a potential gift. Including the first name. A translator of a thousand poems, and not a single one could even be compared to the Marienbad Elegy. The elegy, Excellency, holds us, protects us, unites us. It lives, and we live with it. Your Ulrike.

So: go along, stay until after midnight, study the new first name to see if it's perhaps the final one she wants to carry through Europe like a diadem. He sat and sat, his heart beating in his throat. Apparently, he wasn't supposed to breathe anymore. The agitation of his heart did not allow him to think of anything but the agitation of his heart. To breathe, that was all he asked. But that was difficult enough. The enabling of breath. Walking back and forth was now unimaginable, the window unreachable. He was a piece of butchered meat. Breathing, the most doubtful thing. And yet, this interest in enabling the next breath. Let the trembling in your hands trickle away. There is a trickling through all his veins. It becomes a painful weariness. This weariness prevents any movement. Now you must sit forever and let this painful weariness run through your veins.

Your arms were never this heavy before, nor your head, nor you.

When it grew dark, he called Stadelmann and in a completely calm voice asked him to please fetch some beer, Köstritz beer. Dark or light, Stadelmann asked. Both, and a lot. And some hard rolls. The large ones. Put everything there on the table. And no interruptions. Stadelmann nodded.

He would rather have said very, very much instead of a lot, but then he would have betrayed emotion and Stadelmann would have reported that—perhaps only if they asked—and Ottilie and son August would permit themselves to draw conclusions.

This poem cannot be read, it must be walked, celebrated as one celebrates a holiday. But the aphrodisiacal neck! The plump earlobes! The beauty named Ulrike.

Friday, October 31, 1823

And so the day of the execution has been announced and even a physician with high standards can make known the time of death in advance. Goethe had a week's time to get ready. He could sit and wait, with drooping ears. Waiting—he'd been doing that since his return. He knew as well as he knew anything that nothing could come, nothing from her. He'd known for a long time that knowing something doesn't help when one is condemned—you could say, doomed—to believe. Believing is pure restlessness, continuously thinking that something is possible and thus continuously being disappointed, destroyed. The same game with hope. For weeks he has hoped she would come. After Karlsbad the family was in Dresden. N-C-O-L-W-N. Then in Strasbourg. Wouldn't they have to pass through Weimar? No notification. So they didn't come through Weimar. But he had to hope she would come through Weimar when she returned to boarding school until the note came announcing their arrival in Strasbourg. So they didn't come through Weimar. But he had hoped every day: surely she would not shun the five steps from the posthouse to him, would come through the open downstairs door, would call, call up to him, he would hear her. . . . That dotty crow Bettina von Arnim had annoyed him more than once by bursting in unannounced. That is the law above all other laws: annoying people arrive unannounced. For they are a curse. But those you long for never come.

He had practiced thinking of her absence as a form of presence, practiced experiencing it that way. He had freed this way of thinking from everything that could be considered paradoxical about it. As the absent one, she was present in every second. The result was that every second of the present was weakened. Everything he had done or taken part in during the weeks since his return, had been done or taken part in for show, so to speak. He had always acted in the consciousness that Ulrike was not there, that she would actually have to be there, that only if she were there would the things he did be what they only seemed to be at present. It was all a substitute that only drew attention to what it was replacing: Ulrike. Negative presence, to be precise.

On October 31, a Friday, he was awakened by the sharp little cries he had apparently been emitting in his sleep. He lay there. As soon as he woke up, he had closed his eyes again. In Marienbad he had sprung out of bed every morning, done his exercises—even sung. He admitted to himself that he was idealizing Marienbad. But what else could he do? If you have no present you must idealize the past. Or, how about cursing it? Not yet. At any rate, it does one good not to have to open one's eyes. When he had opened his eyes for a moment he had felt the pain of having to see things. Close your eyes and at once, the warm feeling of not having to see anything. Even his old familiar bedroom did not belong to him but to the world of visibility. Worst was the idea of having to see people. He knew he must combat the temptation to stay in bed. It was not the first time he had had this experience. It was so simple: if he knew when he would next see Ulrike, there would be no necessity to stay in bed and no pain at the visibility of the world. Yet he got up. Without any prospect of Ulrike. Quite the contrary. October 31. It will go down in his history. He doesn't yet know how.

He called Stadelmann to help him into his day. How had Schiller—unsurpassed in elegant formulations of the ordinary—put it? "The human being is made of common stuff, and gives the name of wetnurse to his habits."

He had intentionally neglected to keep this day free of visitors and business. Sir Wylmsen was coming to tea, the captain of the regiment of Scottish dragoons who had fought so valiantly at Waterloo; Chancellor von Müller had heralded him as a combination of Heracles and Antinous. Naturally, the chancellor did not know that Ulrike's father, Friedrich Wilhelm von Levetzow, had been killed in that battle, on a beautiful day in June, as Frau von Levetzow had said in a sepulchral voice. And that was exactly eight short years ago. The program for the evening was a quartet by Prince Louis Ferdinand. In attendance would be Mr. Sterling, who had been in Weimar once before, in May, with greetings from his friend Lord Byron. And Ottilie was over the moon, had immediately become the eighteen-year-old's lover and couldn't stop telling everyone about it. For her sake and, so to speak, to excuse her, Goethe had called Mr. Sterling "the demonic youth" in May. That the twenty-eight-year-old Ottilie ran after an eighteen-year-old could have made her look more kindly on differences in age, but not a chance. No one ever understands anyone but him- (or her-) self.

As, ready to face the day, he entered the study where John was waiting for him, he realized he could not answer a single letter, dictate a single syllable today. At this moment, he couldn't imagine ever again walking up and down in his practiced posture, thinking and dictating. As unobtrusively as possible, he told his secretary that nothing was happening today. Those were his exact words and they made the tone of his voice, so bent on sounding unobtrusive, rather miss the mark. And John didn't even try to hide his surprise. Instead of bowing politely and wishing his master a pleasant day, he stubbornly refused to budge, thus expressing— if only for a brief moment—his opinion of this event, a critical opinion. Goethe could feel his entire history with John. At first Goethe's secretary (and his father had been Goethe's secretary before him), since Kräuter was on the scene, John was increasingly demoted to the role of scribe. He made his master aware of that when-ever he saw an opportunity to do so. And he had just seen one. When John turned back at the door for a final bow, Goethe waved to him more amiably than he had in a long time. But it was high time for him to be alone. In the meantime, Herr de Ror had certainly arrived in Strasbourg, probably already on the previous day. He was likely strolling with Ulrike through the streets Goethe knew so well. Might Ulrike not have suggested an excursion to Sesenheim? Goethe had once talked to her about kissing, but only to give her a quick survey of his most important kisses and really prove to her that she was the greatest kisser of all kiss-ers. It was no exaggeration, not at all. He hadn't lec-tured; it was less a lecture than ever before. He had taken her along on a train of thought that she alone had awakened in him, namely: how kissing happens depends much less on the mouths than—almost com-pletely—on the persons doing the kissing. Ulrike had not just agreed, she had enthusiastically gone him one better: if the souls are not kissing each other, the mouths are dead. Ah, Ulrike, he had said or sighed, but in either case he had once again celebrated the degree of their agreement. In so many conversations and situations, that was always his role: to celebrate the agreement they had once again discovered.

The first time he had done so, Ulrike had said, "Agreement is more than harmony."

And he had replied, "Harmony is terrible, the graveyard of feeling."

"Whereas agreement," she had said, "is the moment when two people, armed only with instinct and battling their way through a labyrinth of distractions, suddenly discover that they have undistractably found each other."

"Ulrike," he had said, "Ulrike."

And she: "Excellency, I think it is kind of you not to notice that I'm imitating you. But I confess it's fun."

And now in Sesenheim, with Herr de Ror. And all at once he knew the first name of that gentleman. Juan—Juan de Ror. Of course. Don Juan de Ror. And in the next midnight he will give up the "Juan" and reveal his ultimate first name to Ulrike. Adam de Ror. As such he will sue for her hand through his patron, Privy Councilor and Austrian Finance Minister Count Franz von Klebelsberg-Thumburg, who in any case will soon become Ulrike's stepfather. Of course. Amalie von Levetzow would have said yes long since had she not wanted to see her three daughters provided for first. Ulrike de Ror, that was a brilliant match. And then Amalie and Bertha in turn, which means that in

two or three years there can be the liberating wedding
so that Amalie von Levetzow at last has a marriage that
isn't a slog through the Prussian aristocracy but replete
with brilliant Austro-Hungarian color. Perhaps the ter-
rific Ulrike—that nineteen-year-old poppet—also a
highly qualified calculating machine for something
called the future. If she doesn't want to waste away as
a boarding-school virgin, she has to get out into
so-called life. And that's where the Oriental non-Oriental Señor Velocifer comes in, straight from Paris-
Vienna in person, master of the hardest brilliance in the
world. You were accused of poetic frenzy; in the case
of Herr de Ror it must be love. It is absolutely foreor-
dained that the earlobe prominences should be furnished with two garnet fireworks yearned for by all the
earlobes in the world. Take her, Señor de Ror, take
what has belonged to you before it was ever born.
Everything in the cosmos has a purpose, and that has
become so evident beyond all subjectivity in those earlobes that we must not surrender ourselves to grief,
especially not personal grief. She has exchanged the
past for the future. One can understand that. All that
is sown today and reaped immediately. Unable to
deliver any sort of future except for a widow's pension,
he must congratulate Ulrike, mustn't he? *Madame de
Ror, je vous félicite cordialement.*

If only he hadn't been so healthy! Why was he so
healthy now! Why wasn't he rolling on the floor and
screaming from pain in his gallbladder and kidneys.
Since her fall, the duchess couldn't take a single step

without shooting pains. A pain please, sharp as knife, so he could roll on the floor and scream and they'd have to close all the windows and doors in the neighborhood and muffle his screams with rugs and the neighbors would have to move out because they couldn't stand his screaming any longer. So that then he would be alone in the world, screaming. Only he and his screaming left. This screaming that he now feels and must not let out because his pain doesn't come from gallstones or kidney stones but from his soul. Because the soul is an organ, too. It hurts. Nothing but hurt. He was standing in the middle of the room. Suddenly he felt that the floor was hot and getting hotter. He lifted a foot and immediately had to lift the other one and then the first one again. The floor was a red-hot plane. The burning on his soles was more and more unbearable. He had to hop faster and faster from one foot to the other. And wherever he hopped, the floor of the whole room was red-hot, the same everywhere. He was long since out of breath from hopping. Perhaps in his initial panic he had begun hopping too fast from one foot to the other. He had to moderate the pace. Maybe his feet were getting a bit used to the red-hot floor. But there was no way he could stop. It occurred to him that it was a dance. A dance on a red-hot dance-floor. Either the floor would stop glowing or soon enough, he would fall down and burn to death. So he simply ran out, over, and down to his bedroom. Which saved him. Once again. He wept. That helped. He would lie down and stay put.

He found it good that he had made a program for today once he had to follow it.

When nothing interested him anymore, he still listened as if interested in what someone was telling him. The Scottish captain went him one better, saying he hadn't come to Weimar because of Goethe, but because of Madame Szymanowska. He had just been in Saint Petersburg, thinking Madame Szymanowska would perform there. Then they told him she was at present in Weimar, so off to Weimar he goes. But to be in Weimar without attempting to see Goethe—Excellency had to admit that that would not be a sin, but a mistake. He couldn't refrain from quoting Fouché, Napoleon's minister of police, who had quipped that it wasn't a crime for Napoleon to have the Duke of Enghien abducted and shot, but only a mistake. This line been passed around these circles for years, and Goethe showed that he was familiar with it and found it to be most pleasantly appropriate on this occasion. And in order to say something his visitor could take home with him, he confessed that it made him happy to be the second choice. One could never practice that too earnestly, he said. It was the sort of exercise that is all the more admirable for being condemned to failure. The captain filed that away as a piece of wisdom from an old man and said they would see each other again at Madame Szymanowska's recital. As he was not listening to the Scottish captain but thinking about Ulrike's father, killed at Waterloo, Goethe avoided twirling his right thumb around his left one. Apparently, he had twiddled his thumbs while Count Taufkirchen was spoiling that last evening with his gossip. Ulrike had told him so on their walk to Diana's Hut. On their walk to Diana's Hut, Ulrike, whose father had been killed on a beautiful day in June during the Battle of Waterloo, had recited Werther's mourning for the walnut trees. And that was never to be repeated? Never again? Ah well. On the redoubt in Strasbourg, that's where my heart grew sore. Hark! Did I hear an alphorn playing?

Before the recital, there had to be tea with Ottilie. She'd ask for that for her birthday; just the two of them, he and she. She was overexcited, more giddy than usual. Her birthday, her recital; she had invited guests. August was already amusing himself in Berlin. Berlin was never mentioned without adding that one could amuse oneself there. But she had brought along Goethe's grandson Walther. Wolfgang had a cold and Goethe could not receive people with colds, not even grandsons. Walther had a notebook with drawings that one could color in, and he'd brought his colored pencils, too. Goethe loved his grandsons but had an aversion to playing the loving grandfather. He had the feeling that his grandsons saw things the same way. Ottilie wanted to negotiate a peace treaty. For too long they'd been circling each other like two strangers or adversaries. Goethe nodded. It didn't interest him. He knew what he needed to say and how he needed to say it: he had returned. He was where he belonged! He never intended anything else! He wasn't responsible for the rumors spread by all the Carolines in the world! He was sorry if some gesture of his had unsettled the family! That was never his intention! So she should please forgive him anything that could be associated with the name of a family who would never be mentioned here again! Done. He hadn't even told a lie. It had been a pleasure to recite this text. Since it had been a pleasure, the text was a kind of truth. Let anyone who likes call it a lie. He always preferred to tell other people what they wanted to hear.

As he rose and made for the door, Ottilie said she was sorry to have to mention his demeanor to him, but he had appointed her to keep track of the impression he made. She paused.

He said, "And so?"

"The forced way you straighten up makes an unpleasant impression," she said. "People can tell you don't want to admit that your torso, as well as your head and neck, would rather tilt forward a little bit. And you struggle against that. Too obviously, in my opinion. Forgive me."

"Not at all, I'm grateful to you," he said, throwing back his shoulders so he was much straighter than before.

And then there was the recital. Since he didn't understand how to hear the music, he watched the listeners, especially Linchen von Egloffstein. But even she couldn't compare with Ulrike as a listener. At the dinner afterward, Ottilie was putting on airs with the demonic youth at her side. He had pulled his long black hair back tightly and held it in place with a huge bow of gold silk ribbon. But later it showed what it was when not held in check: a black explosion. Everything Ottilie said and did, she said and did for him. To celebrate him. Boasted that she was translating Byron's *Don Juan*. She would read from it tomorrow for anyone who wanted to listen. Charles, the eighteen-year-old friend of Byron's, was of course the most desirable listener of all. He was witty and took it all in stride. With fluent flippancy, he pocketed what was on offer. As a parody. But Ottilie didn't notice. Goethe found Ottilie hollow, empty, loveless. Avid only to make an impression but without the capability to impress. But most important: the love she was playacting was a sham, a sham, three times a sham. Love was probably foreign to her. He had to get out of here. His heart was knocking at his chest, trying to get out. You cannot deny your heart anything. It is older than you. He was proud of how he managed to transform his inner haste and hurry and neediness into a cordial farewell. And then he sat down at his desk and wrote and wrote:

A Man in Love

The time has come. How long you have moped around, suffering, pretending to suffer, it was always Frau Berlepsch who really suffered, a god always told you how you suffered or what it was from, it was all an elegy, throw it into the fire, cultural swindle, a practiced forgery, the time has come, midnight with the new or old or in any case the ultimate name, which then she will wear like a diadem, jewelry at last, jewelry forever, the time has come, come at this very moment, now they are doing, in this second they are doing what you may not do, what is forbidden to you, forbidden by the whole world's scorn and derision, they're doing it, the time has come, you did not envisage it, could not picture it, for weeks and months like the stupidest bumblebee you flew against the invisible wall of glass, bumbled into it, fell to the ground, but at once flew up again and again against the glass wall called impossibility, you could not admit that they're lying next to each other, on top of each other, above each other, beneath each other, through each other, in each other, yes, now they're lying in each other at the furious summit of love, the time has come, you could not picture it, suddenly you can picture it, must picture it, cannot picture anything else but them in their finally unleashed fury of love, the time has come, now, to what peak will this baseness drive you, an earthquake, an earthquake all along the Rhine, Strasbourg collapses, the cathedral where it all began, it was all for naught, all banter, a game, pretense, a cocky somersault, without commitment, necessity, destiny, then this, then her, the first, the only, the time has come, at this very second they are still doing it, who will stop first, you two there or you here, you have to write it down until you no longer can, until the earthquake comes, Strasbourg, where my heart grew sore, collapses, the Rhine takes care of the rest, there's no help for you without a catastrophe, it's too late to weep, the time to curse is coming, you can weep, curse, it makes no difference when you're alone if you weep or curse, being alone has no echo, just throw the elegy away, the pseudo-solitude, into the flames with it so the earth is free of the cultural lie, of noble illusion, of the pretense that it's possible to live on paper, the time has come, the elegy unmasked, a buzzing, the most fraudulent limp in the world, claims to be a dance and is a limp, the time has come, the elegy had no consequence except more buzzing, weeping without tears, replaced by words, the time has come, they are with each other, you are alone, you could have known everything, you did know everything, you are the greatest self-deceiver, seducing others to delude themselves, bear their misery, then the time comes, after the catastrophe, now, you cry out, Elegy, where are you, what are you doing, nothing, nothing, nothing, they're lying next to each other without the need for an elegy, life needs no elegy, life despises the elegy, the time has come, how far are they now, right now, yes, I want to know, see, hear, feel, smell, how far now, you two, just in this second and this second and this second, don't feel yourself involved in what is happening there, they are not laughing at you, they are not talking about you, they don't know you exist, and you don't exist, the time has come, there's only him lying in bed with her, raging through the tenderest ruthlessness in the world, the time has come, now there is only the greatest possible pain, my existence is like the greatest possible pain in and of

itself, I'm a day weaker than yesterday, I could use a lie
from Strasbourg, how much more valuable would a lie
be now than this dominant truth which is that they
know nothing of me in Strasbourg, I can invoke you
just as people invoked God, he doesn't exist either,
many found it a help to invoke him, you exist as God
never existed, I've rehearsed every defense, then in a
second you appear from a direction where you never
appeared before, I'm assaulted from behind by imagination, under all circumstances I permit myself to survive, the fact that you're still writing this down is the
reason for your next defeat, don't be surprised, she will
never get to read it, the only reader you have left is the
Devil's grandmother, the tenderest woman in what
is—as far as tenderness goes—a failed Creation, she is
the darling of the futureless, the lonely, the stupid
bumblebees bumbling against the transparent glass wall
called impossibility, colliding and falling and flying
right back up again, the world is abuzz and the Devil's
grandmother the only being ready to take over and rule
the world immediately, she ridicules elegies, they nau-
seate her, the time has come, at last you are writing for
the audience you should always have written for, for
the Devil's grandmother, the tenderest woman in the
world, the Devil's grandmother lives from a single sentence, My heart-and-soul sentence, says the Devil's
grandmother, is the sentence Nothing ends up having
no effect! She is my guarantee, the guarantee of those
who wish for something more, those done in by the
iron-clad world of morality, however, if a certain

someone would write a lavender blue note of pure midnight with a sentence on it, a single sentence, a single word would be enough, nothing but her name, in her hand, would suffice, if she would send off a courier to ride three horses to death so that he would get here before noon, hand over the note, and then fall down dead along with the fourth horse, then . . .

I hope never to hope again, never to fool myself again. If you ever wait again, you should be shot—you should shoot yourself. Tell yourself if you ever wait for her again, expect something from her, you will be doomed, executed with no further ado (to be sure, in the forest), it's trying to start over again, the time has come, nothing will start over again, the time has come, definitely, why was there this word, the time has come, finally, definitely, I expect nothing more . . . And am not master of myself, I promise everything and don't keep the promises. The Devil's grandmother takes me in her arms: pay no attention to the bleating of the know-it-all world, do what's improper, what no one understands, not even yourself. The Devil's grandmother has class I can only admire, class that is not of this world but would do the world good. Without the Devil's grandmother, I would be as impossible as I am. I would have to die of myself as one dies of an illness, I am the illness that does not want to be cured, the Devil's grandmother doesn't believe a word I say, that is why I can still write, the Devil's grandmother knows no pain, nothing ends up having no effect she says, that suffices, she just doesn't know how it is when two people are lying in Strasbourg still in bed, still in bed, I know all about it, she only knows that nothing ends up having no effect, if the effect is an earthquake that crushes Strasbourg that's fine with me, but otherwise I would remain and wouldn't know how to . . .

Chapter Four

Weimar, December 17, 1823

Dear Ulrike,
There is no such thing as a pact or a contract with memory. You can haggle with it for days and nights and agree that for certain locations and times you will only permit blurred, indistinct images and perceptions. You feel that yes, it might work. I can live with this degree of indistinctness and blurriness; it feels like peace. And then you turn around, a door slams, and you hear and see how Ulrike ran from the room in Karlsbad after saying the angriest sentence to her mother and banged the door behind her. All present and sharp again, all bloody again. The whole strategy of avoidance is self-deception.

If I owe your letter not merely to the circumstance that I haven't died yet, I am happy that you wrote to me. *Mon mal n'était pas purement physique.* However, once an illness has assumed command, it doesn't care how it came to power. It starts harmlessly enough, but we know all about such harmlessness. You never have an illness for the first time. This slight cough that behaves as if it's controllable. A day later, it has seized power. Then only the armchair helps. Sit up straight. The straighter you sit, the harder it is for the tickle to clamber up to your throat. The ticklish beast crawls up inside you like an insect and won't leave you alone until it's sitting in your throat and you have to let the cough break out. The cough shakes you, convulses you through and through, throws your hands in the air and your head back. Why doesn't it just tear you apart? What a pointless function of nature, to unleash this storm of coughing that brings not the slightest improvement. Dry, pointed, sharp. Sitting with your legs drawn up. Night has long since fallen. Your chest: a block of heat, a heat carapace. Your breath must struggle against it. The carapace doesn't react. This must be what it was like two thousand years ago in Sicily, when the tyrants baked their enemies in red-hot iron pipes. You have it better than that. At some point, it begins in your arm-pits, on your chest, and soon there is no place where water is not welling up. Then you've become a broad terrain where a thousand tiny springs pour little streams down your sides. For two or three hours, you think your body is weeping, then it stops. You ring for Stadelmann. He dries you off: the purest sense of well-being. Stadelmann is barely out the door when the heat carapace has you in its grip again. And everything repeats. Three or four times a night. You breathe toward the coming day. As soon as daylight occupies your room, the miserable sweating stops. But as long as you're sweating, you're not coughing. Only once you've stopped sweating does the cough return, the cough that wants to tear you apart but never can. You are able to stand it only because there's someone you can think of. Every second is dedicated to you, Ulrike. Thus, I am not alone. Dr. Rehbein attends me day and night, forbids me visitors. Except for Herr von Humboldt, please. He brought Humboldt, warned us against conversing since speaking aggravates the convulsive cough. I had the elegy brought in, gave it to Humboldt, and said, "Tomorrow." Humboldt left. Me in the armchair, half asleep half awake. Then Humboldt again. Ulrike, I'm only writing for this reason: Humboldt said he would speak but I wasn't to speak. The elegy—that very night he read it twice. He was amazed, amazed, amazed. Three times he said he was amazed. Such youthful feeling. Such intellectual and imaginative power. Such vitality. These truly heavenly verses. This gripping passion. There is simply nothing as great, he said, than to completely capture a feeling in poetry. I said that so far, I'd shown the elegy only to one other person. I saw he could imagine who that person is. He couldn't say it, nor could I. A curse upon enslavement to convention. But as Humboldt saw how invigorated I was by what he said, he told Dr. Rehbein who was overseeing the entire visit, "He needs the right kind of company. You mustn't allow him to waste away in the monotony of Weimar." He sounded very stern. Dr. Rehbein started to defend himself, then came the next coughing fit. Humboldt waited until it was over. Dr. Rehbein let him know through gestures that he had to leave now. He took my hand and said, "A divine poem. Not even you have ever written anything better." Cough-free, I replied, "We should leave readers to guess the poet's year of birth. However," I continued, "it will not be printed—perhaps never." And he cried, "Herr Dr. Rehbein, after hearing this I cannot leave." I forbade the doctor to get mixed up in this discussion, pressed to my breast the poem Humboldt had returned, and said without coughing, "I confess I've had to read it so often I know it by heart." Humboldt departed and the nasty cough assaulted me. It got worse. One Humboldt a day, that would have been the right medicine. Instead: fourteen nights in the chair with swollen feet, fever, no fever, leeches and bloodlettings till I couldn't go on, until I screamed for them to give me Kreuz Spring water. Anything but that, they insisted. Nothing but that, I cried. And no more of that awful medicine with anise. Wolfsbane tea? At once! If I'm going to die, then let me die my own way. That worked. They obeyed. I drank a whole bottle of Kreuz Spring at one go. And then a cup of wolfsbane tea. And slept the whole night through again for the first time. After that, Kreuz Spring every day. Afterward they said that my death had already been reported on Sunday. Even in French: *Le Voltaire d'Allemagne est mort.* I hope that charming prematurity didn't reach you, Ulrike. Now I hear that I didn't behave myself at all as a patient. No hero. A whiner who mistreated poor Dr. Rehbein. He wouldn't allow my friend and most gracious sovereign Carl August in to see me. That's how badly things stood. I sent a dispatch over to the palace, however: if I had been His Serene Highness, I would have swept all opposition aside to stand at the sickbed of my friend, possibly for the last time. And as it began to seem that I might recover although I could have had a reversal at any time, my dear Zelter finally came from Berlin. Got the news and hurried here.

"Aha, so you're still alive," he cried, and hauled me entirely back to life with his cheerfulness and love.

He, too, was permitted to keep the elegy overnight. I asked him to read it aloud to me. He did—and how! So cautiously, and then suddenly boldly, and then cautiously again, so that it was a joy to see him being directed by the elegy. When he had read it aloud for the third time—he'd asked to read it to me three times—I said, "You read well, old man."

And he replied, "It's a love poem made of blood and bravery, fire and ire. And I read it well because line for line I was thinking of my beloved. Of her hundred kisses, she told me, fifty were for you. I am supposed to tell you that she was at your side during a state of ecstasy she'd never experienced before or after."

"I feel it. I swear I do. I have the power." That's what I said. Then I said I'd heard tell that all I want to hear are things that flatter me. Everything else leaves me cold.

"Is it true?" asked Zelter.

"Yes," I said.

"Then everything is fine, dear fellow. We do not need to be against ourselves like everyone else."

Zelter stroked my arm. After he left, the cough, the fever, the chest and kidney pains didn't stand a chance.

This illness! Of course: Marienbad, Karlsbad, and the L. family! I could read it in all their faces. My show of renunciation had failed. So he is still suffering from XYZ. Otherwise, how to explain that after forty-nine days of nothing but recovery, he suddenly relapses? Dr. Rehbein, whom I had finally persuaded to read Christoph Wilhelm Hufeland's *The Art of Extending Human Life*, started plying me with Hufeland quotes. He's trying to cheer me up with Hufeland sentences, sentences that might please my lover of machines. "The business of thinking itself," quotes Dr. Rehbein in his best Jena lecture-hall voice, "as actuated in the human machine, is organic." With a sentence like that, he says he is appealing to my capacity for life, which is, he claims, enormous.

We can come together, you and I, in sentences like that, Ulrike. Hufeland! Do you recall our game in the reading room, that rainy summer? In what year was the author of this sentence or this poem born? I contributed the sentence, "Sweet life! The beautiful, amiable habit of being and acting!—must I leave you?" Your mother and sisters hadn't a clue but you, off-handedly, as if you had hoped for something harder: "1749." "Goethe," cried your mother, "really?" I then told you all, not without some pride, that the influential Hufeland had used that quote as the epigraph for his book *The Art of Extending Human Life*. Ah, Ulrike. When I think of you, I'm always shaken by bouts of weakness and strength. The balance I've long been proud of is gone. I confess to a particularly nasty weakness: the desire to do something.

If you don't get everything, how much is enough to make you content? You don't know how much would be the best you could get, but clearly less than everything. How much less? What is the least you should accept without being so ridiculous that she doesn't dare offer it to you anymore? The only person you can bargain with is yourself.

What I could use now, Ulrike, is your practice of turning wise sayings on their heads. Accepting inconvenience by acknowledging its necessity. So I acknowledge once and for all that you need to be in Strasbourg. It is necessary. For you. By my acknowledging its necessity, the inconvenience that you are unreachable has only become sharper. Please turn the sentence around so that something I can live with comes out. I'm playing the role of a man who is beyond it all, heroic and now and then, sentimental. It works. I'm playing the renunciant. I have to, after all. You will recall *The Journeyman Years or the Renunciants*. I'm telling the truth. Comedy doesn't lie, it's just not interested in the truth. On the other hand, I am told that I'm pathologically peevish. You disregarded my question as to whether the Master of First Names thought or felt or knew *quelque chose*. So how could I not be peevish? I am a house of cards that claims to be a fortress. Under observation, I was permitted to look at little almanacs and engravings with you, and that was all!

Dr. Rehbein asked if we should already be preparing for Bohemia next year. I said they should. But do I believe it? I cannot imagine the spruce forest around our blissful valley without you. Four hundred fifty steps is what you said we walked from the colonnades to the spring. I thought you were listening a little as I was talking about how, when Stadelmann brings me the next quill pen, I can only write if it is absolutely indistinguishable from the one I just wore out—I'm talking about how writing is loyalty in practice—and you're counting our steps. And you add that on average, it took us 450 steps, but sometimes it was 430 and other times 470. It depended completely, you said pointedly, on whether you agreed or disagreed with me.

"How so?" I asked.

And you said, "When I disagree, I walk faster than when I agree."

And I said, "Since you always contradict me, we never need more than 430 steps."

And you said, "I had the impression that you've been too seldom contradicted in your life."

Then I had to remind you of the enemies of my theory of colors.

And you, quite sharply: "Forgive me, Excellency, for momentarily forgetting to think about your theory of colors."

"It's absolutely unforgiveable," I cried, infected by your high spirits.

And then you said, with only apparently playful imperiousness, "Change of topic!"

And I, in the same tone, "Coward!"

You almost came to a standstill, but in any case, turned completely toward me and said, "When you make me so addicted to submission."

Then I said, "Ah, Contresse Levetzow."

"Ah, ah, ah, ah," you said. "Now I've said it four times and you can leave it out four times today."

How could that not make me happy, Ulrike! It was the most drastic revival in my life. Returning to life, I wrote to Zelter, the only person I can tell everything to. Almost everything. A postscript apropos the theory of colors: You are the only person, Ulrike, who has ever gotten me to be jocular on the subject.

Weimar, December 18, 1823

Dear Ulrike,
Yesterday I was rudely interrupted. She barely knocked before she burst in. She ran over and scattered a few bits of paper onto the table. Paper with writing on it. Right behind her, little Walther, crying because his Mama had taken away what he was playing with. He had carefully torn up a sheet of paper and was going to make something out of the pieces. You could distinguish: a ship, a tree, a church, a house. He was going

to paste them onto something and then color them. Still crying and blaming his mother, he managed to explain that much. I had no need to put the pieces back together. One glance and I knew what they were: a little poem I'd written down a few days ago. I'd been looking for it, hoping it would fall into my hands again. As we know, a house doesn't lose things, not this one anyway, especially not something like this. Here's how the poem goes:

Her lovely face by day and night
I constantly recall.
She thinks of me, I think of her—
And it does no good at all.

At first, Ottilie was incapable of uttering a word. She stood there hissing, pale as a candle and stretching her arms out toward me, half threatening and half begging. At last, she managed to utter two words: "Tartuffe. Lier." As soon as she got that out, the dam was broken: "Hypocrite. You play the great renunciant for us and in reality you're writing little poems no better than a nineteen-year-old." And more in the same vein. As often, her last words were "You impossible person." I'm gradually beginning to take pride in that. I said, "Come, Walther." He came over to me. I asked him what he was going to make. "Weimar in winter." That made sense, because despite the writing on them, the scraps were white. I always keep some paste in my drawer, so he and I pasted together Weimar in Winter.

We pasted the scraps so the writing still showed, but in a way that created a new text. Walther already knows how to read, of course. Later we added a church and houses and a boat. The scraps said "day and night . . . good at all . . . she thinks . . . of me . . . her lovely face . . . to recall."

Ottilie had screamed her parting, "You impossible person," and left the room. She saw us engaged in sensible pasting. Walther was proud of his work, and rightly so. When I was alone again, I wrote down the poem I could no longer consider "little" since that's what Ottilie had contemptuously called it. And I read it to myself sotto voce:

> Her lovely face by day and night
> I constantly recall.
> She thinks of me, I think of her—
> And it does no good at all.

How could I have misplaced, no, lost that sheet of paper? Now she knows what's going on again. Now all day long, no matter if I again play the sensible, even-tempered person, the patient participant in every-thing, the Sage of Weimar—that simple poem has betrayed me. I must be allowed to write such a thing, mustn't I? I can't destroy myself by swallowing my feelings. But then . . . then I must be careful, much more careful. I'm living in enemy territory. Chancellor von Müller, the only one with whom I can sometimes, in a late-evening chat, come close to the truth about the state I'm in (although he too marvels at how well I've gotten over everything!)—Chancellor von Müller sometimes tells me what's still flitting around in the way of conjecture and rumor. The rumors are fading, he says. What he means is: we can be content. But I cannot spare you the most recent thing he told me, since I found it almost moving. Caroline von Wolzogen, the sister of Schiller's widow and one of the worst of the Carolines, tried to put it about that if Goethe really wanted to take in that young Levetzow girl but couldn't get her past Ottilie, then she—Caroline von Wolzogen—would be more than happy to put up the Levetzow girl at her house. She was obviously ready to take into account that she would thereby become the center of interest for the educated world.

I must really not forget that what I stared at longest in your letter were the last four words. They have burned themselves into my soul. They shine forth day and night as soon as I cast the least thought in your direction, and what a lovely sound they make: "Your devoted friend, Ulrike."

I could write them down a hundred times and read them aloud a hundred times and each time differently. Why don't you come and test me, count the times since you are unsurpassable in counting. And what aren't you unsurpassable in! Your devoted friend, Ulrike. People who laugh at me for not being able to forget you, know nothing about you. They think I've lost my mind over such a young person. For them, it's no more than a comedy by Iffland. Because they don't know the Contresse Levetzow! Don't know her rich repertoire of answers, of disagreements! When I think of our conversations, I know that I had never before experienced the like of them, being either challenged or worshipped. You, Ulrike, you, you—as far as I am concerned, you were born so that I could lose myself in another person and experience how that person gave me back to myself, happy. And am I never to see you again? We must not believe that, you and I. Herr de Ror or no Herr de Ror . . . I must close, otherwise . . . Ah, Ulrike! Could you please supply me with the opposite of one of my pronouncements: If one cannot despair, one doesn't need to live. The opposite, please, Contresse Levetzow. Is it: If you don't need to live, you can despair? Is that true, Contresse? That was the point I had reached yesterday. On the point of despair. And I noticed—I have to admit it—that my hands were trembling. And there is no trembling unless the fellow without a first name has four actors throwing their trembling hands into the air. And I heard those brief little screams coming out of my mouth. It wasn't just my hands trembling—I was trembling up to my shoulders, and from my shoulders it reached for my neck. I raised my hands, put them on Stadelmann's shoulders as if they would get better there. Stadelmann had come in. Perhaps my brief little screams had gotten too loud. But I couldn't leave my hands lying there. I put my arms around Stadelmann, laid my head on the big man's chest (he must be over six feet tall), and wept. And hoped he wouldn't notice. "Excellency," he said.

He led me into my room and put me into the Egloffstein armchair. I needed to let the pain drain off, the pain that was moving from my shoulders into my arms and down my arms into my hands as far as my fingertips. It was not the flow of a fluid but the tug of something immaterial, something, however, that produced a most pronounced physical effect, namely, pain. A hot weight remained for I don't know how long in my arms and hands. I feel it. I swear I do.

The final words remain: Your devoted friend Ulrike. And: You impossible person.

So I will believe Ottilie, dearest Ulrike, and will also close this as Your impossible person. How could I stop writing to you, dearest, when except for you, nothing exists. And you don't exist. *Ecco.* But now there is a New Covenant, the Covenant of the Elegy. Its members are Ulrike von Levetzow, Wilhelm von Humboldt, Carl Zelter, and Johann Wolfgang Goethe.

Chapter Five

SINCE HE HAD received one letter from Ulrike, he waited every day for another. Which had to be even less noticeable than all the other things he kept secret. Whenever he heard Stadelmann or John coming with the mail, he immediately took a piece of paper and began writing so he wouldn't have to pay attention to the one bringing the mail. At the most, he indicated with a gesture where to put the letters. The frozen sea between people. Luckily, we know nothing about one another. When the letter finally arrived, he saw the lavender blue envelope immediately. He also knew he shouldn't open the letter. He knew she couldn't write him the only thing he wanted to read. But he also knew she would always write everything she possibly could. Everything beautiful, good, with the promise of happiness, everything in place of happiness. Ulrike always went further than she ought. She was full of love. She certainly was. It wasn't her fault that she couldn't write, Tomorrow I'll come and put my arms around your neck and whisper something fresh, naughty, wonderful into your ear! So please, no criticism of Ulrike! Don't forget: Your devoted friend Ulrike. When a young woman with a weakness for machines writes something of the sort, she knows what she's writing. Every day that he waited for the next letter, he had imagined what would be in such a letter. He had fooled himself into thinking he was prepared for anything. Another October 31st wouldn't come again. It's simply not fate's way to send the same blow twice, so he could feel safe from a second October 31st. And what he had received from Ulrike since then was soothing, healing. At least that's how she meant it. Your devoted friend Ulrike.

Although he knew perfectly well that one can never know anything ahead of time and that the reality will always outstrip everything—even what one could only guess at—he was once again taken completely by surprise. He could not have guessed what he learned from the letter. Ulrike is now wearing jewelry. An emerald on a golden chain. A deep green emerald that echoes and darkens her eyes. A gift, but not only in the de Ror sense of the word, no, a real gift. A gift she could not refuse because he hadn't given it to her forever, but only to try out. She is supposed to wear the stone—or try wearing it—and the next time he comes through Strasbourg, he'll ask for her opinion. Then they'll see. Let's wait and see. What can she do if she doesn't want to be deliberately impolite? And she doesn't want to be. He didn't deserve that at all, the passionate jewelry-monger. He gives the impression that it actually pains him to look at a woman wearing no jewelry. Actually, at the latest by the age of twelve, a girl's desire for jewelry should awaken. But no norm is universally applicable. However, if a woman is approaching twenty and the desire for jewelry is still slumbering, then it's

the duty of her friends and relatives to put her abstinence to the
test. That's how the conversation went, for a while in the presence of her mother and the count. Let's not forget that he had
particularly bewitched her mother with his mocha gift. Yes, it
was the genuine, one hundred percent mocha coffee, specially
purloined by his connections directly from the harem of the
Egyptian pasha, not yet mixed and blended but selected bean
by bean. When her mother drank some she nearly swooned
with delight.

Then the jewelry-monger requested a solo audience, which
was granted him more by her mother than by her. Probably
because he'd said that when a young woman had such an
outstanding model as her mother (and not just vis-à-vis jewelry), then a kind of delay in the natural wish for jewelry was
quite understandable. He did not speak in a loud voice. He
wasn't exactly presumptuous, he was more pensive. But he
never stopped talking. You had to experience it: he can't help
himself. He has to say that. For her sake. The whole time he
kept his eyes on her, observing or perhaps just inquisitive.
Obviously ready to discover something, for example, the effect
of the talk that was fed by his observation. So it was unfortunately impossible to simply rebuff so much benevolent attention, for example with her wonderfully well-practiced, brusque
announcement on the promenade: Change of topic!
Impossible for her, she had to concede. But the apostle of
jewelry hadn't deserved to be insulted, either. He really had a
talent for amiability and could make one feel he had nothing
but good intentions. A certain someone was already practically
a grown-up woman, and no woman in her circle between
Constantinople and London runs around with a bare neck and

naked ears. In any case, she is soon due to appear at the debutante ball in Vienna and must be ready to answer a hundred questions about her abstinence. And so on and so forth.

I was thinking of you the whole time, Excellency. That is, listening to him I was with you. Goethe had been her great master of conversation for forty-nine days—yes, with his permission she had counted them—for forty-nine happy days she had learned how to talk as others learned how to ride, learned it from him, and so far there was nothing she had ever learned that was so beautiful and so important, so fulfilling, so utterly moving, so enhancing. As for riding, back home at Trschiblitz Castle my bay is waiting for me. We can clear hedges and ditches and feel like a veritable autumn windstorm—I knew how to ride long before I wanted to learn how to read. And now she could both ride and speak. She was in excellent health, she said. When midnight had passed, Herr de Ror had indeed offered his second first name, another name she was not allowed to tell anyone else until she bore his entire name in the light of day. That's where she called Stop and refused to honor a contract she had not signed, which was being imposed on her without her consent. He seemed to be insulted. One confidence deserves another, he said. And so on and so forth. All that to-do about first names was so lacking in substance that she should never have starting telling Excellency about it. But although she had promptly raised an objection, the apostle of jewelry—who then promoted himself to an apostle of life—had put her in such a state with his first-name hocus-pocus that she'd like to know how to extricate herself. But how? Indeed, she now felt herself bound by the so-called confidence into which he had drawn her without asking permission. Especially since he again seemed upset and spoke of a disappointment he had experienced that had almost cost him his life. He couldn't go through that a second time. It had been a betrayal of trust that had brought him to the brink of his existence. And so on and so forth. Now Excellency certainly knew more than she did since Excellency was utterly wise and from his distance could register everything much more calmly than she, buffeted as she was by a whirlwind. Yes, she did feel buffeted. If that was so-called life, she didn't know whether she wanted to participate in it yet. Although there was a sort of adventurousness about it, too, which was—if her feelings weren't deceiving her—not entirely unpleasant. She hadn't worn the emerald in public yet. She had tried it on, but only when she was by herself. She couldn't say anything about it yet. In any case, in color, size, and setting the stone was understated. But according to the apostle of jewelry, its style was comparable to the emerald worn by the Duchess of Devonshire. It had become apparent to her that the entire jewelry offensive had been planned by her mother and Count Klebelsberg. Klebelsberg had just given her mother a chain with Bohemian garnets that she could wrap four times around her neck, the stones more black than red, and along with it two equally heavy, equally blackish-red chains of garnets as bracelets and equally dusky earrings. The count is somehow involved in a garnet mine in Brux and has threatened to bury her under a load of jewels, too, perhaps as an engagement present. She understands: her mother wants to get married, but not with a grown-up daughter in her entourage. So Ulrike, begone! Put some jewelry on her and send her off to the debutante ball. That has certainly occurred to the count.

And Herr de Ror is top of the line. A gold-edged future. But that's all for now, and in the hope that he can hear her calling—as she often does—Ehhhhxcellency. And then once again: Your devoted friend Ulrike.

He knew at once that this salutation was now worth nothing. Her torrent of jewelry talk had invalidated everything. Nothing was left. Now he had been expelled to where he belonged, whence he should never have allowed himself to be lured away. But how was he supposed to have known, in those thousands of moments, that it was all nothing. Nothing but . . . but what? Stop it. There is nothing to understand, nothing more to rehash—where did I go wrong? From what point on . . . ? Throw it away, throw everything away, including yourself. No set phrases, thinking only about what you should do now. It's all just words—words begone! Concealment, nothing else. You are in enemy territory, to expect to produce anything is all in vain. You are the renunciant as never before, you have nothing to broadcast but renunciation! Not loudly, but quite softly, quite wisely, as it should be, the great renunciant, the noblest cultural edifice in Germany, Europe, the entire world, a model of renunciation for ages to come. All the unfortunate should look up to you as to a constellation: here is how to deal with enormous pain, you see, so that the pain is pain no longer, does not hurt anymore, a smile, a cultural grimace that makes your face more beautiful. Pain is an occasional poem, not too light, but much lighter than the elegy. The elegy stays in the safe. Of course, it hurt. Now that it's over, completely over, you can admit that it hurt, since it's all over, it may even have hurt a lot, it depends on its being over, over, over, over. Above all, you must see to it that the news reaches her! She has to see that you are not a writhing worm. It should make her feel better to see that the old fellow has gotten over it. Together you were summer theater. It hurt him—a nice touch that it hurt him. It would have been even better . . . but he's gotten over it. He has renounced, is even rewriting his journeyman novel, again with the subtitle The Renunciants, but now so that everyone can see how renunciation works: Let man be noble, useful, and good. And if things go wrong, a god gives him the power to say what he's concealing . . . no wait, not that . . .

From outside came the clatter of horses, the lovely sound of freshly shod hooves on the hard courtyard, eight hooves in the most unruffled rhythm in the world. And it led him to Karlsbad, where he had lived in the Alte Wiesenstrasse, not fifty yards from the bridge over the Tepl River. Because the hooves pounded on the wooden bridge, Ulrike had called them, "the Ghost Riders." It was in the evening as they sat in front of the Golden Ostrich and watched the moon rise over Mount Dreikreuz. And with her at the mineral spring, silently watching the water spout that didn't rise monotonously to a constant height—because then it would just stand there like a column—no, it shot up, hesitated a quarter-second as if catching its breath, then shot up again. Whenever he stood with Ulrike and all the other spa guests, he didn't know what they were all thinking when they stared in wonder at this spouting miracle. And he found that it was all a mistake! Why couldn't one—why wasn't one allowed to express what one so clearly felt?! He could feel the rhythm in his member, the part that would so much like to be the whole. And what about Ulrike and all the others? When Ulrike then

touched him a little on the way back, he felt completely
happy. Never again would he see the spouting spring with
Ulrike. This "never again" was a force, an annihilating force.
He sensed that he must not give in to the rigidity that was
starting to spread through him. Now as never before, secrecy
was called for. Concealment. If what was dominating him
now should come out, a hurricane of sympathy and triumph
would break out and he would be drowned in a wave of mor-
al-aesthetic dogmatism that would roll in as dreadful compassion. Instinctively, he reached for the list of today's obliga-
tions. It said that Chancellor von Müller and Julie von
Egloffstein were scheduled to come together to present him
with a remarkable painting. Not until five o'clock. At six,
Riemer is going to read his satirical sonnets against the language purists. Then Linchen with Soret, Rehbein, Adele Sch.,
the chancellor, Riemer, Ottilie, Meyer, and Court Chaplain
Röhr. But beforehand, at five, a certain Herr Zeuner, who in
stilted language has asked for a letter of recommendation to
W. von Humboldt and was himself highly recommended by
Chancellor von Müller.

She has exchanged the past for the future. Anyone of
sound mind would do the same. In company, you must not
let the words "sound mind" slip out of your mouth. To be
able to extinguish oneself like a light. You have already
dreamed everything. Just don't admit during the day that
your dream was right. You dreamed you were in a church
with her in Karlsbad, which was St. Jacob's church from
Weimar. Now it was in Karlsbad, high above the city at the
edge of a forest, on the path to Diana's Hut where he had
spent those four *du*-hours with her. In the dream they had

climbed up the steep path without speaking. In reality, during the steep climb Ulrike had already recited Werther's grief over the walnut trees. When they had almost arrived at the forest's edge, they suddenly discovered this church, which he recognized as St. Jacob's. Then they were inside the church, festively illuminated by a thousand candles. It was as overfull as on the day Christiane was buried there. Ulrike smiled as soon as they were inside the church, smiled to one person and another. Who smiled back. Ulrike knew everyone and everyone knew Ulrike. Then they kissed each other, he and she. In reality, it was on their return that they had kissed each other, at the edge of the forest, for the very last time. But as they were kissing each other in the dream, she tilted her head without interrupting the kiss so that she could see beyond him, and watch a young man—clearly an Oriental—who walked past them to the door and, before vanishing out the door, turned back once more and exchanged a look with her.

When he awoke from this dream, he got up at once. He feared that if he fell back asleep, he would have to dream the same thing again. This helplessness in the face of a dream. What ought he to do during the day to be protected from such dreams? He knew the answer: he should assert himself. Against himself. The only thing that had helped so far: work. He could write whatever he wanted about whatever he wanted. As long as he wrote, he was protected. It was practiced, second nature. Writing, he was not of this world but in his own. But if he then tired and had to stop, the past pounced on him with redoubled fury as if because he had turned away from it, it had been recharged, had stored up energy and was now many times more powerful than before.

He got out Hufeland's book and reread the passage he had read and underlined during his illness:

> Boerhaave tells of himself that after thinking about the same thing for a few days and nights, he had suddenly fallen into such a state of fatigue and weakness that he had lain in a death-like condition, feeling nothing, for a considerable time.

Why did he not fall into this wished-for, death-like condition, feeling nothing, since he thought of nothing but Ulrike? Why had he never thought of liberating Ulrike from her refusal to wear jewelry? Because he respected her condition. Because he adored her too much. Because he idolized her the way she was. On the last evening in Karlsbad, he had given her the little golden ginkgo leaf—how absolutely ridiculous. She hadn't even worn it that evening. He, however, wore day and night around his neck the little golden key that led to her glove. They existed in cruel inequality.

Without receiving the fellow, he had John convey to Herr Zeuner the letter recommending him to Humboldt. He felt able to do that because it was revenge for Zeuner's stilted language. Then, the almost longed-for audience with Chancellor von Müller and Julie von Egloffstein. Since Sweet Julie (that was her nickname, and it was appropriate) frequented his house, he and the chancellor competed for her favor, and Julie enjoyed it. But today the two arrived with conspiratorial expressions. The chancellor was carrying a painting covered in a blanket. "Clear a space please, Excellency, and don't look." He obeyed. When he was allowed to look, the picture was hanging on the wall where paintings to be presented were always hung. It was Ulrike von Levetzow. The two of them were delighted at his astonishment.

Julie said it was her Christmas present to him. But since she wasn't sure it would be welcome under the family Christmas tree, she was giving it to him now.

Dramaturgy, thought Goethe. The supreme director, or the Devil's grandmother. He had always known that the word "coincidence" was only an ignoramus's paltry substitute.

"Ehhhhhxcellency," said Julie, drawing out the first syllable as only she and Ulrike could.

It was a touchy situation. He was unable to stand up. He had to assume a posture that the two of them would understand and, if asked, could pass on to others. "How did you come to paint this picture, Julie?" The question sounded intense, but not stunned.

It was the question Julie was waiting for, and she burst out with the answer. In Dresden she'd met a Fräulein Fölkersam who studies art there. As soon as Fräulein Fölkersam, from the Duchy of Courland, hears that Julie lives in Weimar, she runs to fetch her portrait of Goethe and wants to know if it's any good, and Julie, parodying Goethe, says, "Extremely congruent!" The Courlander girl is delighted, starts chattering about how much her friend Ulrike von Levetzow has told her about Goethe and Marienbad. And she has drawn Ulrike, too. Julie bought the drawing and based her portrait on it, part gouache, part watercolor, part chalk, part oil. The greatest thing about it: Ulrike's face in so many colors! He remembered: that's how she looked in the dream. Ah, Julie! She asked him to deliver a death sentence or a reprieve.

"Extremely congruent," said Goethe.

And the other two laughed.

Then he turned to Chancellor von Müller and said seriously, "You know, don't you, that Ottilie and the entire family leave for Berlin tomorrow. 'Berlin is agleam,' Ottilie says. And since she said it, everyone says it. And everyone wants to spend the season and amuse themselves in Berlin. But not everyone can. We poor folks can only mourn as we watch the lucky ones leave, but we are able to look after ourselves. And the first thing that entails is purchasing this picture from the artist, Herr Chancellor. Pay whatever it takes, then it gets taken to my rooms, my armoires, disappears forever. We do not know of any such picture! No gossip, no rumors, we are well-practiced renunciants, nothing leads us into temptation anymore. Herr Chancellor, dear Julie, I see you heartily agree." And he had Stadelmann take the picture down at once and carry it to his rooms. The evening had been salvaged.

When he returned to his rooms much later, he saw a note from the wise Stadelmann telling which cabinet he had put the picture in.

He sat in Mother Egloffstein's chair and let his hands tremble. There was not the slightest danger that his hands would start trembling in the presence of other people, but when he was alone it almost felt good to let them tremble. There was then nothing he had to do. They trembled effortlessly, all by themselves so to speak. He watched them. Looked at his hands, the fingernails Stadelmann had cleaned and polished in Marienbad. When genuine diamonds can no longer compete with imitations, it is probable that with his connections in the Orient, Juan Adam de Ror will become the king of coffee importers. Mocha is the name of the future.

Chapter Six

HE HAD TO get up. Hardly was he on his feet when her absence shot through him, as sharp, fresh, and painful as if the news that he no longer had her had only just arrived. At once, he was overwhelmed by the unsparing feeling of being forsaken. Lying in bed, he had practiced for an unmeasurable time seeing himself without her; had practiced that she no longer existed, would never again exist for him. He was able to feel that he had thrown some sort of impermeable blanket over everything. And now, thanks to nothing but a change of position, all his work at reconciling himself was gone as though it had never been. Every time, memory lunges out and stabs the defenseless. So then, begin again. Practice futility. Now he had Ulrike's picture, now he could go to it at any moment, could look and look at her face in Julie's almost wild riot of color . . . and then what?

He must never look at this picture. And knew that he would tell himself that a hundred times and then run over and take it out and look at it. Look and look and look! A dirty trick of dramaturgy! With this picture, she is more clearly there than if the picture did not exist. So the picture exacerbates his struggle. So he ought to destroy it. He ought to, but . . . He had to do something against this picture. And as fast as he could, he went to his desk. And wrote.

A Man in Love.

No longer a face. A bend in a nose, the tip of a nose, a small mouth that never rests for a second. It twitches, fidgets, a dry insect that will not be skewered by the sharp chin that juts into space. Around these parts, hair flutters inadequately, least of all for the swollen earlobes glowing like two lanterns outside a house of pleasure. The lean neck can only be salvaged by a load of jewelry. Her movements give the impression of having no center point from which they are controlled. An uncontrollable dangle and swing. The voice, shrill, ideal for self-righteousness. The twitching little mouth issues a constant stream of self-righteousness. Never an easy smile. Always a flat giggle tuned to eeee. So much for your picture.

Ah, Ulrike, through you he becomes a dwarf practicing the high jump. Hostility. Without hostility toward Ulrike, he couldn't extricate himself. Apply hostility like an instrument, like a lever with which to increase one's own, inadequate force. But how to cultivate a hostility toward this girl that would convince himself? Hatred? He had survived a long life without hatred. Suffering is the only possibility to hurt her who is making you suffer. But if you realize that everything you suffer was caused by yourself? If something is dreadful and you must admit that you deserve it? If you can say that what you suffer is unjust, you can defend yourself. If you have to say that you yourself are doing what makes you suffer, that you have no one else to blame, then you have to turn against yourself. Disgust? Yes! Increasingly. He was increasingly disgusted by all the clothes he had worn in Marienbad and Karlsbad. He should have done something about them long ago.

And he called Stadelmann and directed him to immediately load into a crate everything he had worn that summer in Bohemia: the Werther costume, the summer coat with a red velvet collar, and all the linen and cotton shirts he had purchased there. The black silk and white silk vests, the white flannel nightshirt, the white cambric scarf and its stickpin, the hose, and the stockings.

"Stadelmann, you were selling my hair again in Bohemia. I should have dismissed you. If you fail me now, I shall have to dismiss you. Everything into a crate, then drive out past the pheasant run into the Webicht Forest and take along some peat and paper and burn it all so that nothing remains. Have we understood each other, Stadelmann?"

The giant Stadelmann, who visibly shrunk at the mention of selling hair, straightened up again and said solemnly, "Yes, sir."

Goethe saw that he could rely on Stadelmann this time. "If I ever happen upon even a handkerchief or scarf that was there last summer, you are dismissed. Is that clear?"

"Yes, sir," said Stadelmann and left.

Ottilie was already in Berlin. This maneuver might be successful. He breathed a sigh of relief. And trotted over to the room with the cabinet where papers were stored. The accounts from his travels, kept and signed by Johann Wilhelm Stadelmann. Wonderful papers in Stadelmann's handwriting, which was as beautifully energetic as his driving style. And he became absorbed in once more reading the summer's words and dates. The moor bath, 30 kreutzer per day; the daily oil, 15; the 4 rolls, 8; the daily wax candles, 1.40. Stadelmann had written down every guilder, every kreutzer: beer, laundry, room, papper (with two p's), gratuities, alms box, ink powder. It did him good to see 3 guilders 20 for the table of Baron von Boesigke; he had always paid when dining at the table of Frau von Levetzow's father over at the palais. He could burn all this himself. Everything, including the bill from the spa inspectors for the cases with 36 jugs of Kreuz Spring water, with cork, delivered to his lodgings. They had saved him. He had to read the bill once more:

> Only upon satisfactorily completed delivery of the goods in the prescribed weight and at the agreed-upon time, please have the kindness to pay the freight to the carter.

No, he would not burn this bill. It should survive as monument to a probity that will someday cease to exist. And he put the bill back into one of the drawers where he kept things to save.

But what about the picture? If he is serious, he has to burn it. But he cannot burn a picture. Not yet. And the box with the glove from August 28, 1823, and the little key he still wears around his neck on a little chain . . . Everything that couldn't be burned must be buried. First, take off the little chain and key, get rid of them now.

He breathed easier. As if this decision had made him much

more able to act, it suddenly became clear to him that his entire show of renunciation, his comical forgoing act, his bogus cultural posing was nothing but a grotesque overestimation of the social environment.

Ottilie was right to call him Tartuffe and reproach him for propagating the idea that the bitterer the cup, the sweeter the face of him who drains it, while in reality, he was as unrestrained, indecent, and unprincipled as the most hopeless opium eater in the slums of London. That's how she shouted at him, and she was right.

As never before, he felt how distant he was from the world of conversation. Was it really necessary for him to expend his most subtle energies to ensure that Bettina von Arnim (a notorious fraud) and all the Carolines and Charlottes talked about him as he would like them to? He should not have concealed Ulrike from them, but from himself. He ought not to have wasted his energy in a charade of renunciation, but in a struggle against Ulrike's presence within himself. He had fought that battle, but not in earnest. Not as earnestly as the battle deserved. He had fought the battle in the consciousness that he could not win it, did not want to win it. In his obsessively positive daily routines he had never submitted himself to a test he knew he wouldn't pass. Giving himself bad grades in life had to be avoided. The moment he thought, with the greatest possible earnestness, that he could make Ulrike disappear within himself, he saw her before him in the park. Under a straw hat secured by crossed yellow ribbons, she stands at the pond, feeding a swan. He had to protect himself from these blows of recollection. Himself! Himself! Himself! What's needed now is ruthlessness toward himself. Or you will croak because of a girl who knows some things about you but guesses nothing. What he felt now was anything but strength. He thought he could be embarrassed, ashamed. Not in the face of the world or morality, of any custom or propriety. Toward himself. He felt that an ability to be ashamed of himself was forming. Ashamed of hanging here, staggering, stuttering, lying to himself as he had never lied to anyone, not even his worst enemy. But to himself, himself, himself he is lying with every thought in which the girl shows up, dominates him and does what she will with him. But it isn't her, it is he who allows insanity to bloom like some fragile, lovely thing. But this insanity of yours is . . . Make no predictions for yourself. Just give in and let the feeling grow that you're ashamed. Ask nothing of this feeling. Let it grow until it brings you to a point you don't need to calculate now. Only the sensibility that brought you to no longer bear the cultural sham—let that sensibility grow. Mercilessly. Let us see, right?

But because anything weighty calls forth its counterweight, a certain feeling would give him to believe that the time when he kept his dependence on Ulrike secret was a blissful time. Out there, the entire out-of-the-question world, and then him, here in the cave of recollection with its inexhaustible treasures shining ever brighter. Now he needed to destroy those recollections. Hiding them, hiding them from himself, just wouldn't work . . . And then there arrived—Oh holy dramaturgy!—a lavender blue envelope containing an equally lavender blue note on which stood "N-C-O-L-W-N. We plan to celebrate New Year's Eve in Dresden. If you would like to do the same, it would please your devoted friend Ulrike."

So it was to be a play by Iffland, he thought. From the doorway, Stadelmann reported the successful incineration of everything Bohemian. Goethe stood up, went over to him, shook his hand, and said, "In the future, you can sell my hair wherever and whenever you like."

Stadelmann said, "It was only when people begged me for it, sir. Girls and such."

Stadelmann was back outside and Goethe sat there, feeling like a field marshal during a battle. Mounted couriers come galloping up, reporting this and that. He must decide what has to be done and give the orders. He was no field marshal, however. If he had been one, he would have been the kind who believes that soldiers must see themselves what works and what doesn't. He had hesitated too long and then in his haste done everything wrong, incinerating the things from Marienbad in the Webicht Forest!

He ordered a cease-fire with himself. Since receiving the New Year's Eve note, he could fulfill his duty to be present without impatience and irritability. He let Chancellor von Müller decide who should be granted an audience for how long, and how they should be received. He had more heart-felt banter with Adele Schopenhauer and Julie and Linchen von Egloffstein than ever before, calling Adele his favorite, which she passed on, so he had to intoxicate Julie even more. With his men, he was a patient companion. In addition to secretarial and copy work, John had a standing special assignment to observe the weather and put his observations down in writing. He was instructed to draw all possible inferences from the thermometer, the barometer, and cloud formations. John reported an imminent spell of warm weather unusual for this time of year. Nothing would remain of the little snow that had fallen so far. He regretted having to say so, since he knew the Privy Councilor enjoyed hard winter weather. Goethe kept his enthusiasm under control. He called for Stadelmann and at once showed himself to be in the cheeriest of moods "because, Stadelmann dear fellow, we may need to dash over to Dresden. What do we have the fastest chaise in the country and the best coachman in the world for anyway, Stadelmann?"

"I'm glad, sir," said Stadelmann.

They were making little daily excursions into the countryside now. But Dresden! Years ago Madame de Staël had sent him a seductively urgent invitation to visit her in Dresden. There hadn't been quite enough attractive power. The lady was magnificent, venerable, and also sufficiently bright, but she was too ambitious for him. He'd felt drawn to her whenever he encountered her. Only a woman can know you the way she knew him. She had provided him with the formula for his kind of masculinity: *Il vous faut de la séduction*. He was the conquered, not the conqueror, and Ulrike was the first one who had refused to conquer him. Nevertheless, that's why he would go to Dresden. W-A-T-F.

On December 28, he had the horses hitched up for another excursion. These days, he found himself unable to work. He was ashamed of himself. But it was no use. More vehemently than ever, he pushed aside anything that threatened to hinder him. He refused to have second thoughts. No matter what that meant! What concern was it of his! This everlasting evaluation! Life doesn't want a grade, it wants to be lived.

Then on Wednesday, December 28, the following happened: As always when they drove into town, they crossed the Marktplatz, keeping to the right of the square and turning into the Schlossgasse to reach the Kegel Bridge and cross the Ilm. On this December 28, he saw a coach on the other side of the river, stopped in front of the posthouse next to the Erbprinz Hotel. Fresh horses were just being hitched up and four persons were standing in front of the Erbprinz, obviously in conversation with the postmaster. Even shortsighted as he was, he could see by the shape of the coach that these were no ordinary mail-coach passengers. The four were of different heights and all wearing fur coats, open because it was not particularly cold. Kerchiefs instead of thick fur caps. The mood he was in since the lavender blue note led him to believe that these four persons he was looking at were the Levetzows. Just as one knows the names of separate peaks that belong together under a single name, he thought he could recognize in the differences in height the Holy Family (as he had occasionally called them, purely in fun). Stadelmann was ordered to turn immediately at the next corner into the Kollegiengasse and drive quickly through the Seifengasse back to the Frauenplan and into the courtyard. He told Stadelmann he was about to give him the most important command he had ever received: to drive as near as he could to the four travelers to see if he recognized them, but not to let them recognize him.

Then he ran back and forth along his six-room course, faster than he meant to. Had he worn spectacles like other shortsighted people, he would have seen whether or not it was them. Field Marshal, you ought to be shot. And it's been just a week or even less since he had been so satisfied with his revision of the passage about spectacles in the *Journeyman Years*. This was his punishment! He had Wilhelm, the enemy of spectacles, say, "Whoever looks through spectacles thinks himself smarter than he is." Spectacles have a bad effect, ethically. I see more than I should. Oh Wilhelm, Wilhelm! Goethe drummed his fists against his breast, not hard, but fast. The battle was not yet lost. If it is the Levetzows, they will not drive through Weimar without paying him a visit. Or are they already late? Is someone already waiting for them in Dresden? Quiet! Not a sound out of you now. He poured himself a glass of port wine and drank it off in one swallow. And then another glass. And a third. His breathing returned to what it should be. All he could do was blunder about and think Dresden—New Year's Eve—Ulrike—New Year's Eve—Dresden. His heart banged in his breast like a prisoner who sees himself unjustly imprisoned bangs against the door of his cell. His heart would beat itself bloody. He felt mistreated. He had been surprised that Ulrike had even sent that note. Yes, there was the formula N-C-O-L-W-N, but then the formal invitation. It wasn't Ulrike's style. It was her mother's. She wanted him as a trophy at her and Klebelsberg's ball. To add some class. He didn't care. The main thing was to see Ulrike . . .

Stadelmann returned, his serious face the very picture of joy. "Yes, sir, yes! It's them. They didn't see me, but it's them. All four of 'em."

"Thank you, Stadelmann," said the Field Marshal, "dismissed," and saluted him. Stadelmann clicked his heels together, turned, and marched out. Goethe had to drink another glass of port. And another. He could hardly stand it. At the end of two hours he had emptied two bottles of port. He could barely walk, but he could sit. And think. Now he was happy that he was the Field Marshal. There had been cowardice, cowardice in the face of friends. The Levetzows had stolen away. They didn't expect him until December 31. In order to increase their prestige. But today was too early. Today they had . . . doesn't matter what they had to do today. But it had nothing to do with him. Nothing more. Ever again. Now he was glad he had tried to surrender to the feeling that had begun to take shape in him in recent days: shame. Now there was no longer any doubt about this feeling. He was ashamed of himself with a vehemence that left nothing else inside him. Now at last, after this latest experience, he was quite sure of his shame. It told him, You have left that behind. His hero's prejudice against spectacles—he no longer cursed it. If you had worn spectacles, you would have recognized the family. They would have had to come to you and that's exactly what they did not want to do. Somewhere (he no longer knew where) he had written, "An animal knows no instruments, it simply perceives what nature makes possible for us." And just think of all it makes possible. Now he could supplement it with, And prevents the impossible. The impossible had been prevented. Was that an ease just now? An ease he had not yet felt? Its name was lovelessness. Yes. Never known, never experienced. But there was no other way to spell this feeling. He was free. No doubt about it, he was loveless. Lovelessness, tangible, a spaciousness as never before, even if it is an emptiness, a non-feeling that surpassed all feeling. He is released, free, this is what freedom is, to be loveless. Loveless, joyless, lifeless, painless. No one will ever be able to torture him again. Not even himself. All living creatures are released. The very first commandment which Moses, exhausted from climbing Mount Sinai, failed to hear (a lapse pregnant with tragedy for all time), he—having arrived at his own Sinai and also exhausted, but not in the least hard of hearing, no, keen-eared as never before—he has heard and understood: Thou shalt not love.

He got into bed. No more thoughts he had to unsuccessfully defend himself against. He felt only himself. Nothing beyond himself. As if he filled up the world. The whole world was him. Bursting with ease. A divine weight. The weight of lightness. At last. His lost equilibrium? Was that it? He thought so. Fell asleep. Slept without interruption far into the following day.

When he awoke, he had his member in his hand, and it was stiff. He knew whom he had dreamed of. W-A-T-F.

The Final Word

FRAU MARIE SCHÄFER, who served the unmarried noblewoman Ulrike von Levetzow as lady's maid for sixteen years, reports the following about the events of November 12, 1899:

When Ulrike von Levetzow went to bed the previous evening, her face was bathed in a cold sweat, and in a premonition that her end was near, she bade me fetch a little packet of letters whose contents were known to no one and to burn them on a silver platter. The ashes were to be sealed in a silver capsule and it was her wish that after her death, this priceless memento be placed in her coffin. This was done. At four o'clock in the morning, she awoke with a cough and at six o'clock she passed away peacefully.

According to the written testimony of her grandniece, they were letters from Goethe.

Notes

14   **"I have no wish to be another Tieck"**: Ludwig Tieck (1773–1853), Romantic poet and novelist.

15   **It dredged up memories of Sesenheim**: The Alsatian town near Strasbourg where the young Goethe fell in love with Friedericke Brion, daughter of the local pastor.

15   **And Charlotte Buff, the great sentimentalist**: The betrothed woman with whom Goethe fell in love while studying law in Wetzlar, north of Frankfurt. She became the model for Lotte in his first novel *The Sufferings of Young Werther*.

15   **And Christiane, the great emotion**: Christiane Vulpius became Goethe's common-law wife in 1788.

15   **And then Marianne, who wanted**: Marianne Willemer, the young wife of an old friend of Goethe's, was the muse for the love poems in his cycle *The West-Eastern Divan*.

42   **He thought of Zelter's setting of the poem**: Carl Friedrich Zelter (1758–1832), master bricklayer and self-taught composer. One of Goethe's closest friends.

45   **A god gave you the power to say how much you suffer**: A variation of a line from Goethe's play *Torquato Tasso*, Act V, scene 5: "And if a man's struck dumb by misery, / A god gave me power to say how much I suffer."

54 **"My name is Lili, but I don't have a park."**: As a young man, Goethe courted Anna Elisabeth "Lili" Schönemann (1758–1817), daughter of a Frankfurt banker. "Lili's Park" is one of the poems he wrote for her.

60 **"You kiss brilliantly, dear sir."**: Charlotte von Stein (1742–1827), lady-in-waiting to the Duchess of Weimar and wife of the duke's head equerry.

134 **Schiller (your favorite), Herder, Winckelmann**: Friedrich Schiller (1759–1805), poet, playwright, historian, and one of Goethe's closest friends and collaborators. Johann Gottfried Herder (1744–1803), philosopher, theologian, and literary critic; Johann Joachim Winckelmann (1717–1768), art historian and archeologist.

144 **"And sitting at the feet . . . for the rest of his life."**: Goethe, *Poetry and Truth*, Book 13, quoting Rousseau, *La nouvelle Héloïse*, to characterize his relation to Lotte Buff.

150 **"The human being . . . the name of wet-nurse to his habits."**: Schiller, *Wallenstein's Death*, Act I, scene 4: *Aus Gemeinem ist der Mensch gemacht, und die Gewohnheit nennt er seine Amme*.

153 **but because of Madame Szymanowska**: Maria Szymanowska (1789–1831), Polish composer and one of the first virtuoso pianists of the nineteenth century.

160 **Except for Herr von Humboldt, please**: Wilhelm von Humboldt (1767–1835), Prussian philosopher, diplomat, linguist, and the founder of Humboldt University in Berlin.

162 **"Sweet life! . . . must I leave you?"**: Goethe, *Egmont*, Act V.